challengers of the dust

challengers of the dust

William Bernhardt

BABYLON
BOOKS

CHALLENGERS OF THE DUST

Copyright © 2025 by William Bernhardt

Cover art copyright © 2025

eBook ISBN: 978-1-964832-24-1

paperback ISBN: 978-1-964832-26-5

hardcover ISBN: 978-1-964832-25-8

praise for william bernhardt and challengers of the dust

"Wow! That was all I could say when I finished devouring William Bernhardt's Challengers of the Dust. Readers beware, hold on tight for this roller-coaster ride that starts and ends in Oklahoma's No Man's Land of the Dust Bowl 1930s. Along the way you will meet con artists, maniacs, daredevils, cannibals, and an array of so many famous and infamous personalities that Forrest Gump's celebrity encounters pale in comparison. Mr. Bernhardt, you have done it again. Don't quit now. More please."

Michael Wallis, author of *Pretty Boy: The Life and Times of Charles Arthur Floyd*

"This was a very unusual book for Bernhardt but written well and it was hard for me to put it down....Please read this book."

Jacquie Robertson, Amazon Five-Star Review

"In this Depression era tale, Bernhardt unleashes his inner pulp fiction, creating cliff-hanger episodes as the protagonist and his cellmate travel from Guymon, OK to Cleveland and back. Ostensibly to find and return a doctor's missing daughter, they encounter a whole gallery of heroes and villains, with appearances by celebrities from Woody Guthrie to Amelia Earhart."

Bill H., *Goodreads*

"William Bernhardt is a born stylist, and his writing through the years has aged like a fine wine . . . ."

Steve Berry, author of *The Kaiser's Web*

Dedicated to Edgar Rice Burroughs, Robert E. Howard, and H.P. Lovecraft.

Hard times call for writers of great imagination.

Don't let nothing get you plumb down.
—Woody Guthrie

one

"YOU DID WHAT?"

"I told the jerk to leave my date alone."

"And that got you thrown in jail?"

"I told him with my fists."

"You hit him."

"Only a few times."

"That hardly seems like—"

"Then I tossed him through a plate-glass window."

"Is there more?"

"The window was on the third floor."

George stared at his grandfather through the filthy Plexiglas divider. He never liked talking on the telephone, but he particularly disliked it when the phone only allowed him to communicate with this person sitting four feet away on the other side of the divider. The person who wasn't wearing bright orange jailhouse scrubs.

"So you were brawling in public. Again. And now you're in

jail. Again." His grandfather had a penchant for repeating the obvious, early and often, in that Western Okie drawl that grated on him like a Thomas Kinkade painting. "Are you trying to put me in an early grave?"

He assumed the question was rhetorical.

"I can't tell you how sick and tired I am of this angry-young-man routine." His grandfather ran a liver-spotted hand through thinning silver hair. The fringes dangled from his buckskin jacket. "And you committed this act of stupidity over some girl?"

"There was a principle involved."

"Oh good, now I feel better. What was the principle?"

"The guy pissed me off." George stared at the concrete walls, wondering what color they were, wondering whether he could reproduce that hideous tint. Somewhere between green and no color at all, like someone had taken the world's most repellent hues and mixed in a little vomit. It did match the cubicle's pungent smell. Body odor, foot fungus, open-air toilets, and poor ventilation did not make for an aromatic environment.

"He offended your knightly sense of chivalry, so you punched his lights out." The tremor in his voice did not disguise the sarcasm.

"The toad came on to my date."

"And who was this alluring Aphrodite?"

The air went dead, all but the pneumatic hiss of the grungy phone receiver. "I can't remember her name."

"How long had you known her?"

"About an hour."

"That long."

"I think. My memory is a little fuzzy." He wanted this conversation to be over. Truth to tell, he never wanted it to begin. For that matter, he did not want to be in the Cleveland County jail wearing grotesque formless clothes. He did not want his lips near this germ-ridden phone, formerly slobbered over by drug dealers and walking repositories of every STD since Adam kissed Eve. But he would happily have accepted all that if he could avoid having this conversation with his grandfather.

He never felt comfortable around the old man. As far as he was concerned, they lived in separate worlds, and he was con-tent to let them remain separate. But when his parents died in a traffic accident twelve years ago, his grandfather became his only living relative, as well as his court-appointed guardian. What little money trickled from the old man's bony fingers always had strings attached. He resented the man's constant efforts to bully him into following in his footsteps—going to college and law school, joining his fraternity, living in dreary red-dirt Oklahoma. The man didn't want a grandson. He wanted a clone.

His grandfather's name was George Earle Jr. And he was George Earle IV.

"Where did you meet this Helen of Troy?" his grandfather asked. "The face that launched a thousand fists."

"At the lake. Thundercloud."

"Thundercloud? Everyone knows there's nothing but trash down there."

He ignored the obvious implications about the lovely woman whose name he still could not recall. "The light is good and it's open to the public. And since I can't afford a studio, I have to paint where I can."

His grandfather pursed his lips. "Don't sing your sad songs to me. You've always had everything you needed."

"What I need is a break.

"What you need is a job."

"I'm a painter. That's who I am. Artists don't work nine-to-five and get a paycheck from the man every two weeks. You give up financial security so you can do something that actually matters. And before you even start, I don't want to be a lawyer. I refuse to spend my life wearing cheap suits and helping felons flee."

"Some lawyers are better than others, true. I hear rumors that a few of those painters have been less than perfect, too."

"Painting is what I love. And if you don't do what you love, you're wasting your life."

"You never know what boots might fit till you try them on. Still not too late to enroll for the fall semester."

"That is not going to happen."

His grandfather arched his back. Even at his advanced age, he remained whippet-thin, not an ounce of fat on him. "Lot of people go back to school later in life. Restart their career. People much older than you."

"Look, I'm not dissing your chosen profession. But everyone hates lawyers. For a reason. I want to spend my life with the people who know what's important in life."

"And you think you know what's important in life." His grand- father pinched the bridge of his nose. He always did that when stressed. It seemed to be his way of containing his temper. "If you want something out of life, you've got to put your nose to the grindstone and stop thinking that your pleasure in the most important thing in the universe. The world won't be handed to you on . . ."

He'd heard the laissez-faire-manly-work-ethic speech so many times he could've delivered it himself. His mind wandered to other topics. Like the bail he needed posted. And the document he'd found in the old man's desk drawer a few days ago.

". . . and if you knew how hard this world could be, you wouldn't be wasting days like you've got an endless supply. You'd—"

"I saw the will."

"You shouldn't read things that don't concern you."

"How can your will not concern me? Well, actually, I guess it doesn't. Since I'm not in it."

"A man needs to make his own way in the world. That's how you learn to respect yourself."

"Then why are you doing this vast disservice to Gordon Irion? mYour designated heir apparent."

"I have my reasons."

"And what little money doesn't go to the tragically now-emasculated-by-your-money Irion creates a nonprofit foundation?"

"It's a tribute."

"To a writer? When was the last time you read a book?"

"I have my reasons."

He turned away, but the coiled steel attached to the receiver yanked him back. "Look, just pay my bail so I can get out of here, okay?"

"No."

He blinked. "Excuse me?"

"Not gonna do it."

"Someone has to post my bail."

"Not necessarily."

"It's five hundred bucks. I'll pay you back as soon as I can. They won't let me pay it myself, even if I have it. Which I don't."

"Guess you're not going anywhere."

"If you don't pay my bail, they'll keep me here forever."

"Nah. I figure they'll keep you a week or so. Then they'll kick you loose. It's only a misdemeanor charge."

"A *week*?"

"That's seven days."

"I know a week is seven days. I don't want to spend seven days in jail."

"It will give us time to talk."

"Visitors are only allowed one hour a day."

"So that will be seven hours. Because a week is seven days."

"I do not want to be in jail for a week."

His grandfather made a clicking sound with his tongue. "Don't see that you've got much say about it."

"Listen to me." He tried to avoid sounding desperate. "This place smells. It's filthy. The food is pure lard. There are no books, no TV. Nothing to do. And the other inmates look at me like they want to kill me because I don't speak in guttural monosyllables."

"You'll survive."

"Easy for you to say. You have no idea what it's like in here."

His grandfather inched slightly closer to the Plexiglas partition. "I was in jail once."

He paused a moment to wrap his head around it. "You? Jail?"

"Once."

"You never mentioned this."

"Never came up before."

"When?"

"Long time ago. In the thirties."

"God help me. Is this another story about hard times during the Depression?"

"You haven't heard this one." Even through the filthy divider, George saw something going on with the old man's eyes, like that steely glint melted into a putty. "Kind of a long story, though. Fortunately, as it turns out, we have some time."

two

guymon, oklahoma, 1935

I **STEPPED** off the westbound Santa Fe passenger train and entered Barsoom.

Four years before, I left Guymon to study at the Massachusetts Institute of Technology and Boston Society of Natural History— what they now call MIT. In the early days, the main campus was in Cambridge and most folks called it Boston Tech. I had great ideas and expectations. I planned to become a civil engineer, to build bridges and skyscrapers. To be a man of substance. Once I went east and shook the red dirt off my shoes, I felt as if I'd been released from bondage. Like I'd shed the chains binding me to mediocrity.

Seemed to me, everything that mattered happened back east. In Cambridge, you could have an intelligent conversation. You could meet someone you didn't know at the diner and end up talking about Newton or Kant or Darwin. For the price of a cup of coffee, you could spend the day discussing that crazy runt in Germany, or whether FDR was smarter than Hoover, or whether

Carole Lombard was funnier than Myrna Loy. Massachusetts provided the intellectual stimulation a man of my cranial capacity craved. Which is why I hadn't been back home for almost four years.

Good thing I saw the sign at the train station, because otherwise I never would have known this was the town where I grew up. The wind hit me hard, slapping me across the face the same way my pa used to, only without the cussing. Dirt blew so fierce my eyes teared up.

What happened? Guymon used to be a sweet little panhandle farming town. I knew there'd been some hard times. I saw the newsreels and occasionally borrowed a newspaper. But this was a completely different world than the one I'd grown up in.

Maybe I should've called home more often. When I left Oklahoma in 1931, it was one of the most prosperous places in America. After the Crash of '29, a lot of big city folks were jobless or homeless. Entire families got kicked to the streets. But Oklahoma experienced an unexpected boom. New farming techniques made it possible to plow and plant land previously thought untamable. While the rest of the country suffered, we had bumper crops. Some folks called Oklahoma "the New Eden."

I clutched a kerchief to my mouth to help me breathe. Right now, New Eden looked more like the seventh circle of hell. Maybe worse.

I passed a few folks at the station. Not many. I noticed they didn't have kerchiefs, but they appeared to be able to breathe. I guess that meant you got used to it after a while. I didn't want to get used to it. I wanted to get back on that train and return to Massachusetts. But I couldn't do that yet.

I had a funeral to attend.

Just after I left the station, I passed a young girl, maybe twelve years old. She was so emaciated I might have judged her younger than she actually was.

"Hey, friend." Her voice was barely more than a whisper. "Got a spare nickel?"

My pa never approved of beggars. They'll just spend it on drink, he used to say.

"A nickel will buy a cup of coffee and a good breakfast," she added, as if answering my unspoken concern.

I gave her the quick once-over. She wore a brown muslin dress, frayed at the bottom and bearing several good-sized holes throughout. Her smudged and dirty face seemed almost hidden under hair stiff with grime. She smelled bad, too.

"Miss, if you need food, I'll bet you could get the local—"

"It's not for me. It's for my brothers." She hitched her dress up some and that's when I saw them. Two boys, no more than three and four, just as skinny as the girl, clinging to her legs like they were a life preserver.

I made eye contact with one of them. Biggest eyes I ever saw in my life, on the tiniest of humans.

I gave her three nickels, one for each. When she kissed me on the cheek, I felt the dirt in her hard-chapped lips.

The walk back to my childhood home would take a while, and I hadn't eaten anything, so I decided to get a sandwich. I thought I'd follow the girl to a diner or some such place, but she disappeared into a cloud of dust and I lost her. That black dirt was everywhere, at times so thick I literally couldn't see where I was going. I didn't think I'd been away long enough to forget the lay of the town, but the dirt made it difficult to navigate. The wind blew so hard that at times it could knock down a grown man. Folks ducked between buildings or clutched a hitching post for dear life when the big gusts came.

I saw a dying dog on the side of the road. Funny how things like that affect you. Just a dog, after all, but for some reason, that dog got to me more than the girl. Seemed like dogs were always happy, even when they had no right to be. But that poor thing couldn't move. It just lay there, tongue out, ribs showing.

I looked around for some water. I had a flask, but it didn't contain water, if you know what I mean. In those days, people would've thought anyone carrying around a bottle of water was a complete idiot. Don't even start on what they'd think about someone paying good money to buy water.

I spotted a hand-operated pump near the general store. I filled a cup, or tried. Dust got into the drinking water. I took a swig. Like drinking mud. Still, I brought some to that poor whip terrier. He wasn't interested. Didn't need any more dirt in his system, I imagine. So, I pulled out my flask and gave him a snort of some medium-grade distilled whiskey. I don't know if that did him any good or not, but he lapped it up.

Truth was, I knew that dog was a goner. All I did was apply a little anesthetic to the situation, so he could pass more gently than would've otherwise been possible.

I made my way home. With all the color drained out of the land, everything looked black and gray. Where was all the green and yellow and blue? Even the sky was a dingy brown.

My grandfather, Gustav Ehrlich, came out here in the 1880s. His folks started in southern Germany, then moved to the Volga River, then to the Cherokee Outlet of Oklahoma. *Russlanddeutschen*, they were called, which technically meant both Russian and German, but really neither. I heard that the treeless stretches of the Oklahoma plains reminded them of their original homeland. These were hard folks, toughened by exile, ridicule, and constant hardship.

My grandfather grew up in the Russian village of Tcherbagovka. His daddy was a leather tanner. They traveled from town to town looking for work. At night, they shackled their horses' legs to their own ankles so the nags wouldn't get stolen while they slept. Eventually my granddad married and started a family. My dad got a draft notice from the Russian czar when he turned sixteen. They knew if he joined the army he would never return. So, they packed up and left.

They eventually made it to Oklahoma. Pa changed his name to George Earle, but they still met with all kinds of prejudice from the "Anglos," especially during the Great War. Anti-German attitudes spread all across the country, sometimes for understandable reasons. Most German-Russian immigrants became conscientious objectors. They had an inclination toward pacifism and a strong distaste for war. Draft-dodging was not uncommon. That only increased the prejudice against them "Rooshians."

We never fit in, even later when I was growing up. We liked high-top *filzstiefel* shoes better than cowboy boots. We liked featherbeds better than hard American mattresses. We liked schnapps better than corn whiskey. We sang "Gott ist die Liebe" in church. We made a bigger fuss over Christmas. I always felt like an outsider, someone trapped between two worlds, never truly a part of either one. An outsider who couldn't wait to go somewhere else.

But we Rooshians ended up being the best thing that ever happened to Oklahoma. My pa said those tough ancestors were why wheat got planted on the dry side of the plains. They brought over Turkey red seeds sewn into the pockets of their clothing. Turkey red is a hard winter wheat, short-stemmed and resistant to cold and drought. They brought the thistle, too—what people 'round here called tumbleweed. Before the Rooshians came, people called this the Great American Desert. Afterwards, it was farmland.

Or used to be. Now I didn't see a square foot suitable for cultivation. I couldn't imagine anything surviving here. Including people.

I soon became aware of two serious problems. One, there were so many beggars on the road that if I'd tried to help them all I would've been out of money before I made my first left turn. And two, people were following me. Just kids, teenagers. But there were three of them and only one of me.

In retrospect, I can see why they caught my scent. When I gave money to that girl—too much—I'd flashed my coin purse, which probably had the same effect as if I'd dangled a T-bone steak in front of that dog.

I decided to take the initiative. I pivoted on one heel and faced them down. "You boys need somethin'?"

They looked to be around seventeen. They wore patched jeans and suspenders. The one in the center, the tallest, wore a newsboy cap with a frayed brim. He was the leader. I judged the others to be brave about as long as he was and no longer. So I figured that if there was any trouble, I'd take him down and the fight would be over.

I'd studied the sweet sport in Massachusetts. Ended up the champion fighter in my fraternity house. These underweight ruffians, I reckoned, wouldn't be much of a challenge.

The leader replied, "Ain't seen you 'round these parts."

"Been away for a while," I explained.

"I'm a little short today," the leader said. He bounced up and down on his toes, unable to stand still. Far more afraid of me than I was of him, I thought. "Loan me some money, will you?"

"How much you want?"

"All of it."

I pursed my lips. "'Fraid I can't go along with that idea."

"Doesn't matter if you go along with it, friend." His bouncing accelerated. "The only question is how bad we got to pound you before we take it."

I didn't say a word in reply. I just raised my fists in the classic pugilistic stance, left fist higher than the right.

That kid grinned. His two buddies glanced sideways at one another, like they knew what was going to happen next.

As it turned out, they did.

"Last chance," the leader said. "Hand over the purse."

"I respectfully decline."

"Shame to mess up that pretty face of yours."

"You may give it your best effort." I returned a steely-eyed stare.

That's when someone hit me from behind. Hit me hard. With a club or something equally solid. I fell to the ground like my legs had been erased by a celestial editor. I hit my head and dirt blew into my eyes.

And then those four boys started killing me.

three

GEORGE STARED at his grandfather through the Plexiglas. "A dramatic cliffhanger. But I'm pretty sure you aren't going to die."

"You never know. Maybe I'm a ghost. Or one of them vampires."

"That would certainly make this story more commercial."

"But that's not what happened."

"And how does this end with you going to jail? Maybe I'm crazy, but it seems like the hooligans should be the ones who get incarcerated."

"Justice doesn't always work the way it should."

He glanced down at his grubby jumpsuit. "No argument there.

But I still don't get how you landed in jail."

"Then how about you shut up and let me tell my story?"

They had me down in the dirt, blind, groggy, winded. No way I was going to win that fight. They didn't exactly observe the Marquess of Queensbury rules. After the first blow came a swift kick between my legs. Nobody ever did that back in Massachusetts. Severe pain radiated through my entire body, guaranteeing I wouldn't be getting up in a hurry.

They beat me up but good. All four of them. Next boot went

into my stomach. Two more followed right behind. Guess I should be grateful they didn't crack a rib, but I didn't feel much gratitude at the time. One of them grabbed my head by the hair and started punching me. Made my nose bleed. Blood trickled into my mouth. And all I could do was lie there and take it.

Those boys weren't just mean or hungry. They were angry. They saw something well-fed and well-scrubbed walk off the train and it made them mad. No telling how many years of misery and frustration got taken out on my face that day.

When they finally got around to stealing my purse, it was an anticlimax. I didn't care anymore. I would've given it to them, just to make the beating stop.

The leader kicked me in the gut one more time, spit on me, then laughed. But I noticed there wasn't much merriment in the laugh. "The Collier family thanks you for a week of good eatin'." He kicked some dirt in my face and disappeared.

I lay there on the rocky ground for what seemed like an hour. I don't know if no one saw me or no one wanted to get into it, but I remained undisturbed for a good long while. I don't think I passed out. It just hurt to move. First time I'd ever been beaten like that—though it wasn't the last. I was so full of myself. I got off that train like the cock of the walk, like I was some alien anthropologist studying these poor farm folk. And less than an hour later, there I was eating dirt.

Something inside my head cried out. *Barsoom. Take me away from this. Take me home again.*

But I was already home. Just not the home I remembered.

I should explain that when I was a kid—well, even after I was a kid—I loved Edgar Rice Burroughs. You know, the Tarzan guy. Those jungle stories were okay, but he wrote other series I liked better. The best was about John Carter, the warlord of Mars— *Barsoom* in the local lingo. Carter is this Virginia cavalry officer trapped in a cave by Apaches. He somehow gets transported to Mars where he has grand adventures, saves a beautiful princess, and becomes a local hero. In the story, Mars is dried up, water is scarce, and the people are dying. In other words, it was much like the place where I now found myself.

Barsoom was in a bad way till that Virginian arrived and straightened things out. At the end of the first book, he suddenly gets transported back to Earth but he doesn't want to go. He's separated from his princess and the world he has learned to love. He stares up at the heavens longing to return. But Barsoom won't take him back.

Well, not till the sequel. *The Gods of Mars*. Even better than the first one.

I dreamed, once or twice, of being transported to Barsoom and becoming a local hero. Winning a princess. Doing some good for the world. But I didn't feel heroic right at that moment, with my tongue in the mud and my eyes so full of dirt it hurt to blink. I felt like the biggest idiot who ever walked the face of the planet. Any planet.

"You all right, mister?"

Took me more than a moment to realize I wasn't hallucinating.

A real person was actually talking to me.

"You want me to call the doctor or somethin'?"

She stood a good ten feet away, that girl, the one I gave the three nickels. I don't know how she came across me, but she tried to be kindly, in her timid way. And she might've been—if I hadn't made the mistake of lifting my head and looking at her.

She screamed. Scooped those two brothers up and ran. That's when I realized how good a number those four boys had done on me. That poor girl ran like she'd seen the Frankenstein monster.

I eventually pulled myself back to my feet. Limped at first, but I walked it out, wiped the blood from my face. My stomach hurt —hell, everything hurt. Head thumped like Mickey Mouse was doing a tap dance on my brain. I could barely see.

I felt pretty damn sorry for myself. Truth was, I hadn't wanted to come home but I did and look what happened.

I made my way down Kingston Row to the three-room house

I grew up in. I shouldn't have been surprised to see how the dirt had changed it. Didn't even look the right color. All the white was a dingy gray. The porch wasn't swept, the gutters were full of muck, and the front screen door clattered in the breeze.

Ma hadn't been dead that long—her funeral was scheduled for tomorrow afternoon—but the house already missed her. It was falling apart like a surviving spouse with no desire to continue alone.

No animals in the barn. What happened to the stock? Where was our horse, our cows?

"Callie?" I called out with as strong a voice as I could muster through my cracked and swollen lips. "Callie?"

No reply from inside or out.

Now that I thought about it, there was no reason my little sister should be home. I telegraphed what day I would arrive, but she had no way of knowing what train I'd be on and this was a school day.

But Pa could figure it out, and he would have no trouble spending the day at the general store waiting for a train to come in. Prohibition ended in 1933, but Oklahoma remained a dry state. Which did not mean a man couldn't get a drink. Just meant you had to know where to go.

Come to think of it, why hadn't Pa met me at the station? I couldn't believe there were many farming duties in this weather. Every farm I passed looked flat and dirty and spoiled.

"Callie?"

Enough already. I pushed open the door.

You'd think the inside of a house would be safe from the dirt, but at best it was a slight improvement. The floor was covered with sand, fine like a powder and the color of blood. The wind howled and rattled the boards in the walls. Sand drifted through the cracks—and there were lots of cracks. The walls were smeared with a flour-and-water paste. Ma's homemade wallpaper, I guessed. Probably supposed to keep the dust out. It hadn't worked very well.

I looked into what we called the parlor. The big chair Pa always favored was turned away from the door. But when I took a closer look, I saw Pa's unmistakable bald spot poking over the top, rising above the cream-colored doily.

"Pa." I walked right up to him, crouched down, and swung the chair around.

He fell forward, gray as ash, dry as flypaper. His head landed on my shoulder, like he wanted a hug. Except he didn't.

I took his head in my hands. "Pa?"

His cheeks were colder than Massachusetts in January.

My first thought was that he was drunk again, passed out, but when I took a closer look, I realized my mistake.

No breath came out of those nostrils. Something black oozed from his lips onto my hands.

I jumped up, wiping my hands on my pants. Pa was dead. And had been. For a long time.

four

I BACKED AWAY, staggering, eyes bulging, bile rising in my throat. The stench overpowered and disoriented me. I fell backward over the coffee table and collapsed onto the sofa.

A cloud of dust rose.

I felt bones beneath me. "Callie?"

She started mumbling. I rolled to the side so I could see her. "Pneumonia got him. Dust pneumonia. Coughed himself to death. Right in that chair."

"Callie?" I almost didn't recognize her. Her face looked near skeletal. She'd lost the pink and plumpness that had made her a right pretty little girl.

"He hasn't been the same since Ma passed. Drank too much. Didn't wash, didn't work. Died right in that chair."

"When?"

"Today. Yesterday. Last week." Her eyes drifted off to the side, glassy and fixed. I wasn't sure she even recognized me, seeing how beat up my face was. She gave off a terrific stench, so bad I had trouble sitting beside her. "I don't think he wanted to live."

"Callie, what happened to you?" She wore a pair of bib overalls—Pa's, I thought—that were way too big for her. Didn't look like she had anything on underneath. She was filthy, but so far, I hadn't seen anyone in Guymon who wasn't. "Didn't anyone come to check on you?"

"People 'round here way too busy with their own troubles." "The day I left, Pa reaped a record crop. Suitcase farmers were making big money. Guymon had dances every Saturday night. We were all dancing the prairie jitterbug."

"That quit." She stared off into space, almost like she was reciting a poem lodged in distant memory. "First the soil got dry and the plants died. You get no rain, everything's gonna die. Couldn't feed the stock so we ate them. No point in both them and us starving, that's what Pa said. Didn't taste good, though. The horse was stringy and sweet. But it lasted for more than a week. And we weren't in a position to complain."

"Why didn't someone tell me?"

She continued like she didn't hear me. Maybe she didn't. "Wind howled like a pack of wolves, all day, all night. Grass-hoppers swarmed in so thick they blacked out the sun and ate the green right off the willows. Hit me so hard I felt like I'd been mule-kicked in the gut. They got in my face, in my mouth. Left bruises and a sour taste. Jackrabbits went crazy, eating everything on the ground. We killed them for food, too, when we could catch them. Everything was all sand and hoppers and dyin'."

"Pa was riding high when I left. I know he tucked some money back."

"That didn't last long. Pretty soon we had nothing to eat but the wheat Pa saved from better years. We ground it up for cereal. Sifted it to make flour for bread. Mixed it with rabbit to make porridge. Then the wheat run out. Pa tried everything he could think of to make money, but it was no good. Everyone was looking for work, and no one had any jobs."

"You should've written me, Callie. Or come out to see me." "Came time I couldn't taste nothing but dirt, all the time, dirt. Dirt in my eyes, nose, mouth, hair, everywhere. Dust rubbed my skin raw like sandpaper. We put Vaseline in our noses to filter the dirt, but it didn't help much. We put wet towels be- neath the doors and covered the windows with bed sheets, but it did no good, just made the sheets an ugly brown. I swept six or eight times a day. It never stayed clean long. Some mornings a big dirt dune would block the front door. Pa would crawl out through a window so he could shovel it off. We taped windows and doors. We covered the sink. Nothing worked. Nothing could stop the dirt."

"I'm sorry, Callie." I knew full well how puny and useless my words sounded. "I had no notion what was going on back here." "Worst of it was that the dust clouds make it so dark all the time. Pitch black in the middle of the day. Pa would tie a rope 'round me before he'd let me go to the barn, so he could reel me in if I got lost. Some days it was so hot the chickens roasted alive." "You shouldn't have been dealing with this. You should've been at school."

"What school? You couldn't even breathe in that school. The Red Cross handed out gauze dust masks. Made you look plumb foolish. Kept the dust out a little but made it hard to get a good breath. After a while, the school just shut down."

I could hardly stand to see my little sister in such a state. I knew she was only fourteen, but the hard lines in her face made her look forty.

"Why'd you stay away so long, George? We needed you."

"I—I didn't know. I read a little about the troubles out west, but I didn't know it hit here." Of course, the truth was I never took the trouble to find out because I was all wrapped up in my big plans. "Ma should've sent a telegram."

"Ma didn't want to bother you. She was proud of her college boy, first ever for this family, with a full scholarship and all the trimmings. She tried to keep things together best she could. The dust would get into her dinners so everything had the same gritty taste. You'd feel it in your teeth. Pa kept on plowing like this might be the year the rains came back and the crops came in. But it didn't happen. Ma fought and fought till her heart gave out. Pa got the cough. I gave him skunk grease like the doctor said, but it didn't help. Made this home remedy of sugar with a drop of coal oil to get the phlegm out of his throat. No change."

"Why—is he still in that chair?"

"That's his favorite chair."

"I know, Callie, but he's dead."

"I didn't know what to do. Some mornings I feel too weak to get off this sofa."

I wondered when she last had something to eat. Probably before Pa passed. "Callie, you do understand that he's dead, don't you?"

"He talked to me this morning."

"I don't think so."

"He did. He said, 'Young lady'—that's what he likes to call me —'Young lady, I think I'll go into town today. Get you one of them penny candies you like so well.'" Her eyes darted toward the floor. "Never done it, though."

I looked at my only living relative and felt tears well up inside. I felt like I'd killed my parents myself, just as surely as if I'd stuck a dagger in their chests. I thought I must be the vilest murderer since Jack the Ripper. Only worse. 'Cause even Jack the Ripper didn't kill the folks he was supposed to love best.

five

I TRIED to get a grip on the situation. I'd come home for a funeral, and now it looked like it was going to be a double-casket affair. Triple-casket, if I didn't get Callie some grub.

"Callie, when was the last time you had a bite?"

"Can't remember."

"Did you eat today?"

"Ain't moved today."

"Yesterday?"

"Weren't my day to eat. Pa's day to eat."

"But Pa's—never mind." I ran into the kitchen and checked the pantry. The cupboard was bare, just like in that old nursery rhyme. Not even the tiniest morsel on the shelves. And judging from the unbroken layers of dust, there hadn't been anything for some time.

"C'mon, Callie. Let's get some chow." I took her by the hand and almost gasped. Her fingers were twigs, and her arms were like the useless appendages of a baby bird. If I tugged much, I feared her arm might come off.

"Too tired," she said.

"You got to eat."

"Not my day."

I assumed hunger made her delirious. I slid a hand behind her on the sofa, easing her to her feet, wondering if she could support her own weight. Not that she had much. Took some doing, but I eventually got her moving.

I needed to formulate a plan. I didn't have an automobile, I didn't have any money, my whole body ached, and I looked like a monster. But I knew that if I didn't get my little sister some- thing to eat soon, she'd die. I wasn't going to let the whole Earle family disappear just because I was too wrapped up in myself to take notice.

Callie could barely make it to the mailbox on her own steam. I ended up carrying her, piggyback style. Put a little strain on her arms, but that was easier for her than walking. Put a lot of strain on my aching back, but at that moment I didn't mind feeling some pain. In fact, I reckoned maybe it was my turn.

We made it back to town without incident, which forced me to consider Step Two of my ill-formed plan: getting food for Callie even though I'd been robbed of my every cent. I saw the Guymon People's Bank was open, but I didn't have an account there anymore. I could wire for some money back east, but I knew it would take a couple of days to arrive. So what was I going to do? Take up a place on the side of the road, begging with all the others? Surely I wasn't that desperate.

And I wasn't even contemplating Step Three: dealing with the minor matter of Pa's desiccating corpse in the parlor.

One thing at a time, I told myself. *One damn thing at a time.*

"You think it's gonna rain today, George?" Her fetid breath crawled across the back of my neck.

"I sure hope so."

"Ain't been no rain in a mess of days."

"I can see that."

"Hard when there's no rain."

I slowly swung her around and lowered her to the ground, right in the middle of Main Street. "I know things have been tough for you, sister. But you ain't alone anymore. Your brother's back in town. I'm gonna take care of you like a big brother's supposed to do. That's a promise."

"You promise?"

"That's right. And I'm a man that's good to his word. You know I am. Always have been."

"Always have been."

I found the telegraph office, but it was closed. I left Callie outside on a bench and went into the general store to inquire.

I knew the man that ran the place, Joe Blades, but he didn't seem to recognize me. Wondered if I'd really changed that much in four years, or if that beating disguised me, or if maybe his memory didn't work as well as it once had.

"You know when that telegraph office opens?"

"Not anytime soon." He was a thin man. His left eye jerked about when he talked.

"Yeah, but when?"

"That place shut down after the crops failed again in '34. Heard Randolph and his family went to California looking for work. Hope they found some. Place's been up for sale, but no one wants it."

One complication after another. Guess Pa had to leave town to send me the telegram about Ma's funeral. "I don't know if you recognize me or not, but I'm Georgie Earle. Big George Earle's boy."

His head twitched slightly. "Ain't seen George Earle much lately."

"Well, there's a reason for that."

"Used to be a good customer. But no more. Ain't no good customers these days."

"Look, I need to get my hands on some money. I got plenty back east. Got me a scholarship and everything. They pay me to go to school and better myself. Thing is, I got robbed. And my sister needs to eat in the worst way."

"Don't we all."

"I know you've got canned goods here. If you could see your

way to loan me some, I'd be much obliged. And I'll pay you back first second I liberate some money from my accounts back east."

"You'll gladly pay me Tuesday for a hamburger today?"

"I'm good for it, mister." I didn't like this at all. It felt like begging, even if I was gonna pay him as soon as I could. "Soon as I got Callie squared away, I'll go into Boise City and wire for cash."

"Wired money takes at least a week these days."

"Well, you aren't gonna starve in a week, mister. But my sister damn well might."

I shouldn't't've raised my voice and I shouldn't't've cussed. I knew that, even as I did it. But it was too late. That man turned his back on me. Didn't even have the courtesy to say no. He just shuffled off somewhere behind the counter.

I must confess I gave more than a moment's thought to stealing a can of beans off the shelves and lighting out with it. What can you do when your little sister's starving? I'd be like that guy in a book I had to read in freshman English who got arrested for stealing bread to save his sister's starving kids. Though as I recall, he got locked up for about nineteen years. There must be a sounder course of action.

I went back to the street. Callie had sunk low on the bench. The sand and dirt blew over her, but she didn't seem to notice.

I couldn't see begging, not in the ordinary way, with my hand out, looking pathetic. But I thought I might target some of the more prosperous citizens. Maybe someone who had an education themselves could understand my situation. I'd be more than willing to work off the debt, if they didn't want to wait for the wired funds.

I spotted one man right away who looked well enough off. Well-dressed, clean, and judging from the size of his gut, not starving.

He walked past me at a brisk pace. I reached out and laid a hand on his shoulder.

"Excuse me, sir. Could you lend some assistance, please?"

He didn't even look at me. "Sorry. I can't encourage bums."

That word stung worse than the beating I'd taken. Maybe my currently gruesome face gave him the wrong idea. "I am not a bum, sir. I'm a college man."

He pivoted slightly. "You're begging, ain't you?"

"I'm asking for help for my little sister."

"Then you're a bum. God helps those who help themselves."

"That may be, but no one can help themselves much when they're starving to death."

"If I give money to one of you, pretty soon my doorstep will be flooded with bums and hoboes and tramps."

"I am none of the above."

"'Sides, most likely you'll spend it on strong drink."

"I need food for my little sister!" I tried to bite back my temper, too late. I didn't like being lumped in with all those wretches lining the road. He started to walk away, but I chased after him. Stopped him right in front of the People's Bank—which was the tragic error that led to the whole rest of this misbegotten misadventure.

"Look, mister, you look like you come from a nice place." *And you look like you haven't gotten your hands dirty in a good long while*, I thought, but I kept that part to myself. "You must have some chores you need done."

"Ain't hard to get chores done these days. People are desperate to work. I got a whole staff to take care of my property. That's mmy way of helping out during hard times. I find it works a sight better than doling money out to bums and drunkards."

I got to admit, I just about smacked the pompous ass right then and there. If I hadn't been hurting so much, I probably would've. But I knew that wouldn't help. I couldn't afford to get into trouble.

And that, ironically, was my last thought before I heard an explosion inside the bank. One of the front windows shattered and a huge gust of wind blew across the street. A woman screamed, followed by a host of shouting and crying.

It's hard to explain just how badly it jangles a man's nerves to hear all this banging and screaming and shouting. One minute the town was quiet as death, the next it was filled with all kinds of commotion. I heard two more explosions—and this time I realized they weren't coming from a train or a motor car.

They were gunshots.

Two men raced out of the bank, both toting heavy canvas bags. One had his face covered with a kerchief, but the other was plain to see. As he streaked by, I caught a glimpse—and I knew why he chose not to cover up, even when engaging in such hazardous activities.

That man had the prettiest face I ever did see on a male member of the species. Not handsome, exactly, but pretty. His whole countenance was soft, maybe even cherubic. His jet-black hair was slicked back and he had big eyes like a china doll. I wondered if that man couldn't charm the tellers even as he robbed their fine institution.

At the same instant the robbers hit the street, someone else pulled up in a shiny Ford. I'd seen some of those new models back in Massachusetts. I guess the robbers had a driver waiting, which seemed smart. Spending a lot of time cranking up the engine would've been ill-advised.

Just as the pretty-looking man slid into the passenger seat, we made eye contact. He winked at me.

What a wink that man had. I think he could've charmed the leaves off a tree.

"Come to make a withdrawal?" he asked.

I wasn't sure what to say. "My sister's starving."

He reached into that bag, pulled out a wad of bills, and tossed it to me. "Take care of your family, son. Always take care of family."

"I will," I said.

"Which way to Boise City?"

I pointed.

He tipped an imaginary hat. "Much obliged."

I stood there like a dumb fool, holding the bills and staring at him like I was comatose. The three men drove away, disappearing into the dust.

Then I felt a hand clamp down on my shoulder. And got a sinking feeling inside my stomach.

"Mister. You're under arrest."

six

GEORGE NARROWED his eyes and peered at his grandfather, wiping a smudge off the Plexiglas with his orange sleeve so he could see better. He didn't want to call the old man an out-and-out liar. But this seemed like a big story to never have come up before.

"You met Pretty Boy Floyd?"

"Not sure *met* is the right word. I like to say we worked together. Certainly that was how the cops saw it."

"And you watched him rob a bank?"

"Mostly I observed the post-robbery phase."

"And I'm supposed to believe this?"

"Might as well. Can't see as you have anything better to do at the moment."

He slid back against the hard-shell chair. "Okay. Proceed."

"Can't. Visiting hour's up. Guard's heading this way."

"Then bail me out!"

"No, thank you. I'll be back tomorrow. I'll continue the story then. If you're interested."

His grandfather left. He drifted through three tasteless, high-carb meals, a fitful night, and twenty-three hours of complete boredom, painting imaginary murals on vomit-green walls, waiting to hear what happened next.

His grandfather returned the next day, as promised. He was never happier to see the old man in his entire life.

———

When that sheriff laid his hand on my shoulder, I didn't know what to do. Everything happened too fast. One minute I was being insulted by the doctor—that's who the high-handed, well-dressed man was—and then the bank got robbed, and Pretty Boy Floyd tossed a big wad of bills into my hand. I could see where the sheriff might be confused as to my role in the affair. I was fairly confused myself.

"Arrest?" That was the cleverest response I could muster. "For what?"

"Grand larceny." I didn't recognize the sheriff, but he looked pretty much like every sheriff I'd ever known—a little on the short side and more than a little overweight, pocketing chewing tobacco under his lower lip and strutting in a way that suggested that he didn't go into law enforcement because he wanted to help his fellow man.

"I was just standing here."

"Looked to me like you were an accomplice before and after the fact. Probably scouted it out for him. Maybe created a diversion, watched the getaway car. And then he gave you your cut. Hell, you even gave him directions. Why'd you do that if you're not an accomplice?"

I shrugged. "My ma taught me to be courteous." He removed the handcuffs from his belt.

I shouldn't have done this next bit. But I knew after he clicked those cuffs over my wrists I'd be trapped. And I knew my sister would starve to death and no one would help her. So I did a dumb thing.

I shoved the sheriff and ran.

"Stop!" he shouted, regaining his footing. "Someone stop that bank robber!"

I raced back to the general store, but Callie was gone. Where could she be? I looked all ways at once, but I didn't see her. I did, however, spot a whole mess of men running my way. Some of them carried guns.

I turned the other direction, not noticing what came out of the general store.

And that was why I ended up getting clubbed over the head. Maybe I was still weak and woozy from the previous beating, I don't know. I like to think so. But all it took was one good shot and everything got real dark and fuzzy. I fell to my knees and the lights went out before my head even hit the ground.

———

I woke up not knowing where I was and wishing I hadn't been quite so rude to that man at the general store.

My head was thick and my eyesight blurry. But it didn't take me long to realize that I was in jail. Maybe I had a vestigial memory of being arrested, not to mention my pathetic attempt to escape, which made the hoosegow the likely place to awaken. Maybe I felt the rawness on my wrists where the cuffs had been. Maybe I sensed the presence of the locked door.

I detected a noise from the other side of the cell. I was not alone.

I tried to focus my eyes. He was a small guy, thin and wiry. Not unhealthy, not starved. But definitely slender. Had a long, drawn face and a way of staring at something that looked like he was trying to poke holes through it with heat rays. At this particular moment, his gaze was focused on a checkerboard propped up on a barrel.

I stretched, started to rise—but that hurt too much. I waited for the kid to say something, but he never did. So I decided I would be the one to break the ice.

"Been here long?"

At first, I got no response. After some time, he looked up, squinting slightly, and shook his head almost imperceptibly. And then he went right back to staring at those checkers.

I tried again. "What'd they get you for?"

The corner of his mouth turned upward. His lips sort of stuck out, not quite pursing. My impression was that he was annoyed at the interruption, but could see we were stuck in here together, so he honored me with a reply.

"Haven't told me yet."

That was a response I did not expect. Nor did I like its implications. I decided to change the subject to something more important. "How long have I been out cold?"

"You slept through the night. Sun just came up."

I couldn't believe it. What had Callie been doing all that time? Had anyone fed her yet? "You seen a young girl? Fourteen, sandy-blond hair, real skinny?"

He shook his head.

Not that I particularly wanted Callie to turn up in the jailhouse. But I wondered what happened to her after the sheriff collected me. I liked to think some kindly bystander might've taken her in, but that didn't seem probable. And she was so starved, I didn't think she could last much longer.

I had screwed up royally. About ten seconds after I swore I'd take care of her, I didn't even know where she was.

"The sheriff here somewhere?"

"Had a meeting. He'll be back."

I nodded my head toward the checkers. "You any good?"

He pulled his arms tighter around that skinny frame. "Best there is."

Now that's the sort of statement that you'd think, if a man made it at all, he'd make with a big grin on his face, to show he was being tongue-in-cheek. Or he'd give you a sort of challenging look, to show he meant business and if you cared to play against him, he'd mop the floor with you. But this kid didn't do any of that. His expression was flat and dry. Almost as if he didn't have emotions, least not about this subject. He was simply stating a well-known truth, like the law of gravity or something. Seemed to me he must be a seriously stuck-up so-and-so, especially given that he could barely be bothered to look up at me.

Maybe this kid was the best player in the panhandle. But he wasn't likely to survive long against a man who got his education in Massachusetts. Might do him some good to get taken down a peg or two. "I'm pretty salty at checkers myself. How about a game?"

His eyes did not move one inch from the board. "Not playing checkers."

"Well, I can see that you are."

"Playing chess."

Did that kid think I didn't know the difference between checkers and chess? "I can see that you're playing checkers."

"I'm using the checkers to play chess. The sheriff doesn't have a chess set."

"How can you play chess with a checkers set?"

"You assign each checker a chess piece." He pointed. "That one's a bishop. That one's a rook."

They all looked the same to me. "But after you start moving them around, how can you remember which is which?"

"I just remember."

This kid was either pulling my leg or he was a tad smarter than I first suspected. Another thing I noticed when I took a closer look—every time he picked up one of those checkers, his hands shook a little.

"You nervous?" I asked.

"Not especially."

"Got a name?"

"Yes."

"Care to share it?"

He hesitated. "People call me Hart."

"George." I offered him my hand, but he didn't see it.

"George Earle. I'm just here for a funeral. I go to school out in Massachusetts."

For the first time, I'd said something that captured his attention. "You're a college man?"

"Boston Tech. 'Bout to graduate. Got into town yesterday."

"How's your visit so far?" he asked, without the slightest trace of irony.

"Could be better."

"Wait till the sheriff strips you down and searches you. You'll think the rest of the day was a picnic."

"Now why would he want to do that?"

"I think he enjoys it."

My whole mouth went dry. I was starting to sense just how much trouble I'd gotten myself into. "What do you do? When you're not playing checkers-chess behind bars?"

I saw that odd, pursed expression again. "I'm a literary agent."

"What the hell is that?"

"I'm a professional representative for authors."

"You mean, you make up stories?"

His eyes darted away. "I don't write them. I sell them. I represent Edward H. Conrad."

"Who's that?"

"Only the best yarn-spinner alive today. You heard of Robert E. Howard?"

"Can't say that I have."

"Conan the Barbarian? Kull the Conqueror? Solomon Kane?"

"Don't ring a bell."

"Well, Edward H. Conrad writes like that. Only a thousand times better. My client writes a series of stories set in another world. You don't know if it's the past or future, this planet or some other. You just know everything's different. So the possibilities are endless. Emerson Babylon, that's what the lead character's called. His stories are hot as blazes. He's like the Tom Mix of pulps. His stories've been featured on the cover of *Weird Tales* three times. Once he even got the cover illustration."

I decided I could meet my new acquaintance halfway. "You ever read anything by that Burroughs fella? The one who wrote *Tarzan*?"

"Of course. He's the progenitor of the whole genre."

"Read any of those John Carter stories?"

"Best work Burroughs has ever done. An American Civil War veteran transported to Mars to settle their civil war. Burroughs has a good imagination, though his prose style is leaden. You read his latest?"

"Are you joking? I'm studying engineering." I paused. "But I've heard some of my fraternity brothers discuss them."

"Too bad for you. Barsoom is an interesting place. Getting better with each installment."

I'd never in my entire life heard another soul say the word *Barsoom* out loud. Till now. "That's just kid stuff. Make believe."

"Is it?" He nodded toward the barred window. "Looks pretty much like old Barsoom right outside this window."

He was thinking the same thought I'd had the moment I stepped off the train. But of course, I was too proud to let on about that. "I think maybe you need to see the world as it really is. It's not like in those storybooks."

"I know plenty about the world as it really is," he replied. "Don't need lessons from anyone else."

"Your pa gonna bail you out?"

"My pa died a long time ago."

"Mine passed away, too," I said quietly. "Dust pneumonia got him. What took yours?"

"His revolver."

I decided not to pursue.

I heard a rattling at the door and saw the sheriff enter, the same bloated good ol' boy who tried to arrest me. And I guess later succeeded.

"Glad you're awake," the sheriff said. "I got some news for you."

"Look, Sheriff, this here's a mistake. I didn't know those bank robbers. Never seen them before in my life."

"Well, I got about twenty eyewitnesses that seen you working with them and getting paid for your trouble."

"They're mistaken. I just got into town."

"I know. But that doesn't mean you couldn'ta been consprin' with Pretty Boy. Maybe you came to town for the express purpose of helping him out."

"Sheriff, I'm a college man. I'm about to get my degree. You can't charge me with bank robbing."

"Don't plan to."

"Then let—"

"Just came from the doctor's. That poor teller who got shot while your friends were making their escape? He died. Real sudden like."

Goosebumps tingled all over my body.

"So I expect you know what that means, being a college man and all. You're gonna be charged with felony murder. I expect to see you dangling from the end of a rope inside of a week, soon as the circuit judge shows up." He tipped his hat toward me. "Enjoy the rest of your day, you hear?"

seven

"MURDER?" I couldn't believe what I heard. "I was just trying to get some food for my little sister."

"Sure." The sheriff tucked his thumbs under his holster. "And your cell buddy just borrowed that car to take his sainted mother to the hospital. Ain't that right, son?"

"I needed to see someone," the kid mumbled.

"And who would that be? Your druggist?"

The kid ignored him.

"Sheriff," I said, "do you know what happened to my sister? She needs some tending."

"Tending? Looks to me like she's about to die."

I threw myself forward, clutching the bars. "You've seen her? Is she okay?"

"She ain't dead yet. But she ain't et, either."

"You gotta get her some food."

"No, I really don't."

"You can't make this thing stick. No one's gonna believe I helped those robbers."

"You've been away too long, son. You don't know how scared people are around here. Or how little they appreciate someone stealing what money they've managed to hold on to. But even if the bank robbin' charge don't fly, guess what? I sent a man around to check out your house. Know what he found? A corpse."

I felt my heart race. "My pa died of the dust pneumonia."

"You would say that. But what a coincidence he turns up dead the day you come back to town. I heard tell there was some bad feelings between you and your pa. Guess those stories were true." He turned his back and headed toward his desk. "One way or the other, son, you're gonna hang."

I felt like frozen sludge replaced the blood in my veins. I couldn't help Callie. I couldn't even help myself. "Please, Sheriff. I can't get hanged. I gotta take care of my sister. There must be some way outta this mess. I'll do anything. Anything you want me to do."

The sheriff gave me a sharp look. "You mean that?"

"'Course I do. You just ask."

The sheriff took off his ten-gallon hat and spun it around in his hands. "Wait right here. Back in a minute."

He returned about twenty minutes later, jingling his keys. "Guess what, boys? We're goin' on a little field trip."

Hart looked up from his checkers. "Both of us?"

"You got it."

"And if I choose not to go?"

"You know, they can hang people for car stealing, too, if the judge is in a sour mood."

"Fine, I'll go."

The sheriff handcuffed us, then put shackles around our legs and chained us together. Then he locked the chain to the end of a long pole. Said the last few people in that cell had lice—like most of the folks in town—and we might've picked some up. Didn't seem too concerned about us, he just wanted to make sure it didn't spread to him. So he pulled us along at a distance, like dogs on a leash. Made it hard to walk, but I thought it might not be advisable to complain. I wasn't so fond of that cell, and I figured that as long as we were walking, he might forget about that strip search.

"See that dirt comin' in?" the sheriff said, pointing at the sky as we stepped through the front door. "That's from Kansas. I can tell because it's black. Black as night. Comes in gray from Colorado or New Mexico. Red, of course, is pure Oklahoma."

We walked down the road in the opposite direction from my house. I noticed as we passed that all the crops in the fields were laid flat, just like I'd seen on the other side of town.

"What happened?" I ventured, trying to be sociable. "When I left four years ago, people were getting rich off the land."

He let out something like a bitter chuckle. "The new agriculture changed everything. Old-timers went from working a few acres by hand to having huge wheat estates, using them big miracle machines to handle their harvest. Making ten times their costs in profits."

He swore under his breath. "Damn fools should've known that couldn't last forever. All those suitcase farmers came to town gambling on the wheat harvest. Trying to hit a crop, they'd say. And before long the whole prairie lost its carpet. Then prices crashed. So the suitcase farmers went home, leaving the land stripped. Then the drought started. Soil got hard and the wind blew that loose dirt all over creation. No more sod to hold it in place, see. So we got them dust clouds, like big mountains floating in the air. Farming went from easy to impossible almost overnight. Foreclosure sales were everywhere—except no one would bid, 'cause they were afraid their neighbors would hang 'em. So the bank ended up with a lot of property and the people ended up broke."

"And the crops are no better this year?"

"Static electricity killed the crops this year," the sheriff explained. "We tried to bring in water to fix the drought, but we didn't see the static electricity problem till it was too late. Nobody's got enough savings to survive so many bad crops. Ain't no family can survive forever on cornmeal and milk—if they can get that."

"Isn't FDR doing something to help?"

"Last year the government rolled in those New Deal programs. Rubs a good man wrong to be taking charity, especially when he's been the breadwinner his whole adult life. But most had no choice. Relief checks, food handouts, whatever they could get. Government bought up a bunch of cattle that were starving anyway. Sent a man out to teach folks about them so-called conservation techniques, but I'm not sure many were listening. They went right on planting crops, even though the ground looked like a desert."

"That's why I went to college," I offered as we walked. "I didn't want my living to be dependent on the weather."

"You might've made a smart move there. Folks gave up, eventually. Some packed it up and headed for California, hoping to find some way of making ends meet. Folks'd pack everything they got onto broken-down trucks. We've lost 'bout a fourth of our population that way. Churches, banks, schools, all boarded up. I read ten thousand people a month move out of the Great Plains. They say it's the largest migration in American history."

"That's why the telegraph office is boarded up."

"Randolph took his family west. Heard he died about three months later. Got caught in one of those big dirt storms. Couldn't escape, couldn't find shelter. So he drowned in dirt."

I thought about that for a moment—but I wished I hadn't. "That how you ended up sheriff?" I asked, as it seemed fairly clear he had not made a career of it. "You one of them failed farmers?"

"I was a doughboy, back during the War. A hero, or so they said. Not that it put any food on the table. So I tried my hand at cattle farming. Had three hundred and twenty acres of land. A windmill pumping water out of the Ogallala Aquifer into storage tanks. My cows drank the water and ate the grass. Had chickens, too, and a little garden where I raised turnips. I did good for a spell. Till the grass disappeared and the beef market disappeared."

He gazed off into the distance. "Then I ran for sheriff. Wouldn't have made it but for the doctor. Thank the heavens for men like Doc Bennett. Or maybe I should just say for Doc Bennett period. 'Cause he's the only man like him left in this neck of the woods."

"Only man like what?"

The sheriff's eyes gleamed. "Rich."

Doc Bennett's house was something to behold. Big two-story spread-out affair with a huge wide-open front lawn. It rivaled some of the nicest houses I've ever seen, even up on Beacon Hill. Had balconies on the upper stories and a great big patio. And it was made of brick, not cast-off lumber. Real red-dirt brick.

The thing that made that house seem most special, though, was the flower garden. Right here in the middle of the Dust Bowl, that man had a garden. He kept it inside a hothouse, a clear glass outbuilding, to protect it from the dirt and the wind. He had two black men taking care of the plants, watering and trimming them. The walls were stacked with potting soils and plant foods. I couldn't help but wonder how much this little indulgence cost.

What kind of person would spend all that money on pretty flowers while his neighbors starved to death?

The sheriff entered as though he was expected, tugging us along on his little leash. That place swarmed with servants. I imagine Doc Bennett could get them cheap, given the circumstances. A maid dusted silver doodads on an end table while three other servants cleared dinner plates. A couple more stood at attention. I never figured out what they were supposed to do. Maybe just stand there and look impressive.

An older woman, perhaps in her late fifties or so, sat on the davenport just inside the big bay window. I thought I smelled alcohol on her breath, and that was saying quite a bit, since she sat a good ways off from me. Her hands jittered, even more than Hart's, and her makeup was uneven. I never understood all the things a woman does to her face, so I can't really go into the details. But I do know that when the woman put her face on that morning, she got it wrong.

There was another female in the room, a tiny slip of a thing. She was everything Callie was not—flush-cheeked, clean, even a little plump. She didn't say a word the whole time I was there, didn't even make a sound. She almost seemed to recede into the folds of her armchair. Her hair was flipped forward so it covered the better part of her face. I got the distinct impression she didn't want to be there. I wasn't entirely sure she wanted to be anywhere. We stood in the parlor for a painful length of time. The sheriff acted as if he was supposed to be there, but I saw nothing that validated his opinion. Finally I heard an outside door slam followed by footsteps on the hardwood floor.

The sheriff tipped his hat. "Morning, Doc."

Imagine my surprise when the doctor turned out to be that geezer I met downtown and tried to hit up for a loan. Imagine my even greater surprise when he didn't appear to realize we'd met before. Did the man never even look at me?

"Howdy-doo, Sheriff."

I thought before Bennett was unseasonably overdressed, given the weather and the dust and all. Now I realized why he dressed up so.

Because he could. And he wanted everyone to know it.

He was all heated up about something. I could see it in his flushed cheeks and wild eyes.

"Sheriff, do you know what an African tiger lily is?" He spit into a nearby spittoon.

"Mmm, some kinda flower?"

"One of the rarest flowers in the whole wide world. And one of the hardest to cultivate." His eyebrows danced up and down. "But I got me one. Bloomed right out there in the greenhouse this morning. Prettiest thing you ever saw in your life."

"Well now," the sheriff said, "I believe I'd like to take me a gander at that." I wasn't sure if he meant it or if he was just humoring the old codger. "Never seen nothing that come from so far away like that."

"You're too late," the doctor said, holding up his hand.

"Thing about the African tiger lily is, it only blooms for one hour. You feed it and nurture it and pamper it like a newborn baby all year round—and then it gives you one hour of exquisite pleasure. You can see why it's so rare."

Who the hell wanted to spend his time raising a flower that's only around for an hour? But I kept my thoughts to myself.

"'Course that orchid did a lot of good in this world," the doctor continued, "even though its time was brief. We got five men employed to look after the greenhouse, working in shifts. And two of them did nothing but watch that orchid. Perhaps that seems extravagant, but it's my way of helping out in hard times. Employ those that's willing to work. Most of these men you hear about in bread lines or taking New Deal charity, they just don't want to work. Expect everything to be given to them. There's always employment for a man who's willing to roll up his sleeves and get his hands dirty. Heck, I had to toil like a slave to get where I am today."

"I know you did, Doc," the sheriff said.

"My father was a barber. Did you know that? Nothing but a plain old barber, one of the most ordinary men ever created by God. He couldn't help me much, and I don't think he tried too hard. But I always knew I was meant to be a great man. I was destined for great things. So I worked my keister off. Took two, sometimes three jobs at a time, picking cotton and driving the school bus and following the harvest. Got into school and made something of myself. Became a public servant, a healer, helping those in need. My Maggie Faye keeps telling me I need to slow down, isn't that what you say, honey?"

The sloshed woman on the davenport raised her glass in an icy salute.

"But I can't slow down when there's those that need me. I've got an obligation to the world. I've been the only doctor in town these past thirty years. Seemed like I spent my whole life running from one operation to the next, working myself to a frazzle."

And getting generously paid for it, I suspected, based on the lavishness I saw around me.

"Then I started a sanitarium for folks with the dust madness. Who knew what a sad business that would turn out to be? The dirt made people plumb loco. I learned to rest in short intervals, using my willpower to shut my body down for a spell. That way, I could go for days without sleep. I did the work of three doctors. And after the dust pneumonia kicked in, I had even more work."

"I think my pa died of that," I ventured.

"I'm sorry to hear that. It's a mean, nasty way to die, dust all through your lungs. It's silicosis, to use the proper medical terminology. Prairie dust has a high silica content. Builds up in a man's lungs and damages the air sacs. Weakens the body's resistance. Coal miners get the same thing. 'Cept it takes years in the mines to build up a bad case of it. Round here, the dust pneumonia can happen in an eye blink."

He lowered his gaze and gave me the once-over. Still didn't see the merest glint of recognition. He sniffed at Hart, too. I didn't know how the kid took the doctor's little oration. He hadn't said a word since we left the jailhouse, and trying to read his facial expression was like trying to decode the Rosetta Stone.

The doctor returned his attention to the sheriff. "The problem with being the man who always helps others is—who's gonna help you when you need a thing or two? You see folks lined up to give me a hand?"

Actually, I saw a mess of servants catering to his every whim, but I guess that wasn't what he meant.

"I'm here to help, Doc," the sheriff said, like the lapdog he was. I never knew what exactly went on between those two. He'd said before he wouldn't have survived but for the good doctor. Did the doc finance his campaign? Slip him money under the table? Send him cheap women from the Sheik of Araby's harem? "You said you needed some men to do a job for you. So I brought you some."

The doctor nodded. "You know my other daughter? Maxine?"

The sheriff's eyes darted to that mousy thing quivering on the high-backed chair.

"No, that's my younger daughter, Stella. Maxie's about thirteen years older." He winked toward his wife, who didn't seem to notice. "We like to take our time about things."

"What's the problem, Doc?"

"Well, Maxie's having a spot of boy trouble."

"Just give me his name. I'll run him right out of town."

"Calm down, Sheriff. See—my little Maxie is with child."

The sheriff cast his eyes down as if the man had just said his daughter was being tortured by Fu Manchu. "I'm so sorry, Doc."

"These things happen. I tried to tell her that boy was no good. I sat her right down and gave her a good talking to. I try to help people like that, giving then the benefit of my wisdom. I explained how hanging out with trash was only going to damage her reputation. People would say she was whoring around whether it was true or not true.' Damn, girl,' I said. 'Cain't you learn nothing from the example your ma and I set for you?'" He sighed heavily. "But sometimes children just don't listen to what's right."

"Ain't that the truth," the sheriff affirmed.

"Anyways, Maxine run off, and for the longest time I didn't know where she was. But yesterday, I got this postcard." He held the card up. The picture looked like a typical town square, and there was green in it. So I knew it wasn't anywhere around here.

The sheriff flipped the postcard around. "Can't make out the location."

"Take a look at the postal mark."

He did. "Oxford, Mississippi."

"Exactly."

"She wrote you. She must want you to come after her."

"You might take the time to read the card before you start theorizing about the case, detective. She didn't write me. She wrote that fool boy of hers. She wants him to come after her.

She's about to have that baby. And she doesn't want to do it alone."

"Is the boy collectin' her?"

"No. I made sure of that. He won't be goin' anywhere for some time." He swiveled around on one heel. All of the sudden, the doc and me were nose-to-nose. "And that, my criminal friend, is where you come in. I want you to fetch my daughter."

The sheriff answered for me. "He will, Doc. I'll see that he does."

"Good. My Maggie Faye wants her whole family home to celebrate her sixtieth birthday. So you've got eight days to find that runaway girl and bring her back home. If you can do that, I'll be very generous. I'll make sure all the charges go away and maybe even help you out a little."

His smile faded. His eyes squinted together. "And if you don't, I'll make sure your dried-up carcass swings from a rope."

eight

I CLEARED MY THROAT. "You want me to get your daughter?"

"You understand the mission perfectly."

"What if she doesn't want to come?"

"I think we can assume she won't. You're going to insist. Forcibly, if necessary."

"Some reason you don't go yourself?"

He tugged at his bolo tie. "I'm getting a little old for hard traveling. And this job needs to be done fast. I hired a detective, but he didn't do nothin' but waste precious time. Tried to hire one of them Pinkerton agents, but they're all busy with labor agitators. They said even if they found her, they couldn't make her come back against her will. I need someone who'll be more insistent. Someone who won't object to breaking rules to get the job done. So who better than criminals? Are you in?"

I thought a moment. I didn't much like being pushed around, but what with the sheriff being his right-hand man, he just might be able to make that hanging threat happen. "Look, I came home for my mother's funeral."

"'Fraid you're gonna have to miss that. Don't worry. We'll make sure she gets buried."

"Right next to your pa," the sheriff added.

"Then I got to get back to school. Finals are coming up soon."

"You know, I admire a man who understands the value of an education," the doctor said. "Went to university in Norman, myself. Didn't need no uppity East Coast school to tell me what I needed to know. You want to hear something I managed to learn?"

Had a feeling I wasn't going to like this much, but I went along with it. "What?"

"A college degree ain't no good to a dead man."

I fell silent. My options here were severely limited. Nonexistent, actually.

"Got a few problems," I said. "I got no money."

"I'll give you all you need and then some."

"No transportation."

"You may have the use of my brand-new Ford Model 48. Take care of her. She's a fine piece of machinery."

"And I got a little sister who's likely to starve."

He pivoted. "Sheriff, could I possibly call upon you to make sure his sister don't starve in the next week?"

"I'll do it."

Doc Bennett smiled. "And if this boy doesn't return by my wife's birthday, kill her."

I swallowed air so fast I actually made a gasping noise.

"But before you do that, Sheriff, round up some of the boys and let them have some fun with her first, will you? No sense in wasting good meat."

My blood stopped circulating and my face felt like stone. The sheriff seemed almost as thrown as I was. "I—sure. I can do that. If you want."

I took a step forward, but the shackles yanked me back. "You better not hurt Callie. You hear me?"

"Or what?" The doctor chuckled. "'Course I'd never hurt anyone. I'm bound by the Hippocratic oath to do no harm." He paused. "I can't speak for what others might do, though."

I bit my tongue and held it all inside.

"I'm not a hard man," he continued. "But I want you to understand that you have absolutely no choice about this situation. You're either gonna do as I say or you and that sister of yours are gonna end up in the graveyard with the rest of your family. Understand?"

"I surely do," I said, staring right back at him. "I'd like to see my sister before I go anywhere."

"I'm afraid that's not possible. No time." He nodded toward Hart. "You and your boyfriend here need to hit the road."

Why would he saddle me with that big-headed twerp? "He ain't my boyfriend. And I don't need his help to—"

"No, I'll come with you," Hart said. I was so surprised to hear his voice I almost jumped. "I don't mind."

"Good attitude, boy. So it's settled then. You bring me back my Maxine." His eyes suddenly got wide, even a little watery. "She's my whole life. Dearest thing in the world to me."

―――

The doctor was as good as his word, at least at that moment. He did give us some traveling money, and he did give us the use of his automobile, one of the nicest traveling machines I ever saw, with five windows and leaf-spring suspension and enough room to fit five people and still be comfortable. The sheriff unlocked the shackles and next thing I knew we were on our way.

Navigation looked easy enough. Travel east and a bit south till we hit Mississippi. But that Ford took some getting used to. I hoped I didn't grind the gears so much I burned out the clutch or tore up the engine. *But then again*, I comforted myself—*this ain't my car.*

At times, the driving was a snap. At other times it was near impossible. When the dust clouds kicked up, it was like driving in a black blizzard. Some of the time I couldn't see more than a few feet ahead. I had to be careful. If I wrecked this traveling machine, we'd never finish our mission in time. For a spell, I hung my head out the window and kept my eye on the ditch just to stay on the road. I was always afraid I might hit someone. Worse, I might plow into one of the dirt drifts, and I knew if that happened, we'd never get free.

I figured the best way to deal with being saddled with an un-wanted partner was to pay as little attention to him as possible. I had to be in charge here, seeing as how my sister's life was at stake. Hart might be okay on a chessboard, but this was real life. We were bound to encounter problems, and a literary agent was unlikely to be much help.

Hart rode in the passenger seat, his eyes fluttering open and shut, like maybe he was half-asleep or daydreaming or thinking about something he didn't care to share. Maybe he just didn't think I was worthy of sharing his thoughts. Sometimes he seemed grumpy or depressed. After several hours of driving, however, I started feeling chatty.

"Boy, that sheriff is one sumbitch, isn't he?" I said. "How does a man like that end up with a badge?"

"He was desperate," Hart replied. "So he took the one job few men wanted, even these days. Sheriff work is dangerous, mostly repossessing farms and throwing people out of their homes. No one wants to do that."

"I think he knows I had nothing to do with that robbery. He needed a patsy to help out his rich buddy."

Hart didn't seem to think it mattered all that much. "The sheriff's been through a lot."

"You mean, losing his cattle outfit?"

"His wife run out on him. Recently."

"Who told you that?"

"No one."

"Then how'd you know?"

"Isn't it obvious?"

I gave him a look out the corner of my eye. "What do you mean?"

"D'you notice those tufts of hair in his left ear? Clearly that man does not live with a woman. He did once, though, or the tufts would be bigger. Socks don't match his uniform, either. Don't even match each other. Something's changed and now he's got no one looking after him."

"That don't mean his wife lit out."

"Notice the ring finger on his left hand? There's a white line at the base. That's where the ring used to be. Hasn't been sunbaked like the rest of his hand."

I wondered if the kid was pulling my leg. "Maybe he left her."

"'Cause he's such a handsome devil he thinks he can do better?"

"Maybe she died."

"No. This happened recently, and if his wife had just died, he wouldn't be working. Judging from his attitude, it hit him pretty bad."

"You're speculating."

"No. But I could. I could speculate that his wife ran off with a younger, more prosperous, better-educated, better-looking man. Which is why he enjoys tormenting a younger, more prosperous, better-educated, better-looking man." He paused. "Case you're wondering, I'm talking about you."

I decided to take the conversation in a different direction. "That true what the sheriff hinted? 'Bout you being a dope fiend?"

"I'm not remotely fiendish."

"You use that marijewana? I saw a movie 'bout that in Massachusetts."

"You shouldn't believe everything you see at the cinema."

"But I notice you ain't answered the question. 'Bout whether you take dope."

Hart waited a long time before answering. His eyes focused on the road ahead—but not really. "I get these moods. Dark, black moods. Don't know what comes over me or what causes them. Just happens. I usually wake up that way, and sometimes they don't go away. And then I do crazy things. Sometimes it gets so bad I just about want to—" He stopped short. "Anyway, I got this drink I make. Little homemade solution with seven percent lithium and a whole lot of cayenne pepper. Seems to help. For a while, anyways."

"If you get these moods so bad, why'd you volunteer so quick to come out on this wayward-daughter hunt with me?"

Again, he hesitated before answering. "Got me out of jail, didn't it? I'm better off when I'm busy. It's when I'm idle that the demons visit."

I didn't really know what he was talking about, but I decided to let it rest, at least for the time being.

———

After a long drive east, we arrived at a town called Boley. It looked about the same as all the other small towns we passed through, except I noticed that every single solitary person we passed on the street had dark skin. Now I don't want you to get the wrong impression. I'd seen men of the Negro persuasion before. Once or twice they passed through Guymon. On occasion I even saw one in Massachusetts. George Washington Carver spoke at our university. But coming across a whole town full of these folk was not an everyday occurrence.

"You know what the story here is?" I asked Hart. He'd demonstrated some predilection for knowledge on arcane subjects.

"This town was founded by freedmen. They used to be slaves of Creek Indians who got forced into Oklahoma—Indian Territory back then—during the Indian removals of the 1830s. Lots of them Indians had slaves. After the War Between the States, the Indians had to let their slaves go free. So a bunch of them settled in small towns here and abouts."

"Don't look like that's worked out all that well."

"Boley was the most prosperous Negro city in the country for a long time. But this Depression hurts them just like everyone else. Crop failures do not discriminate based upon race or religious affiliation. I hear the whole town is on the verge of bankruptcy."

"Can a town take bankruptcy?"

"Apparently so."

"That's a shame." I pointed down the road a stretch. "There's a station. We can stop and get fuel."

I pulled the Ford over and used the good doctor's money to gas up. We attracted a fair amount of attention from the black attendants and a few other rubberneckers. This auto was bright and shiny, and I imagine those folks had rarely seen a machine of its quality. I hate to admit it, but I may have even preened a bit, happy to let those onlookers believe I was the actual owner of that first-class vehicle.

Hart went inside the station while I stretched my legs and relieved myself. When I returned, I found a black man standing by the car.

"Afternoon," he said, tipping the little cap he wore. "My name's Sneed. Jack Sneed."

"Pleasure," I replied, more than a mite reserved, cautious till I knew what he was about.

"I wondered if you might be interested in participating in a game of chance?"

"And what game would that be?"

"That choice is yours. We have many possibilities. Poker. Keno. Kings Solitaire. Three-card monte. The poke board. Blackjack."

"You make much money that way?"

"Have to supplement my income where I can. Gas don't bring in like it used to. Most folks are traveling west, not east. Going to California, not Arkansas. I don't make much off my gas anymore. 'Course, it ain't really a matter of how much I make. Just so's I have a job. So the cops can't pick me up for vag."

"For...?"

"Vagrancy. Been hauled in for that twice, before I came to Boley. Lot friendlier to colored folks here than they are in the rest of the world."

Having been recently arrested myself, I felt sympathetic. "Where'd you get nabbed?"

"Just north of here. Liberal, Kansas. I was rooting around the train station, looking for some scraps of food someone might've tossed away. Bulls cuffed me and dragged me to jail. First time I got four months on a chain gang. Hard labor. Second time was worse."

"What happened the second time?"

"After I cooled in jail for a week, they dragged me in front of this fat-ass judge for what they called an arraignment. Supposed to set my bond, which it didn't matter what amount was set 'cause I couldn't have paid two cents. Them Long Island Railroad bulls told a lot of lies about me and said I was no good for anything but Negro toe-tapping."

He drew in his breath, then slowly released it. "So the judge told me to dance."

"Right in the courtroom?"

"He pointed that gavel at me and directed me to dance, then and there."

I could feel his shame like sunlight on a summer day. "What'd you do?"

He looked down at the dirt. "What could I do? I put this big stupid grin on my face, and I danced. Judge let it go on for several minutes, everybody in there laughing their heads off, till he finally said I could stop."

"And then he let you go?"

"Hell, no. Sent me back to jail for two months." He pulled his cap off and wiped his brow. "You sure you don't want to take a stab at the poke board?"

I was startled by the transition. "Thanks for the offer, but my friend and I are in a hurry."

"Your friend is inside playing a game with my partner."

This was alarming news, not to mention irritating. I hadn't wanted to bring Hart along in the first place, and here he was slowing me down already. "Show me."

Jack took me inside the filling station, then through the back door. We walked for a fair amount till we came to the side of a small mound.

"This here's our home," he said, with an uncommon degree of pride.

Their home was a dugout, and by that I mean a home carved from the surface of the prairie. The walls were boards, mostly scrap planks. There was no insulation, though someone had smeared black tar on the outside.

Following Jack, I crawled inside. They heated the place with an old iron stove. Took one whiff to realize that on cold nights they used cow chips for fuel.

I saw Hart hunched over another barrel, staring at a board. Wasn't checkers this time, though. The board was bigger, and it had little pebbles scattered across it.

"Not so bad a place, is it?" Jack fairly beamed. "I pour boiling water on the outside every now and again to keep the fresh-hatched bugs down. There's a hole not too far from here where we get water."

"Sounds like you've made do," I commented. "Man does what he must."

"He does indeed."

The fella sitting across the board from Hart appeared to be an Indian. I could tell from that sunburnt quality to his skin, although he was made out more or less like anyone else, except his hair was longer.

Hart did not look up when I entered. As before, his concentration focused entirely on the board.

The Indian rose to his feet and extended his hand. "Name's Mo. Folks call me Little Mo."

I thought this unlikely, since he weighed at least two hundred and fifty pounds and towered over me by almost a foot. But it was not for me to argue with someone about his name.

"The Mo is short for Geronimo. I'm related, distantly."

"I've heard of that character."

He nodded sadly. "I'm related to Sitting Bull, too."

"Do tell."

"They're from different tribes, but that don't matter. My grandpappy got around a good deal. You know, Sitting Bull predicted this land would get revenge on the whites, for forcing the Indians off the grasslands. Guess that prediction came true, don't you think?"

I did not offer an opinion.

He continued. "You must be George."

"Well . . . yes."

"Hart told me you two boys were traveling together."

Hart still hadn't looked up from the board.

"I hope you aren't getting impatient," Mo continued. "I've been working on this little problem for days. Haven't been able to solve it yet. Hart volunteered to give me a hand. Could I get you something? Maybe a Nehi Orange?"

"I'm fine, thank you. We need to be moving along. We got a deadline."

"I know. That's why I asked my partner Jack to bring you in."

I thought about the situation for a moment. "So you and Jack here are business partners?"

"That's right. Both our families have been in Boley some time, not like those suitcase farmers looking for a quick profit. Of course these hard times have hit us like everyone else. We couldn't pay for a business investment like this station alone. That's when Jack hit on the idea of teaming up. That's the only thing that's kept us going."

"Which is not to say we're getting rich," Jack added. "But we haven't been driven off by the banks yet."

"And that is a blessing."

I was trying to work this arrangement out in my head without saying the obvious. One of them was black and the other was red. Some folks I knew wouldn't have worked with either of them. But they seemed altogether chummy.

"And . . . this partnership worked out okay?"

Little Mo nodded. "Our families have known each other a long time."

Jack chuckled. "That's right. We go way back."

My forehead creased. "How far back?"

"My family used to work for his family," Jack replied.

"What kind of work?"

Jack slapped Mo on the back. "Whatever it came into their minds to request. My grandfather was a slave. And his grandfather owned him."

"He *owned* your grandpappy?"

"That's right."

"And you don't have any hard feelings about this?"

"Don't much see the point in that, do you? You can't change the past."

"You can, however, change the future," Mo added with a wink. "And that's what we're doing."

"Got it!" Hart sat upright, a small smile on his face. These were the first words I'd heard him speak since I came into the dugout.

Mo's eyes widened. "You're joshing me."

"Nope." Hart reached across the board, picked up one of the small stones, and moved it to a different position on the board, a mesh of intersecting lines. "See?"

I didn't understand what was going on, but that Indian looked at the board like Mother Mary was rising out of the barrel. "That's—incredible."

"Really very simple," Hart said, "once you view the board from a different perspective."

"I've been trying to solve this problem for weeks."

Hart shrugged.

"I'm a mite confused," I said. "I gather this is not some kinda gambling game?"

"Your friend is too smart to fall for those fiddles. So I challenged him to solve this Go problem. Thinking it insoluble."

"Did he win something?"

"My undying gratitude."

"Swell."

"The gratitude of a Creek warrior is a treasure more valuable than gold."

"No doubt. Where did this Go come from?"

"The Orient."

So I had a redskin and a black man playing a Chinese game. This was a part of Oklahoma I had not seen before. "I'm not quite understanding how it works."

"Do you know Mahjongg?"

"Game them old Jewish ladies play?"

"Uh, yeah . . ."

"Don't know anything about it. 'Cept those tiles look pretty."

"Familiar with chess?"

"Some. Is this like chess?"

"Except about a thousand times harder."

"Harder than chess? And you consider this entertaining?"

"For what it's worth," Jack said with a sideways grin, "I'm in your camp. Give me a good stick to whittle and I'm entertained just fine."

Mo laid his hand on Hart's shoulder. "Sir, you are a noble strategist."

Hart shrugged again. "It's just a game."

"And you're a grandmaster who has given me the benefit of your wisdom. I must repay the debt."

"We're pressed for time."

Mo extended his flat palm. "I insist. I will show you the Way of the Arrow."

The Way of the Arrow, as you might have guessed, turns out to be an elaborate name for archery lessons. Which I might've enjoyed under different circumstances, when there was less urgency to our situation.

It didn't help that Hart had so much trouble handling the bow. To be fair, Mo gave him the biggest bow I'd ever seen in my life. It was almost bigger than Hart, and I didn't get the impression the kid had firmly developed arm muscles, since they were primarily occupied with lifting game pieces. He gave it a valiant effort, but every time he lifted the bow, his arms shook and the bow went all wobbly. He hadn't fired anything, and I thought it was just as well.

"Let the Spirit of the Earth infuse you, just as it fills this bow," Mo said. "You and the bow are one and the same. You are connected to it. It melts into your hands and courses through your body."

Which sounded good, but didn't steady Hart's hand one bit.

"Now forget about the bow," Mo continued. "Think only of the target. Block out everything else. Your inner spirit, the one that sees all, is focused upon that target. Close your eyes."

"Close his eyes when he's aiming?"

Mo shushed me. "Close your eyes."

Hart complied.

"And when nothing else exists for you but that target, release the arrow."

A few seconds later, Hart did exactly that. The arrow shot out sideways, closer to me and Jack than the tin can he was trying to hit. We both jumped aside. The arrow struck the back bumper of the doctor's Ford.

"Lord a'mighty, you could've punctured that tire!" The time had come for me to take a firm hand and end the lesson. "Come on, Hart. Time to go."

Hart didn't budge. He had an unpleasant expression on his face.

Mo laid his hand on Hart's shoulder. "What troubles you, my intelligent friend?"

He shook his head. "Nothing."

Mo peered deeply into his eyes, even though Hart looked away. "The black crow rests heavily with you."

"What is that supposed to mean?" I asked.

Mo ignored me. "What is the source of this blackness? Why does it haunt you so?"

Hart shrugged off his hand. "We got to move along."

"I am sorry to hear this. I wish we had more time together. I do not know if I could help you. But I derive great pleasure from your presence. If I can help you at any time, you have only to call."

"There's no need for that." I pulled Hart away from him.

"I am always pleased to see two handsome young men traveling through life together. I know Jack has made my hard life kinder and warmer. I hope the two of you will find the same."

What the heck was that supposed to mean? I decided we didn't have time to ask. I thanked Mo politely and a few minutes later we were on our way.

"Never did understand much about that Indian mythology," I commented as I drove. "The Great Spirit and all that hocus-pocus. Kinda far-fetched."

"But you believe that Jesus walked on water," Hart replied. "And that he raised Lazarus from the dead. And that he rose from the dead himself, after spending several days in Hell."

"That's all recorded in the Bible. A history book. But the Indians don't have anything written down."

"So if something's written, it must be true?"

"If it's the Word of God."

"The Mormons believe Jesus came to America after he was crucified and spent time here converting the savages."

"Well, that's clearly bunkum."

"But it's written down in their book. Which they consider the word of God."

"That ain't the Bible."

Hart hunkered down in his seat and slid his cap forward. "I wonder sometimes if it's possible all these religions are just different roads leading to the same destination. And perhaps what matters is not so much which road you choose as that you choose one." He closed his eyes. "That you find some means of easing the burden."

"I think you need a good tent revival," I suggested.

That kid just grinned. "Perhaps I do."

nine

WE DIDN'T STOP AGAIN for several hours. Far as I was concerned, Hart had already wasted too much valuable time, so once I had him back in the Ford, I never gave him a chance to get out. The more we traveled east, the more the dust let up, which made it easier to travel. Still didn't move as fast as I would've liked, given that my sweet sister's life depended on our meeting a fast-approaching deadline. By late afternoon, we were still in Oklahoma, just coming near the Arkansas border.

We didn't need gas yet, but I thought we should take this opportunity to fill up while we had a chance. Hart went looking for a place to make water. I heard a commotion of sorts coming from just up the road, so I gave it a look-see while I waited for Hart to return. Wandered into what must've been the town square. A big man leaned against the rail of a gazebo. He attracted a good-sized crowd, and they appeared extremely interested in what he said.

"No, sir," the man said, moving about the gazebo with smooth efficiency so he could speak to the folks standing on all four sides of him. "Why would I dare to mention rain, and the lack of rain, and the need for more rain, if I didn't think I could do something about it? Do you think I don't know how hard you folks have been hit by this drought?"

He paused, but if he was expecting an answer, he didn't get one. "No, ladies and gentlemen, I don't need to be told what is obvious to every living soul. How many years has it been since this dry spell began? Three failed crops? Four? I can see the dead wheat fields. I can see the children standing on the side of the road with their hands out. I can feel the dust blowing into your eyes and your mouth and your throat. And what is the cause of all this pain and suffering? What is it that we sorely need but do not have?"

"Rain," a few tepid voices answered.

"Yes, sir, you are exactly and precisely correct. Problem is, no one knows how to make rain. No one, that is," he said, doing a little circle to face all four sides, "except me."

"You can make rain?" some poor rube in bib overalls shouted.

"I can."

"And how much would you charge for this service?"

"Charge?" The speaker pressed his hand against his chest as if offended. "Does the sun charge for shining? Does a mother charge for feeding her young? Does God charge when he brings down his blessings?"

I thought that comparing himself to the sun, motherhood, and God was perhaps a trifle on the arrogant side, but the folks listening didn't seem to have a problem with it.

"You'll do it for free?" a man in the front row asked. He cooperated so kindly that I began to wonder if those two might be in cahoots.

"I will. I don't expect to make anything for doing my duty to my fellow man. I just need your permission, that's all. Your permission and your cooperation."

A matronly woman to his north spoke. She seemed more dubious about this business than the rest of the crowd. "How do we know your method will work?"

"My method? Dear lady, did I ever say anything about this being my method? I don't think so."

"Well then, who—"

"The secret to making rain is almost as old as antiquity itself. How do you suppose civilization has survived so long, dependent as we are on the earth to nurture and nourish us? In ancient Greece, Plutarch noticed there was always rain after a great military battle. The great emperor Napoleon observed the same phenomena. In fact, he had his men fire their cannons at the sky, hoping to muddy the ground that lay before his attackers."

The woman squinted. "You're saying you can shoot the rain out of the clouds?"

"No, ma'am. What I am talking about is the power of concussive force. Concussion theory, as the scientists say."

I did not recall ever hearing *concussion theory* discussed in my many scientific classes back in Massachusetts, but I had to admit his spiel was engaging.

"What is concussion theory?" the man continued, at this point asking and answering his own questions. "This is a field of science so valuable that our great Congress in Washington, D.C., has appropriated money for advanced research. FDR himself hopes to spread the word throughout the troubled regions, to the people who need to hear this glorious good news. Secret testing has taken place in Texas."

"Wait a minute." This came from a young man around my age. "I heard about the tests in Texas. They didn't work. That fella Dryrenforth flopped. They started calling him Dry-Henceforth."

That brought some chuckles from the crowd, but the man in the middle kept on talking, not cowed in the slightest.

"You are correct about that, sir. The tests in Texas failed. Because they lacked the secret ingredient. They had explosions. But making good rain requires more than an explosion. The dynamite opens up the clouds, indeed, but then if you want to produce rain, they must be seeded correctly." He paused, building anticipation. "You need a moisture accelerator."

"And where do we find a moisture accelerator?"

The speaker grinned. "Sir, you are looking at one. I have the ingredients. A secret formula of my own devising. Obviously, I cannot reveal the contents, as my patent is still pending, but I can tell you this: My mixture has never failed. Never once. The explosion opens up the clouds, my secret ingredients seed them, and the rain comes tumbling down."

"Well, then," said the first man, "if it's that easy, let's stop yakking and do the seeding."

"That's what I like," the speaker said. "A man of action. May I ask your name, kind sir?"

"Philo Henry Cantrell."

"Well now, Philo Henry Cantrell, I want you to work with me and be part of the miracle that is about to occur. Will you do that?"

"I . . . 'spose I could do that."

"Fantastic."

"What do I got to do?"

"Nothing much. Just get me a kite strong enough to lift about ten pounds of secret ingredient up to the clouds . . . and two pounds of dynamite, then two pounds of solidified nitroglycerin. Simple as that."

"Where am I going to get all those things?"

"I don't specifically know, never having been in this fine town before. But there must be a place."

"I don't think so."

"Then you'll need to acquire them from out of town. But please hurry. We don't want this drought to last any longer than can be avoided."

The man looked both ways around him, but he didn't see any offers of assistance.

"Couldn't you maybe acquire these ingredients for us?"

"I suppose I could," he said, drawing in his breath. "But I would need funding. You may think I am a man of wealth, and I should be, but alas, as so often happens, the world rewards opportunism rather than genius. When a man devotes himself to pure science, mankind is benefitted, but the pocketbook is deprived."

"So, what do we do?"

He slowly released his breath. "You'll need to raise about two hundred dollars."

A buzz rose from the crowd. "

Two hundred dollars?" the woman said. "I thought you said this wouldn't cost us nothing."

"What I said, dear madam, was that I didn't expect to be paid for my services. But dynamite does not grow on trees, nor do load-bearing kites or secret ingredients. If we are to cook this miracle, we must follow the recipe." He paused, laying a hand across his bosom. "But I will take nothing for myself."

A heated debate ensued amongst the townsfolk. Hart still hadn't reappeared, so I listened in, even though I was getting more than a little antsy. The general gist was that everyone thought it sounded worth trying, but no one knew how to raise the dough. Eventually it was resolved that if they all kicked in a buck, the whole town might be able to raise the necessary funds.

"I've got a treasury bond I could cash," the man in overalls said.

"And I've got some change tucked away in the bottom of a sugar bowl," the woman admitted, and before long everyone talked about giving up their life savings to make this miraculous rainfall. It was not until someone started talking about selling his last living goat that a voice behind me chimed in.

"Don't do that. Don't any of you. Don't give this man your money."

I swiveled around.

Hart stood right beside me.

"He's a con man," my companion said. Small though he was, he didn't have any trouble being heard when he put his mind to it. "He can't make rain. You give him your money and he'll be gone before sunup. You'll have no rain, and you'll never see him again."

A quiet hum ran through the spectators.

"Hart," I said quietly, out the corner of my mouth, "what are you doing?"

"Trying to prevent a whole mess of heartache."

"I don't think it's our place to interfere."

"I think it's every man's place to interfere when he sees a great wrong about to be done." He raised his voice. "Don't be tricked, folks. This man wants to cheat you out of your hard-earned dollars and cents."

I expected the speaker to take offense. To my surprise, it was the townsfolk.

"Who are you, anyway? I don't recall seeing you around here before."

"You some kinda Red? Maybe you don't want the drought to end."

"If you're so smart, why don't you tell us how *you're* going to make rain?"

The folks drifted away from the gazebo and circled around Hart like buzzards sniffing carrion. I knew Hart wanted to help, but he'd gone about it in an impetuous and ill-considered fashion. Normally, I wouldn't much care what he did, but in this particular instance we needed to get back on the road. Judging from the expressions on the faces in this crowd, they contemplated an interruption that might put Hart in the hospital for an extended period of time.

"Look now," I said, stepping between Hart and the accumulating throng, "this boy don't mean anything by what he said. He just gets fired up sometimes, like everyone else in these parts these days."

"Can he make rain?" the overalls man asked.

"No," Hart said, "and neither can that man in the gazebo."

"Prove it."

Hart shook his head. "It's your money. If you want to throw it away, I can't stop you."

I could see that remark bothered the man a bit. "You a college boy?"

"No," Hart conceded.

"Well, this man is. Says his name is Big Hugh Braddock. He's an important scientist. Works for the president."

"So he says." Hart shouted toward the podium. "You got your diploma with you? Or any identification?"

"Don't be absurd," the speaker said, but I noticed his voice was not as loud as it had been before.

"Hugh Braddock is a scientist, not a rainmaker." The crowd came in closer, but Hart went on talking. "An important government official wouldn't be running around the plains like a traveling medicine man. How do you know this person is Hugh Braddock? Surely a government man has some proof of who he is."

"That seems reasonable enough," the woman finally said. "How about it? Can we see some identification?"

All eyes turned back toward the gazebo.

But the man who claimed to be Big Hugh Braddock had disappeared.

ten

WE MANAGED to get out of town without further incident. I suppose Hart did those folks a favor, but I cautioned him about taking any further actions that might endanger our mission. This might be an entertaining outing to him, but my sister's life was at stake, not to mention mine, so there could be no more risk-taking. His whole attitude irritated me more and more the farther we traveled together. I didn't want him here, but if he planned to stay, he needed to understand that I was in charge.

"And that means," I told Hart emphatically, "no more wandering off, no more talking to strangers, and no more game-playing."

"Can I play my harmonica?"

One of the more annoying aspects of this conscripted partner-ship was that I could never tell when Hart was kidding and when he wasn't.

"Absolutely not."

"You have moral objections?"

"No." I squeezed the steering wheel tighter. "I just can't abide the sound of a harmonica."

We were both hungry, so we stopped at this little diner to get some grub. I ordered black coffee and the beefsteak. I felt somewhat extravagant, having narrowly escaped trouble, and since the good Doc Bennett was picking up the tab. Hart asked for hot tea and the short-order waitress looked at him as if he were from another world. Then he asked if they had any catfish. 'Course the answer was no. Then he asked about some kind of salad. Again, big no. Apparently, he had some problem with eating good red meat. That waitress ended up bringing him a whole mess of vegetables, but her expression suggested she didn't think this was how a man ought to feed himself.

"No wonder you got such a pasty-face countenance about you," I said. "A man's got to get some meat in him. Builds up the body. Puts color in your cheeks."

"Speaking of my delicate appearance, do you have a comb I could borrow?"

I passed him my back-pocket comb, though I doubted it could be all that much help. To my surprise, he didn't improve himself at all. He just stuck the comb into his pocket.

"People judge a man by his appearance," I opined, trying to take the conversation back to topic.

"Sadly, some do."

"Back in Massachusetts, we occasionally get some of those Brit fellas in to teach. A scrawnier pack of ghosts you never did see. Skinny, bad teeth, black circles under their eyes. And you know why? Insufficient cow meat."

"Sounds like you've got it all figured out."

"Just trying to help you."

"Maybe you should focus on helping yourself."

"I'm not the pasty-faced one."

"I'm not the one who got arrested seconds after he stepped off the train."

I pursed my lips. "Ain't my fault the town's got a crooked sheriff. Most police officers are honest, hard-working fellas."

"Do tell."

"If a man keeps his nose straight and follows the rules, he should live a good and prosperous life."

"You raised on Horatio Alger stories?"

"I guess I've read one or two. Why?"

"Just wondered. Now where would I find these rules you're talking about?"

"For starters, the church."

"Which church? They're all different, and they've all got different rules."

"I'm talking about a good, honest, American Christian church."

"American Christian, huh?"

"That's right."

"So does that mean no dancing?"

"My church never saw no sin in dancing."

"A lot of them Baptist churches do."

"Well, they're a tad extreme."

"So you're talking about the rules of the good, honest, American, not-too-extreme Christian churches."

I laid down my knife and fork. "Do you know, you can be extremely exasperating to have a conversation with?"

"I'm just trying to figure out what those rules might be. Are you talking about ethics or morality?"

"What's the difference?"

"Morality is a set of arguably arbitrary rules laid down because some authority says you should behave a certain way, probably because it served the rule-makers' interests at the time they made the rules. Ethics is about behaving a certain way because it's the right way to treat others."

"Well . . . I expect I believe in both of those things."

"I don't."

"You say that, but I noticed you spoke up mighty quick when you thought that rainmaker might cheat those folks out of their cash."

"Those people are all but starving. They don't have money to spare. And if they do, they should spend it on food. Not fraudulent schemes."

"So you do have morality."

"No, I have ethics. Cheating desperate people is wrong, regardless of whether it says so in some old book."

"I just don't understand you at all."

He took a big bite of carrot. "You ever read Nietzsche?"

I'd heard that name bandied about back at college, but I hadn't read him and didn't know much about him. Still, I wasn't going to admit that. "What of it?"

"Nietzsche said that what passes as morality is just a mess of rules concocted by the lowest common denominator to pull everyone else down to their level. Nietzsche believed that some men are above morality. He called them supermen. People smart and superior enough to make their own rules."

"How did that theory work out for Mr. Nietzsche?"

A tiny smile played on Hart's lips. "Not so well, in the end." He shoved a big bite of potato into his mouth. "It seems some rules—or perhaps we should say *guidelines*—become rules for a reason. And it's best to know what the reason is before you go breaking the rule. Which doesn't mean you can't. Just means you need to understand what you're doing before you do it. Or you could end up in some trouble. Like he did."

"Was this Nietzsche one of them queer fellas?"

"And by *queer* you mean . . . ?"

"You know what I mean. One of them boys who likes boys?"

"I don't think so. He died of syphilis." Hart's eyes darted down to his plate. "You ever meet one of them boys who likes boys?"

"I had an ol' queer come up to me in the smoking car on a train once. Quizzed me for five minutes about what I liked to do in my spare time. Next thing I knew, he had his hand on my knee."

Hart's eyes crinkled. "What did you do?"

"Called the conductor and registered a complaint. I think they booted that pansy off the train at the next stop. Headfirst."

"Was he hurt?"

"Don't know."

"You think that queer had feelings?

"Ain't given it much thought. Don't much care."

"You think anyone cares about that queer?"

"It's hard to imagine."

"You think his mama loved him?"

"I reckon she'd have to."

"You think maybe he's got a little brother or sister he loves just as much as you love your sister? Or maybe a sister who loves him back? You think he asked to be the way he is?"

I could see where he was going with this, and I wanted to put an end to it. "I have no sympathy for a man who wants to be with a man. It's unnatural."

"Because it offends your . . . morality."

"It just ain't right."

"*Right* being defined as what you yourself like to do. But anything you don't do or that you don't like, that's unnatural." He tilted his head. "You seemed to get along with Jack and Mo all right."

My eyes fairly bulged. "Are you sayin' those two were—"

He shrugged. "I didn't ask. But the possibility crossed my mind."

"Any time you got a black man and a red man so close together, there's bound to be something strange goin' on."

"Because they're different from you."

I shoved another bite of steak into my mouth. "You are uncommonly challenging to converse with."

"You're not the first to say so. Used to have talks with my daddy that went round in circles forever."

"Your daddy . . . who died?"

"My daddy who killed himself. Right after he tried to kill me." Hart took the last bite, then pushed his plate away. "Damn near succeeded, too."

That slowed me down a bit. "Look, I didn't mean anything unkind. I just lost my pa, so I know how bad that feels. There's some things a man can change, and some he can't, and the sooner you figure that out, the better off you're gonna be, right?"

"You know what Emerson Babylon would say?"

"Who?"

"The main character in those yarns by Edward H. Conrad. The writer I agent for. He's the leader of a band of heroes called the Challengers of the Dust who fight for the downtrodden in the barren deserts of the seventeen civilized planets."

"Okay. What would he say?"

He adopted a heroic tone of voice. "So long as my lungs draw breath and my heart pumps fiery hot blood—nothing is impossible."

"I like that."

Hart smiled. "Me, too."

I was surprised how dark it was when we left the diner. It had been one jam-packed day, but I hoped we could still make it a little farther down the road before we called it quits.

Hart tugged at my sleeve. "Take cover."

"What for?"

The kid pointed at the sky. Blacker than black.

"Rain coming?"

Hart shook his head.

"Tornado?"

Hart's expression got grim in a hurry. "Pestilence."

"What's that?"

"The plague. The fourth horseman."

"What are you talking about?"

Hart ran to the Ford and jumped into the passenger seat. "Get in the car and drive. The locusts are coming."

And barely a second after I slid behind the wheel, the black cloud descended.

eleven

I MANAGED to start the car, but we couldn't get anywhere. The locusts were so thick I couldn't see to drive. I couldn't even see the hood ornament.

"Run for cover!" Hart shouted, but the buzzing of the hoppers was so loud I could barely hear him. More bugs than you ever saw in your entire life.

Those grasshoppers came in waves that blacked out the setting sun. They descended like one big cloud and ate the leaves off the trees and everything else in sight.

I crawled out of the automobile and ran back toward the diner, but the bugs were so thick they knocked me to the ground. I felt like I'd been flattened by a battering ram. My face hit the dirt, and bright lights exploded in my head. It felt like they were eating my face. I understood that bit about the fourth horseman, because this seemed like the Apocalypse. My ma used to quote the Bible with great frequency, so I knew in Deuteronomy it said, "The Lord shall make the rain of thy land powder and dust: from heaven shall it come down upon thee, until thou be destroyed."

I heard birds fleeing, ducking for cover, but I couldn't see anything but those bugs. Tried to get up again, but the locust cloud battered me back down. I had no idea where Hart was. That relentless humming sounded like a buzzsaw inside my head.

For a minute, I thought I would go right off my rocker. Seemed like the bugs stayed forever, eating everything in sight.

Hart told me later the locust cloud hovered about five minutes.

I would've sworn it lasted a couple of days.

When they finally moved on, I rolled onto my back and felt myself from head to toe, trying to make sure nothing vital got eaten. After I convinced myself I was still complete, I limped to the car, dipped my kerchief in the radiator and dabbed it on my face. It was cool and calming and stopped my heart from racing. I figure I wiped six or seven inches of crusted bug goo off my face and lips and out of my mouth. I spit and spit, but I couldn't get rid of the sour taste.

That was when I saw him. On the porch of the diner. Some poor slob laying on his back, his eyes wide open, his mouth even wider. Those bugs had gotten in there and completely suffocated him.

That was the second time I saw a dead man in about as many days. This corpse wasn't my pa, but for some reason, it shook me up even more. There are a lot of ways a man can go to his maker —and this had to be the absolute worst.

I hobbled over to where Hart lay in the dirt. He looked pretty shook up. "You all right?" His face was covered with bruises. I expect that was from the hoppers scratching and biting him.

Hart wiped his mouth on his sleeve. "Any man goes through that and feels all right, there's something wrong with him. Is my face as messed up as yours?"

"My face will never be as messed up as yours."

He snorted. "Your face entered the jail cell more messed up than anything I ever saw. And it's worse now."

"I guess one of Nietzsche's supermen wouldn't've had no problem with this."

"Nietzsche would've had those hoppers for dinner."

"I hope you are joking."

"They are edible, you know. Snap off the head, light a match, stick it up the hopper's rear portions. Makes 'em all crunchy."

"Thank you kindly, but I already ate." I helped him to his feet. About the time he made it upright, I felt him go all stiff. "What's wrong?"

He pointed.

Over by the automobile, I spotted a couple, man and a woman, 'bout thirty or so. They looked as if they might've been prosperous once but fell on hard times. Their clothes were nice but tattered, and their faces weren't as hard-etched as some I'd seen today. The man carried a bedroll on his back with a frying pan tied on top. The woman carried a small suitcase. Not too heavy judging by how easily she carried it. They hovered around our Ford, giving it a long look-over. Didn't take a mind reader from Barsoom to know what they were thinking.

"Don't do anything stupid," Hart said. "You're more important than an automobile."

I wasn't sure what he meant by that, but they were getting much closer to my goods—well, the Doc's goods—than they needed to be. And they didn't look all that intimidating.

"Excuse me, folks," I said, making my way to them. "Can I help you?"

They looked at one another, not exactly startled, but cautious. The man spoke first. "This is one fine automobile you've got."

"Yes, sir. She drives like a dream. Even in a dirt storm."

"I reckon so." Up close, his face appeared grimy and sallow. Big dark circles underlined his eyes. My impression was that he hadn't eaten in a while. "Can you get forty miles an hour on this sweetheart?"

"And then some."

"Man alive. A man could cross this state in a day."

"We just about did," I replied. "Where you folks heading?"

Hart jabbed me in the side. His expression basically said, *Keep your trap shut.*

"We're heading for Oregon State," the man explained. "My Caroline's got some family up there. Thought maybe we could stay with them for a spell, till things smooth over some. Where you heading?"

"East. Oxford, Mississippi." I felt another jab in the side, but I ignored it.

The man pressed his lips together. "That's a shame. We're headed in different directions."

"Looks that way." I glanced at his traveling companion. She was a tiny thing, spindly and nervous. Her fingers knitted together, like she was trying to generate heat. "You okay, ma'am?"

"Our baby's sick," she answered. She wasn't looking at me, though. I don't know who she thought she was talking to. "Our baby's sick, and I don't know how to make him well again."

"Sorry to hear that. Is that baby of yours, um, traveling with you?"

"Doctors say he'll never be well, but you can't believe that. A mother's got to believe in her child. No matter what happens."

"I expect that's right. Anyways, we need to mosey. We're under a tight deadline. So if you kind folks will excuse us—"

And then I heard the biggest, loudest, scariest noise I ever heard in my life—and I'd just come through a locust storm. I'm not even sure I can explain it properly. I've read about those banshee wails over in Ireland. All I can tell you is that it scared the bejesus out of me, and I considered myself a pretty stout character at the shank end of a trying day.

I heard rustling behind the car, and a parting of the bushes them bugs had eaten clean. This tiny figure darted out so quickly it was hard to get a fix on it. All I could tell at first was that it was small and ugly. I thought it was a child, but when it got closer, I saw its face was twisted and dark and gruesome. It's expression seemed fixed in a malevolent sneer. Spittle flew out from between its lips. Warts ran up and down one side of its face.

And when I stopped staring at that ugly little face, I realized the homunculus brandished a fork.

An instant after that, the little bastard drove that fork right into my upper thigh.

I'm not ashamed to say I screamed, just before I tumbled to the ground. That hurt. There's something about the soft fleshy part of a man's leg that doesn't want to be disturbed, and that imp caught me completely by surprise.

After a moment, I pushed back to my feet, grabbed that misshapen dwarf by the neck, and lifted him right off the ground. He swung his fork back and forth, trying to stab me. I held him at arm's length, and my arm was a lot longer than his.

"Put down my baby!"

That was the woman. "Ma'am, if this here's your baby, then I surely do feel sorry for you."

"Put him down right now."

"Ma'am, what he just did is called assault and battery, and I believe he has to be held accountable for his actions."

"I said, *Put down my baby!*"

And then I heard a clicking sound that told me the whole scenario had been kicked up several notches.

She held a service revolver pointed at my face.

I'm not an expert on weapons, but I thought that looked like a keepsake from the Great War. I surmised it had been some time since it had been fired. And I questioned whether it would fire today, or if it did, whether it would hurt me most or her. Still, I thought it prudent not to take any risks.

I lowered the runt to the ground.

"You hurt my baby!" Her eyes watered and her gun hand shook. "You shouldn't't've done that."

The man crawled into the Ford behind the driver's wheel. That humanoid baby of theirs jumped in beside him, practically in his lap.

"You think you can get away with anything," the woman said. "'Cause you're big and strong and you've got money. You need to be punished."

I held out my hands. "Lady, I don't think you want to be

firing that gun. It might blow up in your face." I glanced over my shoulder, wondering where Hart had gone.

"Give him the keys to the auto."

I obliged, thinking that the prudent course of action. Her old man got the auto started. "Sit down, Caroline."

She did not comply. She kept staring at me. I noticed her trigger finger tightened.

"You know you can't get far in that vehicle," I said. "Cops'll be on your tail as soon as you pull out of here."

The man pulled out the clutch. "It'll take at least a day of paperwork before anyone's looking for us. We can make it to Colorado. Then we'll ditch the car and look for some other means of transportation." He glanced to the side. "Get in, Caroline."

"Not till this man has been punished," she said. And that's when I knew she was gonna do it. Hard to explain, but I could see it in her face, her eyes, even the way she held the gun. Somehow, she'd gotten it into her head that I was a threat to her kid—and maybe I was. She was gonna plug me to protect him.

Her fist clenched and her eyes narrowed. "You hurt my baby. You can't do that. I'm gonna give you your punishment." I closed my eyes and waited for the bullet.

twelve

OUT OF NOWHERE, I heard a voice shout. "Cops are comin'!"

I opened my eyes. I knew that was Hart, but I didn't see him anywhere.

"Everybody run! Cops are almost here!"

I listened real hard. It was faint at first, but after a moment I could hear a siren. Used to hear them all the time back in Massachusetts. Guess the cop cars out here had them now, too. The siren got louder and louder till at last it sounded like the cops were almost right on top of us.

"Caroline, get in!" the man shouted. With evident regret, she did as he said. He pressed down on the accelerator and the auto shot down the road. A few moments later, they were out of sight. Hart emerged from the bushes. I noticed he had my comb. I thought this was not a time when a man ought to be worrying about his appearance.

I could see he'd been sweating. Guess he was a little worried about me. "Think we should report the robbery to the cops?" I asked.

"Getting involved with cops is almost never a smart idea, in my experience."

"We have to tell them something."

"No, we don't."

"They're almost here."

"No, they're not."

"I heard the siren."

Hart gave me that shy smile of his. Then he brought the comb to his lips. I saw that it had a little strip of toilet tissue strung through the teeth. He blew into it like it was a kazoo, and damned if he didn't make it sound just like a police siren.

"You did that?"

He shrugged.

"Damn good luck you still had my comb."

"No luck to it. I saw this coming a mile away."

"How could you possibly know—"

"Anybody driving around these parts in a machine like that is asking for trouble. I saw that couple inside the diner. They sat by the window, gazing at that way-too-new-and-fancy car. Didn't take a genius to figure out what was on their mind. Judging from their clothes and demeanor, I surmised they were already on the lam from the cops and the best way to make them disperse, should the need arise, would be to convince them the cops were on their way. So, I borrowed your comb and got a tissue out of the diner's bathroom. When the trouble started, I hid in those bushes so they wouldn't see me."

I placed my hands on my hips. "You're telling me you predicted this whole mess before it happened?"

"It's not a matter of predicting. It's about anticipating possibilities and preparing accordingly." Hart drew in his breath. "Okay, I didn't predict the midget. They left him outside for a reason. But I thought they might try to steal the car and I knew you'd try to stop them. Looked to me like they have a lot more experience on the road than you do which meant they were likely packing heat."

It's probably not fair, but his whole attitude rubbed me the wrong way. "If you're so smart, why didn't you come up with a plan that stopped those crooks *and* prevented them from running off with our automobile?"

"Don't be an ingrate. I saved your life."

I supposed he did at that. "I didn't handle that as well as I might've done."

"Your problem," he didn't mind telling me, "was that you saw a woman and immediately assumed she was all frail and inferior, so you acted gallant when you should've been acting cautious. That conventional morality of yours got you into trouble. Again."

I didn't care to get into it with him. "You know what this means? We're either gonna have to hitchhike, or we're gonna have to walk all the way to Oxford, which is unlikely to get us there in time."

"I know that."

"You don't seem too upset about it. These circumstances have got me a bit depressed."

"Welcome to my world."

"We're not gonna catch a ride now that it's dark. We might as well start walking." I pointed my shoes and headed down the road. He followed. We'd traveled a fair distance before I spoke again. "I guess that Nietzsche fella would've known that gal was trouble, right?"

"Oh, Nietzsche would've probably given her anything for a quick one in the bushes."

"He was a horny little egghead?"

"You could say that."

"Well. A man's got needs."

"Indeed."

⸺

Some time later, around midnight, I was done with walking. My legs were worn out. It had been a hard day. But I didn't want to say anything that might make me sound weak. Hart was scrawnier than I was, but I noticed he never complained. He just kept walking.

"Reckon we ought to find a safe place and rest a spell?" I asked.

"If you want." He pointed off the road a bit. A faint glow arose from a grove of evergreens. "See the light?"

"Just barely."

"Let's head that way."

Took us a while to find the clearing. When we did, we discovered a large group of people, most of them huddled around an iron oil barrel. A fire burned inside, and a big cauldron rested over the top. My nose told me they were cooking.

I didn't have to stare very long to realize this was one of those hobo jungles I'd read about in *LIFE* magazine. Most of the people looked like they were in far worse shape than we were, though there were one or two that still had some shine in their britches. These folks appeared to come from all walks of life. Saw one man still wearing a top hat, battered though it was. Another guy dressed like a carnival wrestler. Bunch of young boys, all huddled together. I couldn't tell if they were down on their luck or just on the road for the thrill of it. Maybe a little of both.

The hobo stirring the pot shouted some words at us. I didn't understand him.

"Hello, the fire!" Hart shouted.

"Hello, yourself!" many shouted back. After that, the tension dissipated a bit.

I got the impression they'd exchanged some kind of secret code. Whatever it was, it seemed to work, because from that time on they treated us as if we were one of them and always had been.

"We're fixing a little road stew," the hobo-in-charge said. He had a genteel, smooth sort of voice and a touch of an Eastern accent, not unlike what I used to hear back in school. I wasn't sure where he was from, but I got the impression he hadn't spent his whole life as a hobo. "If you've got something to contribute, we'd be more than delighted to share."

"How about some carrots?" Hart offered. To my surprise, he reached deep into one of his pockets and pulled out a mess of carrots wrapped in a napkin.

"Where'd you get those?" I whispered.

"Saved 'em from dinner."

"Thought you cleaned your plate."

"No, you cleaned your plate. I saved some ingredients for road stew."

"Like you knew we were coming here?"

"Like I've learned to think ahead." He dropped his carrots into the big pot, and everyone cheered.

We met a lot of folk after that, and for the most part they were friendly as they could be. I learned that many had been on the road for a while, some all the way back to the Crash of '29. They liked to sleep in these hobo jungles because if they got caught in town after dark they were likely to be thrown into jail. A few men played poker with a ratty-looking deck of cards, sitting around a stump on moss-covered logs. I thought that looked like trouble, so I stayed clear. Even if we'd lost his car, we still had the good doctor's money, and I didn't plan to lose it gambling.

Off to the side, near the north line of trees, I saw a group of women standing in an irregular formation. They were mostly on the plump side and not the sort of girl you'd bring home to meet your mother. They giggled and acted real flirty-like. Turned out that for fifty cents, they'd go off into the woods with a man and let him do whatever he wanted. For ten minutes. Which was probably more than enough time in most cases.

A skinny-looking fellow several inches shorter than me came amblin' up. He held a guitar in his left hand. "Howdy, partner. My name's Woodrow. Folks call me Woody. Glad you could make it this evening."

"Well," I replied, "our arrival wasn't exactly planned out real good."

"I know what you mean. I'm up from the Texas Panhandle myself."

"What you doing down there?"

"Oh, odd jobs. This and that. Trying to support a family. For a time, I worked a root beer stand, except we sold corn whiskey under the counter, which was far more popular than the root beer. Some ol' boy had a guitar there and I picked it up during my idle moments and learned how to play a chord or two. People seemed to think I was all right. So I put together a few tunes and started hopping trains, playing for bread or water or whatever else I could find."

"Doesn't sound like the worst way to make your way through the world."

"It isn't. We're gonna put on some music in a minute. You play an instrument?"

"Can't say as I do."

"Harmonica? Jew's harp?"

"Sorry, no."

"Maybe you can borrow one. We all share everything here."

"Is that a fact. You one of them Reds I keep hearing about?"

I saw most of the friendly drain out of his face and I was sorry I'd asked. I was just curious, that's all.

"What do you know about Reds?"

"Well, I heard a man at my college say the socialists were trying to destroy the American way of life."

"You believe that?"

"I guess that would depend on how you define the American way of life. If it's what I'm seeing at the moment, a little change might do it good."

Woody's grin returned, and he slapped me on the shoulder. "I like you, friend. You got a funny way about you. So to answer your question, if you define *Reds* as folks who care about their neighbors and think everybody ought to have a fair shake in this world, then I guess I am one. But I'm not interested in stirring up trouble. I think we've got enough of that already."

He took a position by the stewpot so we could all see him by the light of the fire. He played guitar and someone else played the mouth organ. He had a high-pitched warbly voice, almost kinda sissy-like, but I had to admit he had a way with a tune. He sang something about Do-Re-Mi, words I remembered from school, but I got the idea it had more to do with money than it did singing. Then he sang a lullaby about hoboes that was just about the loveliest thing I ever heard in my life.

While he sang some more songs, I wandered around the camp and chatted with folks. Didn't know where Hart had gone to. It was clear to me that most of the men here were not long-time hoboes. Some were family men, former farmers, factory workers laid off. Bank clerks unemployed by the Crash. Storeowners, all broke. Men who couldn't stand to stay home and see their kids starving and running around in rags. Couldn't bear to watch their families die right before their eyes. So they took to the road.

I was surprised at how many women there were. *Must be a horrible life for womenfolk*, I thought. And children, though some of them boys seemed to like it. No school, no parents, no boss—I expect most boys had no objection to any of that. Saw a lot of people with nothing but the clothes on their backs, and not much of that. Worn-out shirts and toeless shoes.

Somewhere behind the musicians, I observed a woman I reckoned to be about my age. She had long dark hair and she looked soft, and I liked the way her green eyes glistened in the firelight. Her shirt was torn and she was dressed like a boy, but that didn't stop her from attracting my attention. Our eyes locked for a moment. I turned away real quick and tried to act casual.

I learned a great deal that night, especially about the ways of the road. I learned the difference between a bum and a hobo, which made what I'd heard earlier in Guymon make more sense (a bum just asks for handouts; a hobo works for his grub). I learned that some of them boys were what they call *kneeshakers*, meaning they'd shake down farmers and housewives for food or small change. Usually they'd be brought food outside, but a *sit-down* was when folks would invite you inside to eat at the table. That happened less and less these days. Some of those young boys started out on the road to get away from a nasty pa or just for the thrill of it, but they ended up panhandling to survive. Most of them never had any experience with women, which was not necessarily their choice, since there were no women who wanted to have any experience with them, except those gals that collected a fee for their educational services.

"I bet you've had a lot of women," one of them boys said, looking up at me. I was pleased he thought so, given how badly beaten up I knew my face was.

"I've sampled me a treat or two," I said. "Back in Massachusetts, the ladies go crazy for college men."

"Do you play football?"

"That don't matter. See, a girl wants to know she's hitching her wagon to a man who's gonna be able to take care of her. Maybe give her a nice thing every now and then, like a new sparkler or some fancy clothes to wear to church."

"Did one ever let you see her privates?"

I found my eyes drifting back to that woman with the torn dress and the long dark hair. "I done more than look at them, if you know what I mean."

They all chuckled at that.

Till one of the youngest chirped up. "I don't know what he means. What do you mean?"

I patted him on the head. "We'll talk about that when you're older, sonny."

"No, I wanna know now. Did you do something to her privates?" His voice was loud and kinda shrieky. I saw heads turning.

"This ain't an appropriate topic for young'uns."

"Education is never a bad thing." I turned and saw Hart standing behind me. He had a mischievous grin on his face. "Go ahead and tell us about your wild sexual encounters, George."

"I'm not one to kiss and tell." I moved along.

Hart was right about one thing—education is never a bad thing, and that night was extremely educational. Some of the folk stayed up well into the wee hours, almost like they didn't want to sleep or were afraid of it. I learned to avoid Weatherford, Oklahoma, where Southwestern College was, 'cause they said the docs and hospitals were denying medical services to transients. When they found a sick traveler, the cops would haul him out of town and dump him on the side of the road. Some cities, even out in California, started putting up blockades and refusing to admit any more travelers. One fella said he thought that violated the U.S. Constitution, but that didn't seem to matter much to the cops.

The main thing I learned that night was that most of the gentlemen of the road were not bad. They weren't stupid, they weren't dirty, and they weren't lazy. Most held down good jobs till the troubles started, and most tried to work afterward. But there came a time when a man, even a good hard-workin' man, got tired of being turned down. Some told me life on the road was all they could manage anymore. Drifting entailed many risks, but it also gave them a certain freedom and helped them heal all that damage inside themselves.

One man told me there were as many as a million and a half hoboes on the road these days. I hoped that wasn't true. I knew these were hard times, but that just seemed like too much misery for too many people to bear all at once.

Hart made him a friend, which surprised me, because he didn't seem all that sociable. It was a kid maybe around sixteen named Jimmy. They were talking about books and writers and a lot of stuff I never heard of before, so I lost interest quick. I didn't know why Hart would want to waste time with a squirt like that, but there's no accounting for taste.

After they finished playing, Woody and his friends moved on. The poker game folded and happily no one was murdered. People gathered 'round the fire and told ghost stories, lots of improbable tales about haints doin' one thing or another. There was one about a man who had a hand replaced with a hook, and another about some hitchhiker who kept popping up on the road over and over again in a disturbing fashion. When that ran dry, Hart told a tale written by that writer he represented.

"Things looked grim for Emerson Babylon. He had the hordes of Old Caldoronia amassing to the north, and the skeleton warriors of Helburtonium to the south. His sword was broken and his potions were dried up. Looked like he was a goner for sure. But did he panic? Did he despair? No. Because he was a hero, and even in hard times, a hero does not quit. So Emerson raised his broken sword into the air, tightened his grip, and he said: 'So long as my lungs draw breath and my heart pumps fiery hot blood—nothing is impossible.'"

I shook my head. It was a crazy story, even crazier than the John Carter yarns on Barsoom, but I had to admit that Hart did a good job of telling it. And the people listening seemed to like it. After Hart finished, his new pal Jimmy offered up one of his stories. It was the most complicated thing I ever heard. The story went on for several generations and had more characters than I could keep track of. His story didn't have so much sword-fighting in it, but he managed to keep it interesting just the same. After that, some of the political types started talking about fascists and socialists and communists and Reds and labor unions. That talk sucked all the fun out of the evening. Pretty soon most folks drifted off.

I decided to pack it in for the night. I tucked the doctor's money inside my shorts so it wouldn't get stolen, and I took off my shoes so I could sleep on top of them. Judging from my observations, there were more than a few there who might be tempted to kill a man to get a new pair of shoes.

Wasn't more than a minute before I fell asleep. Which I suppose wasn't surprising, given the kinda day I'd had.

Next thing I remember that dark-haired woman hovered right over me. She gave me a smile that was unmistakable in its intention.

I wasn't sure what to do. She got down on all fours, right on top of me. She flipped her head forward and all that hair came tumbling down, covering my face and tickling my nose. I could feel the heat of her body and I could smell the scent of her breath. She started moving, and I started moving, and then we were moving together. Something about this was kinda amazing, but kinda disturbing and unpleasant at the same time.

I wasn't exactly sure where the clothes went, but pretty soon neither of us had any on. I kissed her face, and she bit my ear. All at once we were joined. I gasped, then everything got kinda warm and I felt this weird tremor through my entire body. I wasn't sure what had happened, but I'm sure I slept just as peaceful as if I'd been in a big four-poster bed in the kingdom of heaven.

thirteen

I WOKE with the taste of blood and kisses on my lips.

I had to blink several times before I realized where I was. It was still dark out, but maybe not quite so dark as it had been when I fell asleep.

"C'mon, George," Hart said. "We got a train to catch."

I wiped the sleep from my eyes and pushed myself off the ground. "What are you talking about? We don't have nearly enough money to ride the train."

"Who said anything about money? C'mon."

"We must be miles from the nearest train station."

"Would you stop yakking and shake a leg? We got to hurry or we'll be too late."

"I don't understand—"

"Which is exactly why you need me."

"May I remind you that I am a college man, and I don't see what some dope fiend chess player—"

Hart drew in his breath. "What do you think is the quality that makes a man a good chess player?"

I was tempted to say, *Born boring*, but I resisted. "Don't know. What?"

"The ability to think three moves ahead of the other guy.

Occasionally four or six or ten moves. Like I did back at the diner. You have to get to Oxford, Mississippi, and you have to get back by Mrs. Bennett's birthday. You won't get there by walking, and it would be a miracle if you could hitchhike given the way you look at the moment. So I've explored the possibility of other transportation."

I pulled myself together and followed him, running lickety-split to a destination unknown. On the way out of camp, I looked for that dark-haired woman, but I couldn't find her anywhere. Did all that kissing and stuff really happen, or did I dream it? I felt like I hadn't slept at all.

Turned out Hart had stayed up most of the night yakking with that new acquaintance of his. Jimmy'd been on the road some time and he knew all about riding the rails. Hoboes that hitched train rides never went to the station. The station was where train cars got inspected, and they didn't want that. Stations were also where the Brotherhood of the Bulls—the private train cops—were most likely to be found, parading about in their black caps and swinging their nightsticks. They rode the trains, too, so no matter where you got on, you had to be careful. Jimmy said the best plan was to jump aboard at some point after the train left the station and then get off before it arrived at the next one—and not get seen doing it. The only problem was you'd be getting on while the train was still moving. Which is about the most dangerous thing a man could do.

"You want to catch the mail train," I heard Jimmy say, as we raced toward the tracks. "Not everybody knows that. But mail trains are faster than freight trains."

"You've done this a great deal?" I inquired.

"Heck, yeah. I even rode the rods once, just to show that I could."

"The rods?"

"The struts beneath the boxcar. Couple of long poles. You got to hang on tight. Hardest thing is to keep from falling asleep. You lose your grip, you're a dead man."

"And you did this?"

"Liked to kill me. Almost died from the smoke. Coughed it up for close to a year afterwards."

Somehow, none of this made me too excited about the forthcoming opportunity. "Why'd you start doing this? Something happen to your pappy?"

"I wish. He's a mean no-account sumbitch and always was. But I hit the road 'cause life at home was just too boring. These trains are my passport to adventure. Like in those Richard Halliburton books. You read any of those?"

"I'll get to them right after I read Hart's Edward H. Conrad fella."

"These trains've taken me all across the country. I've seen the east and I've seen the west. I've seen the prairie and I've seen the ocean. I liked the ocean better. I saw real-life cowboys. Can you believe that? Like Tom Mix and the other movie cowpokes. These trains have taken me everywhere. Eventually, they'll take me to Big Rock Candy Mountain."

"What's that?"

"It's what all these fellas are looking for. Hobo heaven. A place with no cops, no bosses, no money. Folks just live and let live." Sounded kinda pointless to me, but of course that's in part because I knew I was destined for greater things.

"And what will you do when you've seen everything a train can show you?"

"I dunno. Thinking about maybe joining the Navy. I like the water. I might get shipped overseas. Beats the heck out of hawking papers or shining shoes, which is what most of the boys my age are doing back home. Aren't enough feet in Chicago to earn supper for all the shoeshine boys they got there."

We came to a clearing and I could see the train tracks. Problem was there was no train.

"It'll be here in a few minutes," Jimmy assured us. "You'll hear it soon. Get ready. It'll come in fast. Sometimes I throw a rock or two at them, just to get a sense of how fast they're coming. They say I got the best arm in the county and ought to be playing baseball. But I can't be tied down right now."

I got limbered and prepared to fling myself at a big heavy moving object that could easily crush me under its wheels and never know the difference. After a few minutes passed, I heard the distant rumbling. I had a professor who explained about the Doppler shift and why the train roar gets louder and higher-pitched as it approaches. I didn't recall the details, but it turned out to be true.

A few seconds later, I heard another sound that was considerably more disturbing.

I'd been away from home four years, but that wasn't nearly long enough to cause me to forget the sound of a rifle being loaded.

"Well now. What have we here?"

Somehow, I knew from the tone of the man's voice that he must be one of them railroad bulls. And I hadn't even spotted him yet.

Three men emerged from the trees on the other side of the tracks. One carried a lantern, but the other two toted rifles.

"You boys thinking about doing a little freeloading?" The man with the lantern appeared to be the leader and spokesman.

At first, I was not too concerned. After all, the sheriff back home was responsible for us being sent on this mission. I figured that made us deputies or something. So I tried to explain the situation. "We've been sent here by a doctor back in Guymon. We're supposed to fetch his daughter."

"Do tell." He looked me over once or twice and I could see he was not impressed. I expect I did look fairly rough. Hadn't shaved, and my face was all bruised and beaten. "Did this doctor tell you to steal a ride on a train?"

"No. He gave us his car. But the car was stolen from us."

"Did you report the theft to the police?"

"I didn't see the point."

"'Course you didn't." He came up real close. "You know what

I think? I think you're a bum. And you know what a bum is? A criminal."

When he said that last word, he punched me right in my stomach. Didn't hurt all that much, but it made me mad.

"I think bums are dirty," the man rattled on. "And you know how we treat dirt on this railroad? We wale the tar out of them till they're so broken and sore they can't move. Then we beat them some more."

"You better talk to the doctor before you do anything."

"That doctor, who probably doesn't exist, has no jurisdiction over the railroads."

"That doctor is rich enough to jurisdiction your ass, if that's what he wants to do."

The man hit me again, but I noticed it wasn't as hard as before.

Maybe he was listening, if only a little bit.

"What're you gonna do?" I asked. "Take us to the cops?" "We got our own way of handling things. We've spent years throwing people like you off trains. But you never learn. You just keep doing it. So these days, we favor a more permanent solution."

On that cue, his men raised their rifles.

"Afterwards," he explained, "we throw your bodies on the tracks. That way, no one ever finds you, at least not in such condition as you can be recognized." He held his lantern so high it made his eyes gleam. "You can say your final prayers, mister. Then you're train fuel."

fourteen

MAYBE IT'S because my head still ached, but I was ridiculously slow recognizing that these boys wanted to kill us. Seemed like they could get away with it, too. They had the authority of the railroads, and if they killed someone out here in the middle of nowhere, no one knew about it.

I didn't know what to do. I remembered what Hart said about being three moves ahead of your opponent. But at the moment, I felt sixteen steps behind.

I turned my head slightly, hoping my little chess genius might have a solution to the current predicament. He did not appear to have a plan, but I was impressed by how little our situation seemed to bother him. Was he able to stay so calm because he was courageous, or was it because he didn't care what happened to him?

Jimmy was the first of us to speak. "You better not be messing with me, boys. I'm not just some run-of-the-mill hobo kid. My father is the mayor of Dill City, Oklahoma. He's got friends across the state—and that includes the Union Pacific Railroad."

All three laughed. "Where's that daddy of yours now?"

"Probably at the Pinkerton agency lining up about a thousand agents to track me down. And you know what, one of them might be smart enough to do it. You throw us under the train tracks, you'll swing."

The leader reared back his hand and slapped Jimmy across the face. Jimmy let out a little yelp, but I didn't hold it against him. I might've done the same under the circumstances.

"Listen up, kid," the man snarled. "You know how many railroad bulls have been tried for a crime since this Depression began? Exactly none, that's how many. And it ain't because we're all so perfect. It's because deep down, folks are glad we're here. They might not approve of everything we do or how we do it, but it might not bother them all that much, either. They don't want hoboes riding into their town. They don't want bums on their doorsteps begging for food."

I didn't doubt what he said was true. But I didn't think it was sufficient cause to engage in acts of homicide. And I was distracted, because as the man talked, the train came up the nearest hill and barreled into view. Looked to me as if it was maybe a minute or three away and getting louder by the second.

The leader started harassing Hart. "What's your story, little man? Why ain't you quaking in those stupid little baby shoes of yours? Don't you know you're about to die?"

Hart acted as if he stood six feet tall. "So long as my lungs draw breath and my heart pumps fiery hot blood—nothing is impossible."

The leader's head twitched. A frown line formed between his brows. "You read *Weird Tales*?"

"Never miss an issue," Hart replied.

"You like those stories about the time traveler? The one with the big sword."

The corner of Hart's mouth turned up slightly. "Those are my favorites."

"That last one was something else, wasn't it? Where he went into the future on one of those seventeen civilized planets, and everyone could talk to everyone else through some little thing they kept in their pockets." He made a scoffing sound. "Stupid kid stuff. But kinda fun, when you're in the mood. What's that guy's name?"

"Emerson Babylon."

"Yeah, that's it."

I enjoyed the conversation, especially its lack of attention to the idea of killing us. But the train kept roaring closer. Someone needed to do something.

All at once the leader returned his attention to me. Guess the literary diversion was over. "Don't you be looking at that mail train. You ain't gonna be on it."

And then Hart erupted. Absolutely erupted. Louder than anything I ever heard in my life, especially coming from that quiet little man.

"Excelsior!" he shouted. He fell to his knees. "Excelsior!"

The leader twisted his head around. "That's what that time traveler—"

"Excelsior!" he shouted again, loud enough to be heard over the approaching train. That's when I got it. Hart was creating a diversion. So I needed to take advantage of it.

I stepped forward real quick, using a boxing move they'd taught me back east. I stepped on one man's foot, pinning him in place, then grabbed his rifle and shoved it back into his chin. He fell quick. I got the idea he wasn't used to much opposition. Between the shouting and the noise of the train, the other gun-toter was disoriented. Jimmy ran toward the train, which caused the other man to swing around and point a rifle in his direction. The coward fired at the boy's back.

I took the barrel of the rifle I'd acquired and coldcocked him. He dropped his rifle. I gave him two more right jabs to the face. The second one broke his nose. Blood and cartilage splattered every which way and he went down hard. The leader took off running.

I tossed the spare rifle to Hart. "Come on."

Together we ran after the remaining bull. When he saw two men coming at him with rifles, and both his pals lying on the ground, he quickened his pace. Guys like that might have courage when they're surrounded by friends, but on his own, he wasn't worth much. I fired a few shots into the air, just to make sure he ran far and didn't get the notion to come back.

Hart ran toward the train, which by this time had half passed us by. I followed.

Jimmy targeted a yellowish car with a slightly open cargo door. He ran as fast as he could, trying to match the pace of the speeding train.

I figured out another reason the savvy Jimmy chose this location to jump aboard. When the train came over the crest of the hill, it ran smack into a sharp curve where the track swerved around the forest. The train had to slow down to take the curve. Otherwise, we would never have been able to match its speed. As it was, it presented a serious challenge.

Jimmy boarded so smoothly he looked like Buck Rogers with a jetpack. He took a mighty leap, one foot stretched in front of the other, bounced off the side rail, and flung himself headfirst into the car. He might've been a little guy, but he knew how to move. Hart prepared to execute the same maneuver. I wondered how that would turn out, since I got the idea he'd spent a lot more time with books than he had on the sporting field. Turned out the kid could move when he wanted to. He wasn't as smooth or graceful as Jimmy, but he got up there just the same.

Well, hell. If those boys could do this, it should be a snap for me, right?

The key words in that sentence being *should be*. I regretted losing a weapon, but I knew I couldn't grab the door with a rifle in my hand, so I threw it down. I ran as fast as possible, but I had a hard time matching the train's speed. I expect that since I weighed so much more than the other two fellas, I had a harder time getting up to speed. We approached a severe downward turn on the hill and the train veered. In other words, if I didn't get aboard in the next hundred feet or so, I wasn't gonna make it at all.

Hart stood at the opening. "Jump!" he shouted, reaching out toward me.

I don't know what got into me just then, but I couldn't make my legs do what I told them to do. I kept thinking: *Jump!* But my legs weren't doing any jumping.

"C'mon," Hart shouted. "You're running out of time."

I heard the words, and I knew he was right, but I still couldn't get those legs to cooperate.

"You stupid bastard," Hart shouted. "You think I care whether I hang or not? I'm on this whole cockamamie quest for you. So stop being such a yellow-bellied chicken and jump!"

That did it. I was willing to acknowledge a certain reluctance to engage in a hazardous activity, but I wasn't about to let anyone accuse me of lacking manly courage.

I jumped.

Too short, as it turned out.

My extended right foot touched down just inside the railroad car, but it slipped. I managed to grab the door handle, but my feet dangled outside the car. My arm felt like it got wrenched out of its socket. I hung sideways like a windsock. Gravity tried to suck me under the car, and I knew if that happened, I was dead and gone for sure.

My arm already ached, and I knew I couldn't hold on much longer. I closed my eyes and swore to myself, because I'd gone and botched it this time. I felt bad about abandoning Callie, and I felt stupid for trying this fool stunt. And even more stupid for leaving Massachusetts, because in just a few seconds, I was gonna be dead.

fifteen

MY FINGERS LOOSENED. I couldn't keep a tight grip. I knew letting go would be tantamount to suicide, but I couldn't stop it from happening. My arm felt numb. It was not responding to the urgent commands from my brain.

Took me a few moments to notice Hart leaning out the door, just as far as he could. "Grab my hand!"

How? If I let go of that handle, I would splatter down under the train wheels.

"The other hand, you idiot."

Right. I switched hands on the handle, then brought my right hand around toward him. What with the strong wind pushing me backward, I couldn't extend it far enough, but somehow he managed to get it.

"Now when I say three, you let go of the handle. I'll reel you in."

This did not seem like a sound plan to me. Especially the letting-go part.

"You'll have some forward momentum. Enough to get you inside."

I still did not feel compelled to release the handle.

"You're gonna have to trust me, George. You ain't got no choice."

He spoke the truth, of course. I could see that this was the only way I was gonna end up on that railroad car. But I could also see that if our timing was off by even a hair, my head would be crushed on the rails.

"Count," I said through gritted teeth.

"You let go on three," he said. "One. Two. *Three*."

I let go and he jerked me into that boxcar. Jimmy anchored Hart's feet, making sure he didn't fall forward. Between Hart's strong pull and the momentum of the train, I ended up flying across the car and bonking my head on the opposite side.

The floor of the train was covered with hay. I got a fair amount of that in my mouth. And didn't mind a bit. I felt grateful to be alive.

I guess I took me a little nap, right there on the floor of the railroad car, and Hart and Jimmy let me do it. All I know is that when I finally woke up, Jimmy was saying goodbye.

"You went to all that trouble to get on the train, and now you're getting off?" I said.

"Aw, I just wanted to show you how it's done. This is the Union Pacific. It's gonna take you into Mississippi. I'm headed up to Kansas, so I'll get off and catch a ride on the Santa Fe."

I nodded. "'Preciate what you did for us."

He shuffled his feet. "Heck, that's how it's done out here on the road. Everybody helps everybody else." He winked. "Too bad it ain't like that everywhere, right?" He turned toward Hart. "I'll be looking for those stories by Edward H. Conrad. That boy knows how to spin a yarn."

"And I'll be looking for stories by you, Jimmy."

"You might have to wait a while. I got some living to do first." He grinned, then jumped right off the train, graceful as an acrobat. I watched him land, feet first, but rolling forward, tucking his head in. He did several somersaults till he ran out of momentum, then sprang up and started running away, still grinning like there was no tomorrow.

"Think I'm gonna miss that whippersnapper," I said.

Hart agreed. "Me, too."

My head still throbbed, and I felt exhausted. We talked for a spell about nothing in particular, then Hart taught me this word game called Ghost that actually had nothing to do with ghosts. After a bit, he drew back within himself in that moody way of his and I got bored. I nodded off well before sunset and didn't wake up again until it was dark.

I was startled by a strange noise. Took me a moment to catch enough moonlight to realize it was Hart. He dozed in the boxcar corner opposite mine.

"Stop it," he said, under his breath. His face looked like someone was hurting him, but I couldn't see no one around. "Stop it. Please."

He thrashed and writhed like he was being tortured. Eventually I realized he was talking in his sleep. Must be having some kinda nightmare.

"Not again." He was practically shouting now. "Please don't. Please. Not again."

I grabbed him by the shoulders and shook him. "Hart. Wake up."

His eyes opened real wide. He grabbed my head and dug in with his nails. Looked like he was possessed by a wild frenzy.

"Don't hurt me!" he shouted, and he just about blew out my eardrums.

"Hart!" I shook him even harder. "It's George. No one's hurting you."

Little by little, his eyes returned to normal. His fingernails receded and he got calmer, though his respiration was still going lickety-split. "George?"

"I'm here. We're on a train heading east to Mississippi. Remember?"

He settled down. After a while he said, "Was I talking in my sleep? Sorry if I disturbed you."

"That ain't nothing. Don't worry about it." I didn't like to pry, but at this point, I couldn't help but be curious. "Was that your pa you were dreaming about?"

He seemed confused. "My pa?"

"Yeah. The one you thought was hurting you."

"Oh." His eyes drifted down to some place on the floor. "No. Mother."

"Your *ma*?"

"My mother had a mean streak. Like nothing you ever saw I think that's maybe one more reason my father . . . did what he did."

"I'm sorry to hear that. Wasn't there anyone you could tell?"

"She was careful never to leave a mark, or not much of one. No one in town was interested."

"That why you left home?"

"Not exactly."

"When'd you light out?"

"When I was fourteen."

"That young? What happened?"

His eyes darted about but never connected with mine. "She caught me . . . caught me with a . . . a person . . . and she didn't approve of it. Threatened to hurt me in a way you can't even imagine. Wanted to maim me. I just ran out the door and never came back."

"Least you didn't leave the way your pa done."

"Yeah," he said. "Right."

"I can't figure what would cause a man to do such a thing."

Hart's voice got softer than a whisper. "Some mornings I wake up and everything is so dark I don't know what to do with myself. I feel like I'd do . . . anything. Just to make the hurting go away."

"I'm sorry to hear that." It was a dumb thing to say, but it was all I could come up with. "You deserve better than you got."

"We all do." He smiled, if only a little. He put his hand on mine, then pulled it away real quick. "You're a kind man with a generous heart. You just don't know it yet."

"That so?" I laughed, trying to melt away the awkwardness. "Does this mean we're friends now?"

"Hell, no," he replied, shoving me away. "Why would I want to be friends with a polecat like you? You can't even play a decent game of chess."

We both laughed and settled back to our corners. I don't know why I was so tired, but it wasn't a minute later I fell back into a deep black slumber.

——

Next time I woke, it was because a big ugly monster had his hands around my throat. Not Hart. Not anyone I'd ever seen before. Took me more than a moment to register the fact that I couldn't breathe. My head felt like it was about to explode and the expression on that monster's face made it clear that he did not intend to let up until I was good and dead.

sixteen

I **LEARNED** how to break a headlock in those boxing classes back in Massachusetts. So even as feeble as my mind was at that moment, I managed to reach out between his extended arms and punch the sides of my hands into the soft parts of his underarms, real hard. His grip slipped. I slapped his hands away.

"Who the hell are you?" I bellowed.

"I am the rain," he said, his eyes all weird and squinty.

"Then you shouldn't be here. 'Cause these parts haven't seen rain in years."

"God took away the rain because his children were sinners."

"I expect they always have been. But that ain't stopped the rain before."

"The time of reckoning is upon us."

"And that explains why you were trying to strangulate me?"

His voice dropped a notch. "I just wanted your boots."

"Guess what? They ain't located in my throat."

"I didn't think you'd agree to a loan." He swung his fist back and aimed a haymaker at my face. It was so dark in that boxcar I didn't see it coming till it was almost too late. I managed to duck, and the fist slammed into the back wall of the train car, sending splinters flying. I scrambled out from under him and jumped to my feet.

I don't know if it was because he saw those precious boots getting away or what, but he came at me like he was on fire. He roared like an animal and rushed me. I tried to get away, but I moved too slow. He knocked me to the floor.

That was where he nailed me. Maybe I was still sleepy, but he landed one on the side of my head that made me hear bells that weren't coming from a chapel. After that, everything slowed down. I tried to get off a good one, but he always managed to knock it away. He put another one in the side of my neck, and that took all the fight out of me. I'd been involved with a fair amount of conflict these past few days, and I think it was catching up with me. He hit me again and blood trickled into my mouth.

Somehow, that acrid taste roused me. I thought about Callie and the promise I'd made to her. I couldn't keep that promise if I got killed by some behemoth just 'cause we had the same shoe size. I kicked him off and staggered to my feet. He came at me again, but I managed to push him away. Hurt my arm, though. It was still sore from dangling off the side of the train. He managed to slip another one onto the right side of my head. He opened a wound them boys had started back in Guymon, and I felt seriously woozy. I knew I wouldn't survive another hit like that.

He made a fearsome growling noise and rushed me. I wasn't planning anything—I just knew I needed to get out of his way. I jumped to the side, and he couldn't stop in time.

The door of the railcar still hung open. He stopped at the brink and started tipping. He waved his arms around in circles, trying to keep from falling out.

"Help me!" he cried. All the mean drained away, and he looked more pathetic than anything else. I reckoned he was seriously messed up, but he surely didn't deserve to die in a big splat on the side of the train tracks.

The suction was getting him. "Help me!"

I reached out a hand. I had almost grasped him when I got knocked back onto my posterior.

Hart had tackled me.

I scrambled up again, but it was too late. That poor monster who thought he was God's own rain tumbled into the darkness. I heard a grotesque crunching noise that made my eyes water. I still don't know if he fell to the ground or got thrown under the wheels, but either way, I doubt he walked away from it.

I stared at Hart, my eyes wide. "What the hell was that for?"

He didn't answer.

"Do you know what you done?"

"Yeah," Hart said quietly. "I saved our lives."

"You executed that man."

"And you almost executed us," he shot back. "You and your idiotic conventional morality. That man tried to kill you, and it would only be seconds before he tried again. Did you think because you saved him he'd get all sweet and kindly? Like he'd be Androcles's lion and turn all nice because you pulled a thorn out of his paw? That man was plumb crazy. He tried to kill you once and he'd do it again. Probably kill the both of us. He was twice as big as you and three times as strong. I don't know if you noticed, but you were losing that fight."

"I held my own."

"You were getting beat to a pulp, and I'd be next. So I did the only sensible thing."

"You let a man die."

"I let us live. You gonna complain about it? I had the idea you wanted to collect that doctor's daughter and get back to town and help your sister. Did I have that wrong?"

"No," I had to admit.

"Then don't die satisfying some two-bit Sunday-school notion of right and wrong."

He went back to his corner. I don't think he actually slept, but he acted like he did.

I settled into my corner, but I had a hard time sleeping. Just when I was almost warming up to that kid, he did a thing like that and made me uncomfortable just being around him. Sure, what he said made some sense, but it left me feeling unsettled, too. We didn't have the right to pick and choose who lived and died, did we?

That's when I realized exactly what the difference between the two of us was. Hart wasn't mean and he didn't hate folk. He saw a choice between that brute living and me living, and he chose me. Maybe that was wrong. Or maybe he was willing to make hard choices other folks backed away from.

———

I dreamed about my parents. It's a hard thing, living all your life as someone's child then suddenly realizing you're an orphan. The world's a harder, colder place once your parents are gone, no doubt about it. Like your security blanket got burned to a frazzle. Probably just as well I was too busy to think about it much when I was awake. I wasn't sorry when morning arrived.

Somehow, Hart managed to keep track of time and distance. He reckoned that we were near our destination. And he reminded me that we had to disembark before we arrived, because if we rode the train all the way to the station, the local bulls would arrest us. Or worse.

We waited until the train hit a slow spot, going 'round another curve, then we jumped for it. I tried to execute that same duck-and-cover somersault landing I'd seen Jimmy do. Mine was not as pretty as his, but I managed to get off the train without killing myself.

Hart did not do so well. He didn't break his neck, but he did hurt his ankle. He could walk, just barely, when he held on to me. This was bad news, as I knew we would have to walk a while before we got into town. Hart managed it, and to his credit, I never heard him complain once.

That left some navigational challenges, because neither of us was precisely sure where we were and there was no one to ask. After a spell of walking, we spotted a dirt road. We hiked down to it, then followed in the general direction we wanted to travel, judging by the position of the sun and the time of day. After a couple of hours, we encountered a road sign that read: OXFORD 5 MI.

That brought a smile to my face. Much more so than the next sign we saw. A great big billboard that read: JOBLESS MEN KEEP MOVING. WE CAN'T TAKE CARE OF OUR OWN.

Nonetheless, we had made our way to Oxford.

Oxford reminded me of the towns I visited growing up. The houses looked well-kept, and the streets were relatively free of horse dung and dust. I knew they must have their unemployed and bums and drunks like every other place, but they did a good job of hiding it. After a mile or so we hit the town square, a nice little setup with a big grassy lawn and a park. Everything was much greener here than in Guymon. I could imagine a band playing in the gazebo on Sunday afternoons and kids horsing around. Maybe sweethearts having picnics and sneaking kisses when no one was looking. Wouldn't be the worst place to live, I reckoned.

Since our only clue to the location of the doc's daughter was a postcard, I thought we ought to find the post office. I knew I looked beaten and grimy, but I hoped I appeared respectable enough to amble about town without getting stopped by the cops. Hart's ankle still hurt him, so I set him down on a park bench in the square. If the ankle wasn't better soon, he might need to see a doctor. I figured I'd let him take the weight off it while I ran errands, and we'd see how it felt after that.

I found the post office, but it was closed. Found a doctor's office, too, but no one was there, so I hiked back to the town square.

To my surprise, I found that another gentleman had joined Hart on the park bench and the two were chatting up a storm. I hoped Hart hadn't revealed anything that might incline the man to report us as transients. I didn't have time to get thrown in jail again.

Hart's companion was a skinny man with a thin little mustache. He had an easy way about him that made words flow smooth as ice. As I got closer, I noticed that his eyes were somewhat bloodshot. When I got even closer, I smelled the strong odor of whiskey about him.

I didn't want to interrupt, so I sat quietly on the end of the bench. I didn't really pay much attention till I heard the word *Absalom*. That was not a word you heard too much in these parts, even at tent revivals. I suspected there weren't many folks around here who would even know what it meant.

"It is the nature of man to rebel against authority," the stranger said. He had a slow Southern drawl, but I had no trouble understanding his words. "The new generation always rebels against the old."

"It doesn't have to be that way," Hart opined.

"It is the progression of the species."

"Progression or evolution? Darwin showed us that species evolve. How can we not expect social evolution as well? Kant did. Wittgenstein did, in his way. When Nietzsche wrote about the new morality, he contemplated a form of social evolution. Casting aside the religious and moral values of the previous generation."

"Which the previous generation will nevah agree to."

"They have no choice in the matter. All those Old Testament shalls and shall-nots worked for the patriarchal Hebrews wandering around the desert treating their women like slaves. But they make no sense today. A new way of thinking is required."

"Which is exactly what the old guard will nevah permit." The lanky man stretched out on the bench and crossed his legs at the ankle. "The urge to rebel is inherent in our species, but the patriarchs will try to crush it. Just as David sent his general to crush Absalom, his only son."

I will admit, I encountered some difficulty following the conversation. It seemed to veer from Bible stories, which I knew reasonably well, into abstract philosophy and naturalists like Darwin, who I had been taught preached apostasy and did the work of the devil.

"Post office is closed," I informed Hart.

Hart's companion arched an eyebrow. "That would be because today is Sunday."

"Oh. Right." I realized I'd completely lost track of time. "You boys wool-gathering?"

Hart made the introduction. "This here's Billy. He lives here."

We shook hands. He had a light shake and a tremor, which confirmed my feeling that he'd had a snort or six.

Hart jumped back into the conversation. "You know, I could see a story being made out of that David and Absalom yarn. Maybe taking place on another planet. The young prince revolts against the stodgy ways of the alien warlord."

Billy batted a finger against his lips. "Or maybe right here in the South. Maybe in Yoknapatawpha County."

"Billy's a writer, too," Hart explained.

"Too?"

"Like my client, I mean. Edward H. Conrad."

Billy turned slightly. "You read Conrad?"

"Over and over again."

"*Weird Tales*?"

"Get it every month."

Billy seemed pleased. "There's a lot of creativity going on in those pulp magazines. 'Course it isn't serious literature, least that's what they say at Ole Miss. I wonder sometimes which is harder though—telling stories about the people and places you know, or inventing stories about people and places that never existed. Whole worlds created pure out of the imagination."

"An interesting question," Hart said.

"'Course it all comes down to language, at the end of the day. It's not the story so much as the words."

"I'm not entirely sure I agree with that."

"Hardest thing in the world, trying to come up with the right word. You think and think and think till you're sure your head is 'bout to bust. You hear those voices in your head yakking all day long, ready to drive you right out of your mind."

"Man could go crazy."

"And some have."

"But when that word finally comes, it's the greatest feeling in the world. Nothing else like it. A man can do a lot of different things, trying to get that feeling back." I saw Hart's eyes get kinda glassy and fixed. "But nothing does it. Nothing else comes close. Hardest thing in the world, this writing game."

"You got that right. There's no shortcuts and no formula. It's just work. Hard damn work. Every day you start from scratch, like you'd never written anything before. You cross your fingers and pray something good comes out of it. And that it does a little good in the world for folks."

"How long's it take you to write one of your books?"

"There's no telling. I wrote one in a month. But I was under a deadline, and I'd had some . . . health complications that prevented me from getting a proper start. I don't think that was my best work. Did have some points of interest, though. Sold well, and then Hollywood bought it. Those screenplay writers don't know nothing. Spent some time out in Hollywood trying my hand at it. Glad to be back home."

"Hollywood can't touch Conrad," Hart said. "All that other-worldly stuff is too expensive to film."

"You read Howard?"

"Robert E. Howard? Everything the man ever wrote. Without exception. Now George here," Hart said, obviously trying to lighten the mood, "he likes Edgar Rice Burroughs."

Billy nodded. "That right, son?"

For some reason, I felt defensive. "I read some of those Mars stories when I was a kid. Found the magazine lying around some-where. Think it was in a doctor's office or something."

Billy nodded. "That ol' boy's got a good imagination. Don't think he knows so much about people, though."

"Maybe people are different on Mars," Hart suggested.

"I suppose that's a possibility." Billy took out a cigarette and lit it with a match. He puffed a few times to get it started. "I don't think he's so well-informed on British aristocrats."

"John Carter was a Virginia cavalryman."

"I'm talking about Tarzan. He's the offspring of a lord and lady. That's the whole point, I guess. Blood will out. Leave a lord in the jungle, and soon he'll be runnin' the place. You believe that?"

I said yes and Hart said no simultaneously.

"People rise to the top for a reason," I said. "Hard work. Determination. Ambition."

"Yes, but those qualities don't get passed from one generation to the next," Hart replied. "You put a pampered lord out in the jungle, the most likely result is that he's some wild animal's supper."

"Well, I don't know about that," I said.

"George here is a great moralist," Hart explained. "Except he got all his morals from what other people told him when he was about three."

I'll admit that stung. Me and Hart weren't exactly friends, but we'd shared some adventures and I didn't like to hear what seemed like unkindness. "I can think for myself," I insisted. "I'm a college man. But I also believe there's right and there's wrong and a man should abide by the rules."

"See what I said." Hart gave Billy a wink.

"Every man's entitled to his opinion," Billy said. The clock tower sounded in the town square. "Looks like it's time for me to head home. Post office will be open tomorrow. Doctor's office, too."

"My ankle's feeling better already," Hart said. "I just needed to stay off it a spell."

"Be that as it may, why don't you two boys come home with me to Rowan Oak? Estelle don't mind strangers. She might even welcome you. Especially if she thinks you'll keep me on my best behavior. Only got one spare bed, but one of you can take the sofa. I think you'll fit on it just fine, Hart."

I don't like to impose, but it seemed like a reasonable offer to me and beat the heck out of sleeping outdoors with cops prowling around locking people up. So I figured we should probably accept.

Billy had a nice two-story house in a shady grove near the edge of town. His wife seemed a mite startled to have visitors, but she adjusted well. I saw her give her husband a close look-over, but apparently he passed inspection. Turned out she and Billy had known each other since they were kids, but he'd hesitated a bit and had uncertain job prospects, so she ended up marrying some other guy. After several years she kicked him to the curb and Billy stepped into the breach.

Dinner was fine, a little flank steak and grits, cornbread on the side. I guessed that money didn't run too plentifully, but Estelle did the best she could with what she had. Later he introduced me to the new addition, a tiny little sweetie named Jill.

After dinner, the menfolk retired to what Billy called the sitting room. He offered pipes or cigars to everyone. Hart took one, but I declined, since I was convinced smoking was a noxious habit that could never do a man any good. Hart didn't disagree. He just didn't seem to care. After that, Billy brought out what he said was his best scotch whiskey, though the jug was so big he must buy it by the gallon, which made me wonder just how great it could be. Billy poured a huge glass of it for himself when, to everyone's surprise, Jill appeared out of nowhere.

She threw herself down before him and pressed her cheeks against his knees. "Daddy, I know you finished a book, but please don't get that way. My birthday's coming." She looked up at him with big wide eyes. "Please?"

'Course, I knew Billy was already well into his cups, but I was still surprised when he looked down at her and murmured, "No one remembahs Shakespeare's daughter."

She started crying and ran off. Billy took such a long draw from his glass I was surprised he was still conscious afterward. "I do have some bad habits," he explained. "I don't drink when I'm working. Never. Well, almost never. But when I'm between projects, I figure I'm entitled to relax a little. Is that so unreasonable?"

I tilted my head to one side. "A working man's a human being, just like everyone else."

"Yes indeed. Okay, not just like everyone else. Least not in my case."

We had a long and animated conversation that lasted well into the night. Most of it was about books and writers, and some of that I didn't follow. I knew a little, about that Hemingway man in Florida who Billy apparently thought was overrated, and another guy named Scott that Billy liked better but thought had ruined himself by becoming "domesticated." They also talked about philosophy and natural history, which I had an even harder time following. I only got comfortable with the conversation when it turned to politics. Everybody talked about politics back in Massachusetts, so I could follow this part with ease.

"Hoover wasn't such a bad fellow, you know," Billy opined. "He had a good heart. People forget all the charitable work he did during the Great War. I don't think he's to blame for this Depression. Is it his fault the cotton crop went rotten? Did he stop the assembly lines? They stopped 'cause there was no demand, 'cause no one had any dough to spend. He thought the economy would fix itself, laissez-faire and all that. Perfectly understandable. It had worked for about a hundred years. But not this time. So Hoover, the progressive, was perceived as some kinda arch-conservative."

"Roosevelt made him out to be the villain," I ventured.

"That's politics for you. Blame the other guy. Hoover was a humanitarian."

"I heard he sold off all his stock just before the crash."

"That's as may be," Billy said, "but it don't mean he knew what was coming. I don't think anyone knew nothing. Just a lot of speculators who got hoisted by their own petards." He took another swig. "Thank God I never saved anything."

"Most of my school chums back—"

"—in Massachusetts?" Billy interjected.

"Yes . . ."

"Lucky guess."

"Most of them think Roosevelt is a socialist."

Billy leaned back in his chair. "When you're living like a dog and eating out of a rusty tin can, socialism sounds pretty good. We got men who want to work but can't, desperate for some way to get themselves out of the mess they're in. You can't make decisions based on abstract philosophical positions when you're in pain. You got to make decisions based on what you need. It's people that matter ultimately, not ideas."

"What do you think about this so-called New Deal?"

Billy lit a pipe. I could see his eyes getting rheumy, probably the result of all that supposedly high-grade scotch. "Let me tell you a story. I knew a boy 'round these parts. Probably known him since I was knee high to a grasshopper. Good man. Proud, like most folks here. But this Depression came, and he couldn't find work. Too proud to beg, wouldn't take handouts. And when those New Dealers showed up with that Civilian Conservation Corps camp—he wouldn't have nothing to do with it."

"I understand the sentiment."

"Until he saw how much good they did. People working who hadn't worked for years. That gave a man pride. A sense of accomplishment. If he passed the physical and had a letter from his parents, even a kid could get work, and that's a far sight better than riding the rails."

Hart and I exchanged a look.

"Boy could make ten bucks a month, enough to get by on. Those CCC people only stayed for nine months, but they did a lot of good. Built parks. Built that town square where I found you two. Hadn't been for that New Deal program, I 'spect my friend would be dead now."

"I think Roosevelt is all charm and no substance," I said. "Hoover was smarter. Hoover wrote his own speeches. Roosevelt has a staff of writers."

"He needs better ones," Billy replied. "We have nothing to fear but fear itself? Where's he been all his life? Truth is—we got a lot to fear. And we ain't gonna fix it by ignoring it." His eyelids fluttered. "Not sure we can fix it. But I'm trying."

That last remark caught my ear. I wasn't sure what he was talking about. "You're trying? Excuse me, but—what exactly are you doing?"

"Writing my stories."

I didn't want to be rude to our host, but this struck me as strange. "And how exactly do you imagine your stories are gonna help people?"

"Stories have helped people since the dawn of time. Why do you think folks like them so much?"

I shrugged. "They're . . . entertaining."

"So is a dog chasing its tail, but one doesn't keep going back to it over and over again. People love a good story."

"Some people, maybe. I'm not gonna spend all my time reading silly tales. I'm going to college so I can do great things. I'm gonna build skyscrapers and bridges."

Billy puffed a couple of times on his pipe. "Why do you think you like them Mars stories so much?"

I didn't recall ever saying I loved them that much, but I went along with the flow of the conversation. "They pass the time."

"You have any trouble passing your time?"

"Not normally."

"I didn't imagine so. In my experience, time can generally pass just fine on its own. So why did you read those stories?"

I thought a moment. Couldn't come up with a good answer. "You ever wish you could just get away from everything? Stare up at the sky and travel someplace far, far away from where you are now?"

"You mean like John Carter. Sure, maybe. Once or twice."

"Were you inspired by John Carter's deeds? Did you get a thrill every time he saved his princess from the evil monsters of Mars? Did they make you want to be brave and heroic? Did you learn from his mistakes?"

"I guess."

"That's why we read stories, son. And that's why people like Burroughs and Howard and Conrad and me write them. Because they make people feel a little less lonely and maybe even a little smarter about things than they were before. Because they show us the way."

"Bridges help people," I insisted. "And skyscrapers."

"True enough," he said. "Least for a while. And then they fade away, like everything else man builds." Another puff and a pause. "Everything except stories. Stories last forever."

━━━

I got up early the next morning so I could be at the post office the moment it opened. There was only one clerk on duty, but it didn't appear that there was a great demand for his services. I explained who I was searching for and showed him the postcard.

"Maxine Bennett. Oh, I remember her. She picked up her mail here on a regular basis. Got it General Delivery."

I noticed the man used the past tense. "You mean she doesn't pick her mail up here anymore?"

"She don't live here no more. Sorry, friend. I think you just missed her."

I felt my heart sink into my shoes. I didn't have time to chase her all over the country. We only had one lead—and it just hit a dead end. Which meant in all likelihood I would end up swinging from a rope. And Callie's future might be even worse.

seventeen

I QUELLED my rising panic and asked the clerk some semi-intelligent questions.

"Where'd she go?"

"No idea."

"Where was she staying when she was here?"

"She stayed at Miss Sally's, just outside the city limits. Tall Sally's pretty generous about taking in strays. Long as they're willing to work."

That didn't sound so good to me. I could just imagine what kind of work Maxine might be doing and I didn't imagine her doctor daddy would care for it.

"Did she leave a forwarding address?"

"Let me check." He retreated to the rear portion of the post office. I heard him pulling out drawers and slamming down stacks of paper. He emerged a few minutes later shaking his head. "Nope. No forwarding address. Not a trace of her."

I thanked him and asked if he could give me directions to this Sally's. Took me about an hour walking around, but I eventually found the establishment in question. From the outside, it looked like a normal two-gabled two-story house, the kind you saw all over the town. It was painted a bright yellow and looked innocuous enough. I strolled up on the porch and knocked on the door.

I heard giggling inside. I knocked again.

After a few moments, a woman came to the door. She had ample flushed cheeks and curled yellow hair and about the friend-liest smile you ever saw in your entire life.

"What can I do for you, cowpoke?" she said, still giggling.

I wondered what I had done to merit being called a cowpoke. It had been some time since I'd had a bath. I'd been in several scrapes, some of which were having a negative impact on my countenance. And after sleeping in jail and at the hobo camp and on the railroad car, who knew? I tried to wash up a bit at Billy's house, but I guess I didn't do as good a job as I should've.

"I'm looking for a young girl."

"So is every man who comes down this way," she replied, still smiling and giggling. I did not doubt but that this was so.

"I'm looking for a particular lady." "Just any ol' gal won't do."

"No, it won't."

"So you wouldn't settle for me, for instance?" She pushed forward her ample bosom in such a way as to practically thrust my nose into her cleavage. I have to admit I got more than a trifle embarrassed at that point. I took a step backward and tried to convey my lack of interest without being rude.

I suppose Maxine had to survive somehow. But I wondered how appealing she might be, given that she was with child. Still, these professional colleagues might protect her from strangers. I had to work out how to get this gal talking to me.

"I'm looking for Maxine Bennett."

"She ain't here no more."

"So I hear. But might you, or perhaps someone else in this establishment, have some idea where she's gone?"

"You expect us to give away her whereabouts to any cowpoke who saunters up to the door?"

This was where I had to suck in my pride. I had one bullet left in my holster, and now was the time to fire it. "I can pay you."

She fluttered her eyelashes. "Can you now?"

"Let me buy an hour of your time." I had read that these girls of easy virtue were willing to do anything for money and that they sold their time in one-hour increments. That's how it always worked in *Spicy Western Tales*, anyhow. I figured they'd be relieved to spend an hour yakking and not having to take any clothes off or pretend like they enjoyed what they were doing. "What's your going rate?"

"That depends on what you want." At that, a mess of other girls rushed up to the door, five altogether. Some were prettier than others, but none of them were altogether homely. They giggled and batted their eyelashes and pressed up against one another. "Now which one of us do you want? We're all available."

No doubt about that. They probably all recognized that I was a cut above the usual customer. I didn't want to hurt anyone's feelings. But I thought they'd be more garrulous if I got them alone. One-on-one, so to speak. My budget didn't permit me to hire them all. I just hoped they didn't expect me to sacrifice my virtue and engage in a carnal act or two. I abruptly realized I didn't want to be here any longer than necessary. "I reckon I'm having some trouble making a selection."

"Maybe you should take all of us."

"You mean, one after the other?"

"No, honey. All at once. You can handle it, cain't you?"

This comment led to such uproarious laughter that I began to smell a rat. I gave those gals a more in-depth inspection. I realized that every last one of them had those full flushed cheeks, and come to think of it, they all had pretty full bosoms, too.

Then I finally looked low enough to detect the significant swell each and every one of them had in the tummy.

This was not a den of iniquity, or at least not the one I thought it was. Every single one of these young ladies was with child.

"Girls?" I heard a stern voice behind them. Their eyes widened and they scattered.

A short, squat woman in a black lacy dress appeared. "May I assist you?"

"I'm looking for a gal by the name of Maxine Bennett."

"And why would you look for her here?"

"I was given this address at the post office."

"And why do you seek her?"

I felt like I was being cross-examined by one of those Massachusetts lawyers. "I was sent by her daddy. He wants her to come home."

"Well, isn't that nice. After all he's done."

"He says she's the dearest thing to his heart and he's worried about her," I explained.

"This presents a sticky situation," the woman said. "Should I send her back to the father I don't approve of, or leave her in the hands of a man I don't approve of? Well, truth is, I don't have any say in the matter."

I didn't quite grasp the dilemma. "Ma'am, is this place . . ."

"This is a home for young ladies in the delicate condition." She raised her chin and drew herself to her full height, which was almost five feet. "We do not make moral judgments. We accept the girls as they come to us and try to help them as best we can."

Those girls at the door knew what my mistake had been. They were having a little sport with me. And I fell for it. It would almost be funny—if I hadn't been such a chump.

"Maxine came to you for help?"

"She had nowhere else to go. She'd come to Oxford to meet some boy, but he hadn't shown up. She sent a postcard to some other boy, but he didn't show up."

"That's 'cause her daddy waylaid him."

"The first boy finally appeared, and she ran off with him. I didn't think she should travel, close as she was to her time. But she didn't listen."

"Where'd they go?"

"Don't know."

"Catch the boy's name?"

"I did not."

"See him?"

"Tall, lanky fellow. Loud voice. Seemed a little nervous."

Not terribly helpful. "Anything else?"

"Well, not that I was nosing into other people's business. But I helped Maxine get what things she had into the boy's automobile. And I noticed some of the signs in the rear seat. You know, the kind those labor agitators carry?"

"Placards?"

"That's just it."

"What did the placards say?"

"I don't recall the details. Don't cotton to that Marxist doggerel. But I recall they were all stamped with the name of an organization. IOOP."

"What's that stand for?"

She put her fists on her hips. "Do I look like a communist?"

"No, ma'am." I tipped my hat. "And you have no idea where she went?"

"Sorry, son. None at all. If you see her, tell her Tall Sally sends her best."

This was Tall Sally? "I will, ma'am."

"I didn't have her here as long as I have most of my girls, but I love them all dearly just the same. Remind her about testing the bottle on the wrist."

"Uh . . ."

"I try to offer instruction when I can. They think having the baby is gonna be the hard part. Only later do they realize that's when the hard part begins."

I made my goodbyes and headed back to the center of town, crushed. Maxine had slipped through my fingers once again. I tried to think rationally, like they taught us in school. The problem was, we didn't have enough time to do a global search. If we didn't meet the doctor's deadline, I didn't doubt for one minute that it would be the end of Callie, and as soon as they could lay their hands on me, the end of me, too. Probably Hart as well.

I tried to apply the logic that I had learned, but the Aristotelian syllogism and the Socratic method weren't solving my problem. I was ambling toward Rowan Oak when I felt something cold and hard dig into my side.

"Stop right there, stranger. You're under arrest."

eighteen

I **WHEELED AROUND** and found myself staring at two cops, both wearing uniforms so shiny I figured they must be newly minted members of the law enforcement community.

"Under arrest? For what? I just got into town last night."
"That's the problem. We don't want no strangers here in Oxford."

"There's no law preventing a man from traveling from one town to another. That's in the U.S. Constitution."

"You some kind of communist?"

"No, sir. I don't hold with any form of radicalism. I think a man should stand on his own two feet."

"You got work, buddy?"

"'Course I don't have work. I am a college man. I go to school in—" Just for the moment, I decided to withhold the location. These nimrods might think Massachusetts sounded communistic. "Got me a full scholarship."

"From where? Russia?"

"From the Rotary clubs of the *U S* of *A*."

"My daddy was a Rotarian."

The more aggressive of the two was a tall man with eyes that seemed to be in a perpetual squint. Since he had a badge and the other man did not, I assumed he was in charge. "You got a place to stay? We can't have you sleeping on park benches or public alleyways."

"I'm staying with my friend Billy over at Rowan Oak." I decided not to mention that I'd just met the man the night before.

"Rowan Oak?" They both looked at one another and shared a chuckle. "You must enjoy a tipple or two."

"Not especially."

"I don't think much else goes on at Rowan Oak."

"Billy's a writer."

The smaller cop made a snorting noise. His voice was high and somewhat nasal. "You ever read any of his scribbling? Hell, half of it don't even make sense. Where'd you come in from?"

"Guymon, Oklahoma, if you must know. It's in the panhandle."

The little fella's eyes retracted into his skull. "Hey, that's where Pretty Boy robbed that bank a few days ago, isn't it?"

I wished now I'd given them a different place of origin. "That's what I heard. Am I free to return to Rowan Oak now?"

The little man couldn't seem to take his eyes off me. "You stay out of trouble, hear? We might check in on you later."

"Suit yourself."

They turned to go, but just before they did, the big one gave me another jab with the point of his nightstick. "And when we say stay out of trouble, we mean trouble of all kinds, understand? No organizing."

I nodded my faint comprehension. I knew I shouldn't be disrespectful to law enforcement sorts, but those two were just bullies, plain and simple. Worse—bullies with too much time on their hands. And I hate bullies. Always have.

━━

I suspected I'd find Hart in a black mood with no lithium to be had, so imagine my surprise when I found him up-and-at-'em, commanding the attention of Billy's whole family, not to mention a comely gal with short hair I'd never seen before. His audience hung spellbound on his every word.

I should've known he was telling one of those stories.

"Things looked awful dark for that Kennubian princess. She hung by a slender thread over the Sorrowful Slime of the Dark Lord, with no weapons on her and barely a stitch of clothing. Her handsome warrior Emerson Babylon and the rest of the Challengers of the Dust were nowhere to be seen. The fate of the seventeen civilized planets hung in the balance, for with her life would go all those who believe in freedom and hope for a better tomorrow. She closed her eyes—"

He looked up abruptly. "George. When did you sneak in?"

"Don't stop!" the woman said, and the others echoed her sentiment. "Don't leave us hanging."

"Be patient," he said, waving them down. "George, what you been doing?"

"Taking care of our business."

"Did you find that girl?"

"'Fraid not." I gave him the short version, just so he'd realize how desperate the situation had become. "I don't know what we should do next."

"I've heard of that IOOP," the new gal said. "Some kind of union, I think. They operate out of Cleveland."

"Cleveland?" I said. "There's no way we can get to Cleveland and back in time."

She shrugged. "Sounds like you're dangling on kind of a slender thread yourself, friend. Just like that Kennubian princess." She stuck out her hand, so strong and forceful that I checked to make sure she wasn't a man. "My name's Amy, pardner. Yours?"

"George," I replied. "You a friend of Billy's?"

She grinned. She had freckles and a gap between her two front teeth, but it didn't make her any less attractive. I couldn't shake the feeling that she looked familiar, but I couldn't quite place why. "We've shared a drink or two when we bumped heads. I keep thinking if I hang around him enough, some of that literary smarts will rub off."

Billy waved a hand in the air. "I'd say you're doing all right on your own. How many copies did *The Fun of It* sell?"

"Who cares? The critics hated it."

"The people loved it. You and your husband have got them buying anything that's got your initials on it."

She tilted her head to one side. Her curly hair was parted in the middle, so the tilt made it flop right in front of her face. Seriously cute, in a boyish way. "Just once I'd like to read a review from the critics like the ones you get. That sort of thing must make a soul proud."

"Yep," Billy said. He took a sip from his mug. "A man can be proud all the way to the poorhouse."

I didn't want to get waylaid on another of those literary discussions. "You just get into town, Amy?" I asked.

"Flew in this morning."

I raised an eyebrow. "Flew?"

"Parked my plane in the town square."

"That right?" I'd heard about these aviatrixes before, but I'd never actually met one. "Long flight?"

"Compared to what? Flying across the Atlantic? No. Crossing from Honolulu to California? Definitely not. I'm in my little Lockheed two-seater. Sleek little bird with low wings. Nothing better to fly in the world."

"You're making this up."

"She's not," Billy said. "She got the Distinguished Flying Cross from Congress for that Honolulu flight. Only woman to ever get one."

"Well, ain't that something. It's a pleasure to meet you, ma'am."

"Congratulate me later. I'm hoping to set a new world record for crossing the globe. You ever been up in a plane?"

"Can't say that I have."

"Ever want to?"

I thought about that. Part of me did and part of me did not. "Might be willing to do it once. You still get the jitters when you take off?"

"I get a thrill like nothing else on earth. I live to fly. I'd fly in my sleep if I could. I once played tennis on the wings of a biplane."

"You did not."

"Did. Didn't work all that well though. Wind tends to carry the ball off."

I hesitated. "You think . . . maybe . . . you'd be willing to show me that plane of yours?"

"I suppose I could be persuaded to do that. If you could persuade your friend to finish his damn story!"

"Later," Hart said.

"Why not now?"

Hart pushed out his chair. "A good storyteller always leaves his readers wanting more."

———

Hart and I decided to go into town to see if we could rustle up more leads about Maxine Bennett and the IOOP. Hart thought there might be someone who knew something. We tried speaking to folks when we could catch their eye or as they rested their feet for a moment. Most knew nothing. A few seemed put out to be questioned and resented the suggestion that they might know anything about a single woman in a family way.

Only after several hours of fairly futile conversation did we come across one young gentleman with useful information.

"I knew Maxine a little." He was a round fellow in suspenders who looked as if his spare time had gone to his gut. "I knew the boy better. Duke, they called him."

"Was that his real name," Hart asked, "or a nickname? Or a title?"

"I don't know. I reckoned it was a nickname, but I could be wrong."

"Did you get a last name?"

"Sorry, no."

"How did you know this Duke?"

"Met him at the bar at Al's. Little drinking hole on Park Street. Spent a couple of hours with him getting royally snockered. He didn't mind hanging around as long as I was buying." He pressed his hand against his head. "I stayed longer than I shouda."

"What was he doing there?"

"Said he come to collect that girl, Maxine. Planned to take her away the following morning."

"Was he the father of the child?"

"I don't think so. But he was all messed up in those people's business somehow. Said he knew a secret that was worth a lot of money. If it didn't get him killed."

Now here was an interesting wrinkle. I knew Hart thought so, too, because he leapt right on it. "Did he give you any idea what this secret might be?"

"No. And not for my lack of trying. He liked to tease, especially as the liquor loosened his tongue, but he didn't come across with much information. Most of the night he talked about politics."

My heart sank. I didn't see how this could be relevant, or even interesting. Some people liked to go on and on about politics, but I'd had more than my fill the night before. "Like what?"

"I got the idea he was pretty pink. Said once he collected the girl he was heading north to Cleveland."

There it was again, plain as day. If we didn't get to Cleveland, we had no hope of finding Maxine. Made me wish I could turn back the wheels of time like that fella in Hart's stories, 'cause I didn't see how we could get there and back before my time expired.

"Cleveland's a big city," Hart said. "Any idea where in particular they might be headed?"

The fella thought for a moment. "Well, I think that's where the Midwest Garment Workers factory is located, ain't it?"

Hart nodded. I myself had no idea.

"He talked about how that outfit abused its employees, taking advantage of the hard times to pay folks starvation wages. Forcing them to live in a company town and they had to shop there too so there was no chance they could ever get ahead. No chance they could ever leave. Like slaves, practically. That outfit he worked with hoped to do something about it."

"That outfit . . . ?" I said, kinda suggestive-like.

"The IOOP. International Organization of Occupational Protest." He shook his head. "Even the name sounds red, don't it?"

I did not express an opinion on the matter as I had none to express. I pumped him for any more information he might be able to provide, but we'd pretty much worked our way to the bottom of that well. While we stood there jawing, I heard shouting rise up behind me.

"*Stop!* Both of you! Police!"

I felt a sudden coldness, like I had sleet oozing through my veins. I turned and spotted those two cops I'd met earlier. 'Cept now they looked angry. They ran toward me. One of them had his pistol out.

"Stop that man!" the gunslinger shouted. "He's a bank robber. Works with Pretty Boy Floyd. Get him!"

nineteen

I DIDN'T KNOW what to do. As I've said before, I'm normally a law-abiding citizen. But I didn't have nothing to do with that bank robbery, and I'd already dealt with one set of cops on the matter. I later learned that the sheriff in Guymon filed charges right after he grabbed me and issued a report saying I'd escaped after I left town. Seemed like a crazy thing to do when I was on a mission he'd arranged. But this whole situation was a good deal more complicated than I recognized at the time, and I guess he was covering his tracks in case I didn't return. That little scrawny Oxford cop recognized me and confirmed his suspicions when he got back to the station. Now they'd decided to round me up and see if they could collect a lucrative reward for capturing a notorious bank robber, namely me.

So I had two choices. I could stay and get arrested, in which case I'd never get to Cleveland or help Callie. Or I could make a run for it, in which case I still probably wouldn't complete the mission in time. But at least I wouldn't be in jail.

I turned tail and ran.

Hart followed right behind me. Guess that ankle healed up, 'cause he moved at an admirable clip.

"Stop those men!" the taller of the two cops shouted. "They're fugitives!"

He kept hollering and running, but I didn't see none of the townsfolk taking much interest. I didn't know if that was a sign of the times or an indication that this sort of thing happened none too infrequently.

We stayed consistently ahead of our pursuers, but I realized there was a long-term problem. Hart said the same thing.

"What's our endgame?" he asked, panting, as we raced side-by-side down Park Street.

"Don't know," I huffed in reply. "Can't get back to Billy's. Can't keep running forever." Truer words were never spoken, because I was already running out of steam, and we were nowhere near the city limits. And we had no guarantee the pursuit would end at that imaginary line, anyway.

"You play a game with no plan for the ending—you lose," Hart said. I had already come to much the same conclusion, though I was formulating it in less elegant language.

"Maybe we should just let them arrest us."

"You do that, your sister's dead," he said bluntly. "And you, too."

"You think that sheriff will hang me?"

"I think these two jokers might do it. Then they get the glory and reward for taking down a wanted criminal."

I managed to find a little more energy and increased my speed. We rounded a sharp corner.

The lead officer fired his pistol.

I don't know how close it really was, but I could swear I felt that bullet graze the side of my head. I know I saw it smack into the brick wall to my immediate left. If my head had been any larger, I'd be a corpse.

He fired again and this time Hart cried out. He kind of tripped and turned sideways, and I could see he was going down. I grabbed him by the shoulders and kept him steady, but there was no way I could keep running in this position.

It seemed the chase had come to an end. And we were dead as drumsticks.

That was when I heard the noise. Sounded like nothing I had ever heard before. Kinda like a tractor but much louder. I wondered for a moment if one of Hart's stories was coming to life. Was this some kind of machine from Mars?

"I'm coming, boys!"

I turned my head and saw a sight I never imagined I would see, not before nor after. You're gonna think I made this part up, but I didn't.

That thunderous sound emerged from a small two-seat plane. Except it wasn't flying. It was rolling down the main boulevard of Oxford.

Amy was in the pilot's seat, of course.

Those cops took one look and ducked for cover. I think they were no more used to seeing such sights than I was. The fact that she steered a beeline right toward them possibly also added to their consternation. After they scattered, she shot right past them and came up near me and Hart.

"I can't stop," she shouted over the noise of the engine. "Jump on as I pass by."

This seemed like a dubious proposition in the best of circumstances, which these were not.

I glanced at Hart. "You up for this?"

"We got no choice." I admired the way he could cut to the heart of the matter, even when he was hurting.

I started running, pulling Hart along, trying to keep the same pace as the plane. This was not unlike running to jump on the train, except that time I wasn't toting Hart and I still almost didn't make it. But I could see that this street was about to bottom out and lead straight into a dead-end alley, which suggested to me that either the plane had to be in the air before then or we were all goners.

I hoisted Hart upward. He grabbed the rim of the open seat

and pulled himself in headfirst. I continued to keep pace with the plane. Soon as Hart was situated, I jumped in after him.

There was only one open seat, and it was none too roomy.

Fortunately, Hart was a small man. "Inhale!" I told him.

I guess he did, because I managed to slide into the seat behind him.

"Hold on!" Amy shouted, and a second later we were in the air. I'll admit my heart shot right up into my throat. There was something unnatural about the feeling of leaving terra firma, especially when your top quarters were exposed to the open air. Men were meant to have dirt under their feet, least that's how I felt about it.

I could hear those two disappointed cops behind us, shouting and shooting, but there was nothing they could do.

"Deus ex machina," Hart said.

"What's that again?"

"The machine of the gods. The gods swoop down from the heavens to resolve the conflict. Makes for an unsatisfying conclusion to a story. But in this instance, I'm not complaining."

"Nor me."

Amy had this big grin on. Her whole face lit up. I think right then she looked more alive than anyone I've ever seen in my entire life, before or since. That girl loved to fly.

"Thanks for the rescue," I shouted.

"You seemed to be in need."

"We were. But you may be in for some trouble now."

"I doubt it. I got me lots of friends in high places."

"I hope you're right. Much appreciated."

She turned back toward the sky. "Well, I couldn't let those cops arrest you. Least not till I hear how that story ends."

As it turned out, Hart was not much wounded. He had a little scrape along the hip and it bled for a bit, but it stopped eventually and he didn't seem the worse for it. The bullet went clean through and didn't leave a mark. I had a suspicion that it stung, but Hart didn't let on. I've said it before and I'll say it again: he was not much of one for complaining.

Amy asked us where we wanted to go and of course we said Cleveland and she said that suited her fine. She allowed as to how she was an excellent pilot but not that great a navigator, but she thought she could get us somewhere in the general vicinity. This was good news, since by flying we could get there before sunset, which meant there was just the slightest chance we could complete our mission and get back to Guymon in time.

Hart took a little nap, which normally I wouldn't've minded, but in this case, when we were wrapped all around one another, it was less than convenient. How he could sleep when we were up in the air like that, I'll never understand. He was only out an hour or so, but when he woke, he was in a black mood.

"Have another bad dream?" We had to shout at each other, since we were so high up and the engine was so loud. But we got used to it.

Took him a while to answer. I got the impression he was still deep within wherever it was he went, and it took some while to get himself back. "Yeah. I was playing chess with my pa."

"That don't seem so horrific."

"You weren't there."

"If he played chess, he couldn't have been too stupid."

"He was very smart. Like me. But my ma never gave us a moment's peace. I couldn't do anything to please her. She said chess was for sissy boys. She wanted me to play football. Can you imagine? Look at me. She always wanted something that would make her feel all bloated up and important, but never seemed to give one tinker's dam what I wanted for myself."

"Didn't go in much for sports?"

"I was sick a lot when I was a kid. Docs weren't sure what was wrong with me. Always bedridden. So I was nothing but a big disappointment to her. And I was the only son she had. So she never let me forget how disappointed she was."

"Your ma sounds like a handful. And your pa was no walk in the park."

"He had the darkness, like me. A pervasive case of the melancholy, that's what he used to call it. I heard him say once, 'They think this is the Great Depression? The Great Depression is right here.' And then he'd thump himself on the chest."

"And eventually . . ."

"He got to the point where he couldn't take it no more."

"I hope you realize that was a damn fool thing to do. No disrespect to your bloodline intended."

His eyes drifted. "Some mornings, when I'm lying in bed, and everything hurts and I'm all alone . . ." He didn't finish the sentence, and I was relieved he didn't.

I couldn't entirely comprehend everything he was saying, but I did get two things out of the conversation. First, this boy was a heck of a lot smarter than I was. And second, maybe being so smart wasn't always a blessing.

Hart cleared his throat. "I, uh, wanted to thank you for what you did back there."

"Meaning?"

"Tossing my carcass into this plane. I wouldn't have made it on my own."

"You've helped me more than once since this journey began. I wish I could help you more. Pull you out of your funk." I paused, and the image of the woman with the dark hair flashed into my head. "You know what you need, Hart? You need to find you a girl."

He gave me a look that was hard to describe. But I didn't think he was appreciative of my suggestion. "That's the secret to happiness, huh?"

"Beats a swift kick in the pants, that's for sure. I had a little encounter back at the hobo camp that did me a world of good."

His eyes narrowed. "I did notice someone prowling around your spot late that night."

I whistled. "She was a sweet little number, I'll tell you."

"That was a girl?"

I felt like he'd socked me in the chest. "'Course it was a girl. Why would you think otherwise?"

"Did you notice the clothing?"

"That didn't mean anything. I 'spect that was all she could find to wear."

He did not appear convinced. "What happened between you two?"

I suddenly felt extremely uncomfortable. "Nothing worth speaking about. You need to find you some pretty little thing who'll take care of you. Settle down. Get a steady job. Does wonders for a man."

"Think you've got it all figured out, huh?"

"Well, there's some things I think I know, yes."

"Just repeat all the trite aphorisms you've heard other people say, because they heard them from someone else, and go on believing everything you hear. Deny your true feelings. Pretend to be what everyone else is pretending to be."

"I didn't say anything about pretending. But living a good clean Christian life works."

"How do you know?"

"Well . . . look around you. Look at the normal people with successful children and no troubles 'cause they live the way you're supposed to."

"Let me tell you something, George. If there's a family you think doesn't have any problems—that just means you don't know them very well."

I shook my head. "I don't think you and me are ever going to agree on much. But I still appreciate your help. You didn't have to join me on this fool mission."

He shrugged. "Beats sitting around in that jail cell all day."

"I think there was more to it than that."

He shot me a quick glance.

I added, "I'm just sayin' I appreciate it. That's all."

"When I was growing up, guys like you always picked on me. Bullied me 'cause I was smaller and smarter. But you were never like that. You've been nothing but nice, in your own way."

"Aw, hell. Anybody'd do the same."

"I know from experience that statement is not true." He twisted around and looked at me, straight in the eyes. "I never knew a guy like you who was actually my friend."

⎯⎯

After that, I guess I took a nap, too. Didn't mean to, but it had been another trying day.

And when I woke, I stared straight into the abyss. The plane plummeted so fast it pulled my cheeks back to my ears. Near as I could tell, we were on a straight line to the earth traveling way too fast. I saw Amy pulling on her stick and flipping switches, but none of it seemed to make any difference.

We were going straight down, and at this rate, I figured we had maybe thirty seconds to say our prayers before we were squashed flat as the prairie.

twenty

"HOLD ONTO YOUR SEATS!" Amy shouted. As if we had any choice about the matter.

"What's happening?" I shouted back.

"Got a little off course," she replied. "It happens. Caught a tailwind."

"Can you pull us out of it?"

"What do you think I'm doing up here? Playing the piano?" She leaned back as far as she could, tugging insistently on what I assumed was the throttle. Hart was awake, too, and he saw what was happening. As always, though, he had a strange calm about him.

Eventually, Amy flattened the plane out. When I say eventually, I mean it seemed like it took two or three years, but in retrospect it was probably more like twenty or thirty seconds. She leveled off, then cruised about looking for a suitable place to land. Once she found her strip, she touched down and rolled to a stop.

I was appreciative for the lift, but in all honesty I must say I was not sorry the ride was over.

I squeezed out of that seat and lay down on the ground. It felt good to be on solid earth again, and it felt even better to stretch out.

By the time I got back to my feet, Hart and Amy were palavering, but in such quiet voices I didn't even know what they said. Imagine my surprise when I saw her lean forward and plant a big juicy kiss right smack on his lips.

Hart appeared just as astonished as I was. He kinda clinched up, but he relaxed a moment later.

"Now see," Amy said, her arms akimbo, "that wasn't so bad, was it?"

"No," he allowed. "But I don't plan to make a habit of it."

I guess she could see the astonishment plastered on my face as I approached. "Are you shocked, George?"

"I guess it's none of my business . . . but ain't you a married woman?"

"It's a practical arrangement. Nothing more."

Didn't seem like much of a marriage if the gal was running around kissing other men. "Was there something Hart did to earn this gift?"

"'Course there was. He told me how that story ends."

"You coulda bought the magazine."

"I liked this way better. Besides, a gal doesn't need an excuse to kiss a man like him. Nothing more attractive than a smartie."

Maybe it was just the dying light, but I think Hart flushed up some.

Amy climbed back into the cockpit and strapped on her leather helmet. "Cleveland is just about a mile due east, if my navigation is correct—which is far from certain. You should be able to find it without much trouble."

She started up the engine. "Remember what I said, Hart," she shouted over the noise. "You ever decide you need a woman for anything, just give me a call." She blew him a kiss. "If you two boys get tired of dating each other."

What the tarnation? I wanted to follow up on that, but I didn't get a chance. She was in the air and gone before I could say another word.

We found a nice place in a grove of trees and hunkered down

for the night. Once the sun rose, I figured we'd be able to determine which way was east and find our way into town. I gathered some leaves and pine needles and made some beds. I was thirsty, but I figured it could wait till we got to Cleveland. The weather turned cold after the sun went down, but all things considered, I was glad to be there and not in some stinking cell. Or swinging from the end of a rope.

I couldn't fall asleep right away, so I gazed up at the stars. They seemed incredibly bright, brighter than I'd ever seen. Maybe I just never looked that hard before. I got this idea in my head that those stars were like sentinels, or shepherds, watching over us. Then it occurred to me that since I left Guymon, I'd met a lot of good people who didn't have no one to protect them. I wondered how many others like that were out there, lost and lonely and hungry with the world seeming dead set against them. Seemed like someone should be doing something about it, I thought, as my eyelids started to weigh on me. Right then everyone was too busy trying to survive the day. But there ought to be a shepherd, not up in the sky far away, but right down here in the dust and the dirt. A shepherd in the sand who kept an eye on folks and made sure they were safe and loved, no matter what they done or how bad things got.

———

Next morning Hart woke in a foul mood, worse than usual, and I had a tougher time sorting him out. I gathered he'd been dreaming about his folks again. Eventually, I told him to start walking. Whether he was in the mood for it or not, we had no time to waste. I thought he was better off once he got his legs moving and his blood circulating. But even then he muttered to himself. I tried to ignore him, but it presented a challenge. He chattered under his breath, like he was talking to someone who was there, except they weren't.

"You wanna hear a joke?" I said at last.

"Because you're desperate to tell it?" he snapped back. "Or because you think you're gonna brighten my spirits?"

"I think you could do with some brightening."

"Better than you have tried."

"Well then, what would work?"

"I wish to God I knew."

We walked in silence. Then I tried a different approach. "Look, Hart, we've been through a lot together, and I don't like to see any man suffering the way you do. Maybe you ought to see some kind of doctor."

"They don't make a pill for what I got."

"I was thinking maybe . . . one of them head doctors."

"An alienist? An acolyte of Dr. Freud?" He actually laughed a little. "You think digging around in my childhood is gonna help anything?"

"You do seem to have a few difficulties in that department."

"The past is the past, George. We have to focus on the here and the now."

"I agree. Problem is, I don't know what you have in the now."

He turned his head abruptly. "I have you, right?"

"Well . . . sure."

"And you've got your sister. And you want to do right by her."

"That's true."

"So let's just do that, okay?"

I nodded and let it go. We walked the rest of the way to Cleveland without the benefit of conversation.

—⊏⊐—

I expected Cleveland would resemble Boston, subscribing to the theory that all big cities must be more or less alike. As it turned out, Cleveland was something different altogether—crowded and dirty, and I disliked it almost from the moment I stepped into town. Everyone was in a hurry, but I couldn't figure out what the hurry was all about. We crossed a bridge over the Cuyahoga, and it stank so bad I could barely breathe. I glanced at newspapers with half-page headlines about organized crime and labor racketeers and the sharp increase in juvenile offenders. Seemed that even outside the Dust Bowl, folks still had plenty of problems. One paper claimed some crazed maniac was running around killing people and hacking them down to their torsos.

On the other hand, Cleveland did have electric streetlights— that was new. And traffic lights, which was good, because they had the worst traffic you ever did see. I didn't know there were that many automobiles in the world, much less one city. Cops rode on little two-wheel motorcycles. Everything appeared very modern. The movie theaters had shows that talked, and one even claimed they had a show in color. Restaurants served seafood and other fancy stuff shipped in by train. Over and over, I heard this record with a high-pitched boy singing "Life Is Just a Bowl of Cherries." I wondered whereabouts he lived that he could think such a thing.

I got some directions and headed toward the center of town. About all we had to go on was the IOOP and that Midwest Garment factory they were protesting against. The company had several factories, but the largest was in the center of town and people allowed as to how that was where all the trouble was. So of course we headed that way hoping it would take us to Doc Bennett's daughter.

We were only a few blocks from the factory when I felt Hart tugging on my shirt. He pointed toward an open door. Music streamed from inside. I thought it might be a waltz.

The sign on the door read: DANCE-A-THON. DAY 92.

"I heard about these," I commented. "Never seen one, though. You?"

"Oh yeah," Hart replied.

"Can't understand why people would torture themselves like this."

"They're hungry. Or poor. Or bored. What I can't understand is why people would think it's entertaining to watch. But they do."

I poked my head through the door. In the center was a wide hardwood dance floor with maybe twenty or so couples on it. But there were hundreds of people watching in the bleachers behind the dance floor. They gabbed and ate snacks and talked amongst themselves. A few shouted at the dancers, who hung on one another and mostly looked as if they might drop dead any moment.

The announcer was a goofy guy with red hair. He liked to work his way through his collection of silly expressions and comical voices.

"Let's go inside," Hart said, and he did just that, without waiting for my response.

"We don't have time to waste on—" But my protest came too late.

"Let's hear it for little Mabel Rae, everyone." A spattering of applause followed from those who paid attention. The announcer made a funny high-pitched laughing sound not unlike the braying of a donkey. "She's on her third partner now, but she's still hanging in there. And what about Bobby and his betrothed, LuluBelle? They still say they want to get married, folks, but they can't do it unless they get the prize money. And then there's Flynn."

All of the sudden, spectators hissed and booed.

"Now, let's not be too hard on him. Sure, he cast aside that pretty little brunette when her feet gave out, and there's some folks think he tripped Abie during the derby round yesterday, but we still want to give him the same support we give everyone else, right?"

More booing, more catcalls, which I gathered came as no surprise to the announcer. His job seemed to be turning the dancers into characters in a melodrama. And this Flynn character was cast as the villain.

Some of the spectators threw trash at Flynn. He ducked, but

some of the garbage still smacked him. He kept on dancing, but he didn't look too happy about it.

"Let's not forget about our lovely engaged couple," the announcer continued. "Is there anyone out there who wants to help them out? Shall we give them a silver shower?"

One man in the back threw a coin at the feet of the couple in question. Pretty soon others did the same. It really did look like a silver shower. Twinklings of light against a dark backdrop. "Like a starry twilight painted by Vincent van Gogh," Hart murmured.

"Who's that?"

"Dutch painter. Painted the everyday in bold, vivid colors. Did what all great artists do. Let us see things we'd never seen before."

"You meet him somewhere on the road?"

Hart smiled slightly. "No. He's long gone. Tragic end." Pause. "As so often seems the case."

I hoped the poor couple on the dance floor profited by this silver shower, but I noticed that the money got scooped up by someone who worked for the marathon. The dancers just kept on dancing.

"I don't get the appeal," I said. "So the folks running this gather people together and put them in a stupid game and play up some of the participants as sympathetic and some as villains and create a melodrama. Who would want to watch something like that?"

"You might be surprised," Hart replied. "You pay a dollar and you can stay here for hours. Better than radio or movies. Least some folks think so."

"You think these dancers have really been at it for three months?"

"Heck, that's nothing. I saw one that went on for nine months in Chicago. Everybody wants to set a new world record. Even if it's a record for doing the stupidest thing imaginable."

I thought about that a moment. I'd seen some of those flag-pole sitters trying to set records, and I'd be hard pressed to explain what the point of that was. Or goldfish-swallowing. That Gertrude lady swam across the English Channel, even though there were plenty of perfectly good boats in the area. For that matter, I recalled reading about a guy who wanted to set a record by stuffing peanuts up his nose. Maybe it would be better, I mused, if folks channeled all that energy into something useful. I thought again about that shepherd in the sand I imagined the night before. Sure seemed more valuable than this.

"It's not strictly speaking a marathon," Hart explained. "They do get breaks. Fifteen minutes every hour, generally."

"But why would anyone do it?"

"Because they feed you. Five, six meals a day. Got to, to keep the game going. And you get a place to sleep—fifteen minutes at a time. Beats homelessness, for as long as you can hold out. And the announcer keeps it interesting. Sometimes they stage weddings for the dancers. One time they encased one of the dancers in a block of ice."

My eyes narrowed. "How do you know so much about this?"

"I did it a time or two."

My eyes fairly bulged. "You? A marathon dancer?"

"I'm light on my feet."

"Why?"

"I was hungry."

"So you danced with a girl."

"They wouldn't let me dance with a boy."

I chuckled a bit, but he didn't. "How'd it turn out?"

He smiled slightly. "I never saw a game I couldn't figure out a way to win." He leaned into the room and pointed. "See the woman in the frilly white dress?"

"Yeah. What about—" I stopped short. There was something distinctive about her that a man didn't have to look too hard to notice.

She was several months gone with child. "You think that's Doc Bennett's gal?"

"Can't tell for sure. There's probably more than one pregnant lady in Cleveland."

"I would imagine so. Geez Louise, what a poor mother. All that dancing can't be good for the baby."

"Neither is starvation."

We waited until the dancers took their next break. A woman named Anita came out and sang a song. She sang about as pretty as anything I ever heard in my life, but I didn't have much time to enjoy it. Hart talked to some man who didn't want the dancers disturbed during their brief rest time. Hart slipped him some of Doc Bennett's money and before long we were talking to the gal who was in the family way.

"Are you Maxine Bennett?" I asked.

Up close, I could see how sweat-soaked and tattered that white frilly dress was. I wondered how long she'd been wearing it. Her eyes were red and surrounded by such dark circles she resembled a raccoon. "I could be anyone you want me to be, if there's food and I don't have to dance for it."

She looked plumb tuckered, which made me feel bad about taking up her rest time. "But are you Maxine?"

"Are you fellas cops?"

"No. We're just regular folks."

"Why you want Maxine?"

"It's not us that wants her. It's her pa."

"That's so sweet. Pa always had a good heart."

Hart and I exchanged a look. He wasn't sure, either. We'd both seen the photo, and she resembled it somewhat, but not entirely. How much of that was due to sheer exhaustion and pregnancy, I couldn't say.

I started to speak again, but Hart jumped in. "You got any problem coming back with us?"

"Is there a reward?"

"No. We're just supposed to bring you back."

"My baby could use a good home." She patted her protruding tummy.

"And would your pa's home be a good home?" Hart asked.

"I expect it could be worse. Can you loan me some money so I can get fixed up? I wouldn't want Pa to see me like this."

"He might want you to work in his law office. Maybe be his legal secretary or something. After the baby's born."

Her eyes brightened the moment he said the word *lawyer*. "I reckon I could do that. But I'd probably need some new clothes, don't you think? And we'd need a wet nurse to take care of the baby. Maybe we should go shopping."

"So you wouldn't mind working in your pa's office?"

"I've always loved being around my daddy."

"Then you are not Maxine Bennett," I said. Hart had exposed her for the fraud she was. "And might I add that you could go to prison for impersonating another human being."

"I wasn't impersonating! I just want out of this dance. Can you blame me?"

I could see she was in a difficult situation and had fallen on hard times. But I had no sympathy for someone who would steal another woman's birthright. In any case, I had no time for her. So I turned my back real abrupt-like and marched out of the dance hall.

Hart did not move so quickly. Their hands touched, and I'm pretty certain he slipped her a little of the doctor's money. Not that we had much to spare at that point. But I guess maybe since he had done this dance himself, his heart ached more for this almost-mama wearing herself to a frazzle.

If I'd been a better shepherd, I might've felt the same way.

When I reentered the main part of the dance hall, someone else was singing. I could swear I'd heard that voice before. I walked out front and saw to my great surprise that ol' boy Woodrow from the hobo camp, this time singing about how the land belonged to everybody or something like that. I assumed he was speaking about the land in general and not Cleveland in particular. Least I hoped so.

He sang in that same high-pitched voice, but I noticed the

crowd paid attention to him, even better than they'd paid attention to the dancing. He did have a way with a song. He took a break between verses and spoke direct to the people.

"I don't like songs that make a man feel low, or like he's not any good anymore," Woodrow said. "I don't like songs that tell folks they're worthless or kick a man when he's down. I like a song that tells people that this is *your world*."

The crowd hooted and hollered in response.

"I like a song that says that this is your world, and you belong here. You've got a role to play and a part to fill and a song to sing. So let's all join together and sing this next verse and remember that we're all one people. And this land belongs to all of us, not just the rich people or the factory owners, but everyone."

I saw more excitement and enthusiasm generated by that one song than from all the politicking and proselytizing and belly-aching I heard on that whole journey. I wondered if maybe ol' Woodrow was a shepherd, of sorts. Using his songs to help folks that he couldn't help any way else.

———

Before long Hart and I were back on the street. I saw a young man leaning against a post, scribbling into a notebook. I thought he might be able to give us directions to the factory.

"You a reporter?"

He was short and a bit plump, with round owl glasses and bushy, hard-to-manage hair. "No. Well, not for real. Maybe someday." His voice was high-pitched and a bit nasal. "But I created a reporter. Two of them, actually."

"You...created them?"

I could tell he was naturally shy, but on this subject, he was enthusiastic. "I'm a writer. That's why I'm here. Thought I might get some ideas."

"Another writer? We just left a novelist—"

"Nah. I want to write a comic strip. And I've got a super-idea.

This will be the most thrilling adventure feature ever. My character defends the weak and oppressed, like some of these people fighting for their rights today. My character can lift entire—"

"Stop." I had to grin. He got so excited when he talked about his work. But I didn't have time to chat about the funnies. I managed to redirect his enthusiasm and get directions to the factory.

We were only about a block away when we heard what sounded like a strangely familiar voice.

"I tell you, ladies and gentlemen, there's money to be made. A whole lot of money. And there's no reason why you folks shouldn't be the ones to make it."

I stared up in disbelief. "You have got to be kiddin' me."

"Seems we're not the only ones who made good time to Cleveland," Hart observed.

The man perched up on the balcony spoke to a good-sized crowd. "You may have seen other so-called scientific solutions come and go. You may have known in your hearts that some of those were the crackpot schemes of men of deceit and false witness trying to part you from your hard-earned dollars. Well, I have no sympathy for that kind of man. None at all. These are times when men of good faith must stick together. These are times when it's not enough to take care of yourself, without a thought for the needs of your fellow man. This is a time when we all stand together or we all fall. And that is why I'm making this very special opportunity available to you."

This was of course the man we had first met back in Oklahoma, the man trying to convince the folks at the gazebo that he could make rain. This pitch appeared to be a variation on the same, except tailored for a more upscale audience.

"Ever since the greed of man brought the stock market crashing down on itself, folks like you have searched for legitimate and prosperous means to invest your money, to turn your God-given manna into more manna, to see your earnings go forth and multiply. Well, congratulations—you have found the promised land. This is, quite frankly, the investment opportunity of a life-time. Certain men of science in the great state of Texas have discovered how to end the drought that plagues so much of our nation. Once that technology becomes widely available, do you think there might be folks willing to buy it? And if so, do you think there might be a profit to be made for those who own it?"

"'Course there is," a man shouted from the crowd. "Any fool can see that. Simple supply and demand."

I wasn't totally sure, but I thought the respondent was the same man who had stroked this speaker back in Oklahoma. Most likely they traveled together.

"That's exactly right, good sir. This is a free economy, which means that those who own what others want stand to make good money. This is your chance to get in on the ground floor of something that's going to change the face of this nation. This is what's known as combustion theory—the secret to making rain."

At this point, he proceeded to give the whole spiel about Napoleon and Alexander the Great and how loading a kite with dynamite was going to make rain. Stupid as it sounds, that man did have a way with words. He held his audience spellbound, and some of them were giving serious thought to what he said. I suspected that unless someone interfered like Hart had before, a few would soon be opening their wallets.

"Think we ought to break this up?" I whispered to Hart.

"No."

That caught me by surprise. "Why not?"

"Don't see that it's any of our business."

"That didn't stop you before."

"That was an entirely different situation." Hart thrust his hands deep inside his pockets. "Those folks back in Oklahoma were dirt poor. He was exploiting their poverty and their lack of education and most of all their desperation."

"And he's doing the exact same thing here."

"No. Look around you." I cast my eyes into the crowd. "These folks aren't poor. They aren't rich, but they aren't desperate. These people have jobs and some money in their pockets. They probably should invest some of it. And if they're stupid enough to invest in something this crazy without proper investigation, just because they heard some fast-talking charlatan shouting from a balcony—that's their own fault."

Hart made his way down the street. I started to follow, then stopped.

"Yes, ladies and gentlemen," that speaker continued, "just five dollars will earn you ten shares of stock in the All-American Combustion Company. I guarantee that stock will—"

His eyes darted. He saw me in the back of the crowd. I could tell he recognized me.

I pointed my finger at him, like I was making a little gun, then popped my wrist, like the gun fired.

"—on the other hand," he stuttered, "perhaps I shouldn't use the word *guarantee*."

I gave him a long look.

"And . . . perhaps I should advise you that any investment naturally entails some degree of risk."

I put my fists on my hips and kept staring.

". . . So if you're low in cash and can't afford a loss, by all means do not give me your money."

I nodded, then turned and joined Hart.

"On the other hand, for those men of prosperity who understand the risks but still have the courage to take a gamble on the possibility of a high future return . . ."

We'd traveled maybe two miles farther into town, getting close to the lake, when I heard a thunderstorm of footsteps. The whole ground shook. Before long, a tidal wave of people surged our direction. I never saw so many people in one place in my life. I was certain if we didn't get out of their way, they'd trample us dead. "What's going on?" I shouted as I pushed Hart to the side of the street.

Someone at the head of the pack answered me. "They're killing us! The cops are killing us!"

twenty-one

WHEN I SAW that wall of people heading my way, I have to admit that I completely lost my nerve. Hordes of plain folk running in a blind panic. People tripped and fell, then got trampled upon. Men and women screamed and shouted. Some of the men carried signs, but that just caused more confusion.

The street spewed forth this human avalanche, one wave after the next. We ducked inside a shop to get out of the way. Reminded me of that swarm of locusts, except this was worse, because these were human beings. And you couldn't just spit out a human being.

Pockets of fighting broke out here and there, which only made matters worse. I heard a rifle shot, a sound with which I was getting entirely too familiar. The shots were somewhere up the street, behind the flow of traffic. But it helped explain what sent all these folks scurrying. Seemed those cops were supposed to protect the factory, but they'd left their post to hunt down their prey—the protesters.

Turned out there had been considerable labor unrest in this town for some while. The union wanted to organize the workers, and the factory owners were doing everything they could to prevent it. They had a sweet deal, with employees working for the company all day and living on company property, shopping in company stores, never getting paid enough. They ended up in debt and that trapped them in the company town forever. Roosevelt's National Industrial Recovery Act permitted collective bargaining, so labor unions had a right to organize, which led to the first-ever strikes. And some of them proved successful, which led to even more. In Chicago, over four hundred and twenty thousand textile workers walked out, bringing production to a standstill. After that, the big companies got worried. If it could happen in Chicago, it could happen anywhere. Maybe even Cleveland. The strike started earlier that morning, and the owners had retaliated with paid thugs toting shotguns. It started with shouts and threats, and before long seven people were dead. That's what started the strikers running.

Problem was, the shooting didn't stop when the people dispersed. There's arguing to this day about what orders were given, but there's no dispute about what happened. Those cops chased right after those folks and managed to shoot forty more of them. In the back.

Once I saw those cops advancing with their rifles, I became seriously nervous. We hadn't been in the strike, but I doubted those cops could make the distinction. We looked dirty and bedraggled and poor. They might gun us down before we got a chance to explain.

I wasn't sure what to do—till I saw something that settled it for me.

A pregnant woman, being tugged along by a tall young man wearing an IOOP badge.

I recognized her from the photo, no doubt about it. We'd found the doctor's daughter.

And she ran right past us.

She tried to hold onto the boy, but they got separated in the mad rush and she careened sideways in my general direction. Next thing I knew she'd tripped over a body and spiraled forward, face first. She held out her arms, trying to protect the baby. That meant she took most of it on her hands. She cried out and covered her head to shield herself from the onslaught of fast-moving feet.

Then this cop appeared behind her. His rifle was aimed right at her back.

In retrospect, I have to assume the cop didn't realize he was about to plug a pregnant girl. They'd been told to teach these strikers a lesson, one that would be heard clear across the country, but I doubt if that was meant to entail shooting expectant mothers. But all the panic and running started, and the bloodlust rose up, and people lost their senses. I'm not even sure the cop had a clear view of what he was shooting. It had turned into a turkey draw, and the winner was gonna be the guy who bagged the most game.

He loaded another round. I saw him pumping the action, squinting his left eye, standing so close it would be impossible to miss.

That's when I tackled him. The rest of the crowd had mostly passed on, giving me a little room to maneuver. I grabbed him around the waist and knocked him to the ground. He hit with a solid thud. The rifle fired, but the shot went wild.

He seemed winded by the fall. I knocked the rifle out of his hands and popped him one on the chin. I would've been content to leave it like that, but as I got up, he grabbed my foot and yanked me back down. It seemed he wasn't done fighting.

I hit the pavement, and he managed to get a solid kick into my gut. That should've knocked me for a loop, but I seemed to be operating on steam above and beyond my usual allotment. I whacked him on the side of his head. This was an old boxing move, and even if I didn't have gloves on, it still worked pretty well. The only difference was, it hurt my hand. I winced, trying to shake off the pain. Which gave him the opportunity to get me rock solid in the neck.

That one almost knocked me cold. I saw his big boot coming my way and I figured what happened next was gonna be none too pleasant.

Just before his boot connected with my face, he cried out. A moment later, he crumbled to the ground.

A dark-haired man in an expensive coat stood over him. "Knew those jiu-jitsu lessons would come in handy one day."

I blinked several times. I wanted to sit up and see what was happening, but my abdominal muscles weren't working right. I couldn't place the voice. It didn't sound like Hart. I finally managed to roll over onto my side so I could get a better view.

He was a tall man, good-looking in a movie star kind of way, with his hair slicked back and parted down the middle. He had a somewhat high reedy voice, but his body seemed strong and sturdy.

"Give you a hand?" He pulled me to my feet. My stomach ached at the exertion, but I tried not to let it show. He appeared to be some kind of authority, so I tried to offer an explanation. "He was about to plug this pregnant woman."

"I know. You averted a tragedy."

"I didn't mean to hurt him. I just—"

He held up his hands. "I'm sure you didn't, and maybe it wasn't your fault. But the man is a law enforcement officer, and you did strike him, so I'm bound to bring you in."

"You can't do that."

He grinned slightly. "I'm fairly sure I can."

"No, you don't understand me. I got to get this pregnant gal back to Guymon, Oklahoma, or they're gonna kill my sister."

He squinted a bit. "I think perhaps that blow to your head left you somewhat disoriented."

A new voice joined the conversation. "That man on the ground is no cop."

We both turned and saw Hart, finally making his appearance. "I watched the whole thing, sir. That man on the ground is not a police officer."

The slick-haired stranger glanced at the body on the ground. "He's wearing a uniform."

"Not exactly." Hart hitched up the man's trousers. White socks.

"Not regulation," the jiu-jitsu man commented.

"No police officer would dress that way, sir. Especially not on a day when he was likely to attract attention. Let me show you something else." Hart picked up the rifle and turned it butt first. "That regulation issue?"

"It is not. He's a ringer. I'll have him brought in." He glanced up. "You've got a good eye on you, son. Ever thought about becoming a detective?"

"Thought about it. Not sure I'd get along so well with my fellow officers."

"I don't get along with them all the time myself. But I get the job done."

That remark caught my attention. "You . . . some kinda detective?"

He shot me a quick grin—broad and oozing with charm. "Name's Ness. I'm working with the local police."

"I think they need help."

"You're not alone." He helped the girl back to her feet. "How's that baby, ma'am?"

"I—I think we're okay."

"I can get you to a hospital. My Ford and driver are not far from here."

Her eyes darted about in a nervous manner. I got the idea she was looking for someone—or perhaps looking out for someone. "No, I'm fine. Just a little shaken up."

"Understandable. Well, I'd best move on. My associates are trying to quiet this catastrophe down." He offered Hart his hand. "Appreciate your assistance. If I can ever do anything to return the favor, just let me know."

"I will," Hart replied.

Ness tipped his hat. "I hope this incident won't put you folks off Cleveland. It's still a good town—and it's about to get better.

If we had more concerned citizens like you, this town wouldn't need a safety director."

That man grabbed the fake cop by the collar and whistled for his automobile.

I turned my attention to the girl. "You Maxine Bennett?"

She appeared horrified, like someone had exposed a dark secret. "How'd you know that?"

"I've come all the way from Guymon to collect you. Your pa sent me. He wants you back home."

"Well, I ain't going. And you can't make me."

"I beg to differ."

"This is a free country. You can't make me do nothing if I don't want to. I ain't broken any laws."

She did have a point. But I was in no mood to be reasonable. "Your pa is your legal guardian. If he wants you home, his word goes. I would prefer not to use force. But if I have to, I will."

"You a Pinkerton agent?"

"No, ma'am."

"'Course not. They're all out helping the factory owners break up the strikes. So what are you?"

"Just a concerned citizen." She didn't need to know everything about me, or Callie. At least not at this moment.

"Do you know why my pa wants me back?"

I thought that an odd question. "I expect he's worried, you being out in the world all on your own and in an expectant state."

"I'm not on my own. That's what he doesn't like."

"He doesn't approve of your boyfriend?"

"He doesn't approve of any boyfriend. Other than himself."

I was getting confused, at a moment when I couldn't afford to be confused. I had a mission to complete, and I didn't need any unnecessary complications. "Look, you can work out your problems with your pa when you get back. My job—"

"We'll hear you out." That was Hart. All of the sudden he'd decided to inject himself into the conversation. "Maybe we can step into that drugstore and get a soda."

I glared at him. "Hart, we don't have time—"

"There's always time for a man to make sure he's doing the right thing." He took her by the arm and steered her toward the store. "Come along, ma'am. I reckon a little Coca-Cola will settle your stomach real nice."

———

Hart had a never-ending ability to surprise me. At times, he could be withdrawn and moody. Other times, he seemed entirely self-centered and like he didn't care about anyone. He'd gab on about Nietzsche and how only fools gave in to sentimentality and morality. And yet, every time we ran into someone in need, which was quite a lot, he was the first to leap to their aid.

We all got fizzy drinks. She ended up wanting hers with a scoop of ice cream in it. Didn't take me long to see that this Maxine might be almost a mother, but she was nothing but a little girl herself. She giggled, she gossiped, and she had a fondness for silly jokes.

"Do you boys know why your nose isn't twelve inches long?" I informed her that I did not.

"'Cause then it would be a foot!" And she cackled at her own high humor. There followed a whole string of jokes, many involving elephants.

"We traced you to Oxford," Hart explained. "But by that time, you'd moved on to Cleveland."

"Oh, I couldn't stand that Oxford. So many snippy people passing judgment. Tall Sally was all right. But I only went there because I had no money and needed a place to sleep. I sent a postcard to my boyfriend to come fetch me. He never did."

"That's because your pa stopped him," I explained. "And sent us instead. But you got you a new man now." Hart gave me an ugly look, but I continued. "I saw him, running in that mob." Come to think of it, I hadn't seen that boy since. Where was he?

Why hadn't he come back for her, now that the shouting was over?

"Oh, that's just Clyde. He don't mean nothing to me."

"He doesn't?"

"He's one of them labor organizers. He thought I was cute so he offered me a ride. Kept tryin' to pry information out of me about my pa."

"He must've liked you a bit. Or he wouldn't have offered."

"He bought me a drink and I got to talking. I always get to talking when I drink. Some folks think you shouldn't be drinking when you're carrying a baby, but I don't see nothing wrong with it. Mama's got to keep her head together, right?"

"Do you know where this boy is now?"

"Nah. It's okay. He gave me a place to stay, but he's been getting kinda fresh lately. I wouldn't have none of it. I noticed when things got sticky, he ran off without looking back once to check on me. Probably just as well we've been separated. Especially now that I have you two boys to take care of me."

"I don't know that we're gonna take care of you exactly," I said. "But we're definitely taking you back to your pa. You've got some explaining to do. And I imagine he's gonna want you to marry up with that boyfriend of yours."

"Marry Duke? Why?"

I looked at her with considerable disgust. "'Cause he's the pappy of that there papoose you're about to give birth to."

"No he ain't."

"Didn't you say he was your boyfriend?"

"Yeah."

"Well—then—"

"We fooled around a little. But never nothing like that."

If I sounded confused, it's because I was. "If he's not the father, then who is?"

"My pa, of course. That's why he wants me back."

twenty-two

I WAS THUNDERSTRUCK, but I noticed that Hart took it more in stride. Maybe he was better at masking his emotions than I was. Or maybe he was just the usual three moves ahead. I was never sure which it was and, as it turned out, I never got a chance to ask him.

"Are you tellin' me—" I don't know why I bothered starting that sentence, 'cause I sure didn't have the courage to finish it.

"Oh, Pa and I started up a long time ago," she said, so matter-of-factly that it couldn't help but make a man sick. "He told me that he and ma hadn't been getting along for some time. She couldn't satisfy him, he said. You know, she does drink a bit."

And I could see why.

"She and pa got into some terrific rows. She can be kind of a shrew, if you know what I mean. Pa works hard and needs some comforting from time to time. That's why he came to me."

"And—you're okay with this?"

"I was at first." Her eyes turned away and her voice dropped. "In fact, I felt honored that Pa chose me. But it started happening all the time, over and over again. Like he couldn't get enough. He'd be back in my room every night, sometimes twice a night. Ma would weep and wail, but he'd keep comin' just the same. He

hurt me! Hurt me bad. I started to realize this wasn't the way
other families were, but there was nothing I could do to stop it.
Pretty soon Ma started behaving nasty toward me, like somehow
this was my fault. I didn't know what to do. An obedient
daughter is supposed to obey her pa, ain't she?"

"Up to a point," I offered.

"Well, no one ever sat down and explained that point to me.
Pa said if I didn't do as he instructed, he'd take the switch to me,
and I didn't want that. Ma might've disliked what was going on,
but I noticed she never disobeyed him. So how could I?"

This story got more and more appalling with each sentence.
And the worst part of it was—I realized I was acting in the service
of a monster. Even though I was doing this to save Callie, I liked
to tell myself I was doing a good thing, reuniting a daughter with
her pa. Now I realized it was anything but a good thing. That man
had turned us into accomplices in his foul scheme. He charged us
with returning a victim so she could be victimized some more. She
was little better than a sex slave, and we were pimps working
for him.

"Miss Maxine, you should never have sent that postcard. He
wouldn't've been able to find you, or send us after you, if he
hadn't gotten that postcard."

"I know. But I was lonely and broke and desperate. Pa wasn't
supposed to find out." She pushed her soda away. Tears trickled
out the corners of her eyes. "I was miserable at home toward the
end, sure. That's why I left. That last night, he come at me three
times. Three times in the same night. He'd go away, but he'd come
back an hour later. And I was already with child! I couldn't stand
it anymore. So I ran off in the middle of the night. But I left in
such a hurry—I never thought about the consequences."

"The . . . consequences?" Something told me I didn't want to
know, but I asked anyway.

"Yeah. Like with me gone . . . he'd go after Stella."

That sent a chill down my spine. All at once I remembered
that tiny, frail girl who sat in the corner of the parlor like a mouse,

never saying a word, acting like she was afraid to show her face in public. I began to understand why she might be such a shrinking violet.

Hart cleared his throat. "You sent the postcard so she'd come join you." He drew in his breath. "You were afraid that with you gone, your father would satisfy himself with your sister."

"My daughter."

He blinked. "I thought Stella was the doctor's daughter."

"She is."

"You mean—" Hart's lips parted. This time, even he was surprised. And I felt like I was gonna throw up on the countertop. I thought this story couldn't possibly get any worse. And then it did.

"Stella is not your ma's child?"

"No. Mine and Pa's."

My hands shook. "Then . . . this has been going on . . . a long time."

"Yeah," she said. "A real long time."

twenty-three

I PULLED Hart back into the street for a powwow.

"We cannot take that girl back to her sick bastard of a daddy," I said.

"We don't have any choice."

"He'll just start in on her again."

"I know that."

"Plus there's a new baby coming. What if it's a girl? Is she gonna be the doctor's next sweetheart?"

"I don't know. That's not our immediate problem."

"How can you say that?"

Hart laid a hand on my shoulder. "George, I don't like this any more than you do. But we've got no choice. Do you want your sister to die?"

"'Course I don't."

"Then you've got to get Maxine back to her pa. Quickly."

"There has to be another way."

"There isn't."

"There must be."

"Then you tell me what it is."

I couldn't think of a thing. "You're the chess master. You're always three moves ahead of everyone else. Think of something."

"Believe me, I've tried. But there's no solution to this problem. If we don't return Maxine before the deadline, your sister dies, you hang, and I probably hang right beside you. So we got to take her back."

"And then what?"

He shook his head. "I don't know. Let's figure out one thing at a time, okay?"

I somehow let him convince me to continue participating in this vile scheme. But every step I took made me a little sicker and a little more hurt inside. This journey had been hard all along, but at least before there was a certain adventure to it. A sense that we were on a valiant quest, like those knights that sat about the round table. Now I knew this was no quest and we were no knights. We were monsters. Or maybe something worse.

Before I even knew what was happening, Hart had dragged that girl out and stuffed her into the back seat of an automobile. She cried and wailed, but he shoved her in just the same. He took care not to hurt that baby, but he made it clear she had no say in the matter.

It wasn't till we were outside the city limits that I thought to ask where in tarnation he'd gotten this vehicle.

"Borrowed it," he said curtly.

"From who?"

"Didn't ask."

"Are you telling me you borrowed this car in the same way that you borrowed the car that got you thrown into jail?"

"More or less."

"Are you a crazy man?"

"That's a matter of opinion. But I'm definitely a man who doesn't want to see his only friend swing from a rope. Now shut up, will you?"

I let it go at that.

We drove for the better part of the day, switching off driving and stopping for gas when we had no choice. This old Dodge steamed a bit from the hood, but it hadn't broken down yet so we kept pushing ahead. Hart found a map in the glove box and, applying my college geometry skills, I calculated that we could be home just before time ran out, if we didn't take any unnecessary breaks.

Maxine continued to be unruly, griping and hollering and complaining and saying she wanted to go back to Cleveland or Oxford or anywhere but home to her pa. She offered us money to collect her little girl Stella and bring her to a safe place where they could live together. There were just two problems with that plan. First, Maxine didn't have any money. And second, that plan would end with Callie dead.

So we traveled with a screaming, griping pregnant woman who kept threatening to jump out of the automobile. Not the most pleasant situation in the world. Fortunately, she looked to be about fourteen months pregnant, so her mobility was limited and her ability to fight was almost nonexistent.

By the middle of the next day, I calculated that we were somewhere in Missouri, but the roads were not well marked and it was a long stretch between towns. I was tired from all the struggling and my eyes were blurry from not getting enough sleep. All of which was just me making excuses for getting lost.

"I thought we were on Route 66," Hart said.

"I thought we were, too. But if we were, we'd have hit Kansas City already."

"I'm not liking the sound of this. We don't have any time to waste."

"Maybe you could apply your chess-playing intellect to figuring out where we went wrong."

"I don't think chess has much application to map reading. Especially when I'm not the one reading the map."

Hart started looking around for a place to pull over, maybe to get directions or perhaps a better map. But we went a long way without seeing anyone. Not a filling station, not even a house. Just long stretches of road and trees. I began to fear we were seriously off course.

"A fine pair of kidnappers you two are," Maxine said.

"We ain't kidnappers," I replied.

"You're holding me against my will. That makes you a kidnapper."

"Not when we're acting at the express direction of your pa. Look, I don't want to have this debate again, all right? Sit quietly and—"

"Look!" she screamed, right in my ear. I just about hit the roof. She leaned across the front seat and pointed toward the left side of the road.

Two big cargo trucks were parked on what little shoulder there was. When I looked a bit farther, I spotted people in the fields. Looked like we'd come across some kind of farm, someplace outside the reach of the Dust Bowl. I thought they were picking peas.

Hart pulled the auto over, hoping to ask for directions. A big burly guy ran up to the car, dripping with sweat. I'd seen men like him before.

"Help you folks?" His eyes almost immediately moved to the female.

"We're lost," Hart said. "Can you steer us back to Route 66?" "Man, you are a long haul from where you want to be." His eyes remained on Maxine. "It'll be a couple hours before you're back on track and there's nothing at all between here and there. Why don't you get out and stretch your legs? We could spare you some water and maybe a chunk or two of bread."

I could tell Hart had concerns about this proposition.

"I'm thirsty," Maxine said. "I want water."

She opened the door and pushed herself out. We had no choice but to stay close to her.

That guy's eyes fairly bulged when he saw how pregnant she was. He still chased after her like a hungry dog, though.

I'd heard about these migrant farm workers before. Saw a

spread in *LIFE* magazine. Lots of men and women and even small children worked in that field. Most of them Mexicans, but not all. The Mexicans traveled with the boys in charge from one farm to the next, barely making enough change to stay alive to pick the next day. Some of the white folk did the same. A few locals came in to make some extra bread.

Someone rang a big bell. All the workers lumbered to the side of the road. They formed a long line and one at a time they got a drink from a ladle of water. Just one ladle, that's all. Didn't matter how young or how old. One ladle. I could see that some folks needed a lot more. Hell, they all needed more, but they didn't get it. After the water they each got a chunk of bread. Some of the small fry got half a chunk. The bosses said that if folk got too weighed down with food, they became unproductive. What I later learned was that the bosses ensured that they would be starving by the time night came. That guaranteed they'd spend their meager wages on food—and still not get enough. Which guaranteed they'd be back the next day, working for the same slave wages.

We were also given a ladleful and a chunk of bread. In fact, that boss gave Maxine two, saying something about how she was eating for two. I didn't like the look in his eye and I wondered how he could be so generous to her when he was so stingy to his own employees. I was preparing to suggest that we depart when the incident occurred.

"You trying to rob me? Is that what you're doing?"

It was that same boss who met us out at the car, screaming his head off at a boy who couldn't have been no more than twelve.

"No, sir. Of course not."

"Are you denying what you did?"

I could see the lad was torn in the usual way of kids that age, debating whether the cover-up will be worse than the crime. "I—I don't know what you mean."

The boss grabbed the boy by the shoulders. "You stole from me! You're a thief!" He shook the boy hard, then slapped him across the face so strong the kid fell to his knees.

Maxine gasped.

"It was just a pea!" the boy squealed, rubbing his face. He looked like the slap had knocked him silly.

"You stole from my crop."

"I picked about a million peas. I didn't think you'd miss one."

"You think stealing is okay if no one notices?"

The boy didn't answer.

"You admit you done wrong?" He raised his fist way over the kid's head, threatening to bring it down.

"Y—Yes. Sure. I'll admit it."

He pulled the kid up by the scruff of his collar. "Good. Your punishment is that you'll work the rest of the day and tomorrow, too. For no wages."

A tiny woman watching let out a small sorrowful cry. I assumed that was his mother. "He can't go without food."

"Then someone else will have to feed him." The boss shoved the kid away. "I'm tired of putting food in the mouths of them that steals from me."

That mama cradled her son and cried. I felt sick. I even checked my pockets, but I could see that I had so little cash left I couldn't afford to part with any of it. It was only later I learned that Hart had been less selfish. He'd given her everything he had.

Seemed that boss had barely finished tearing at that boy but what he was back to leering at Maxine. I cut in and tapped the man on the shoulder.

"I want to thank you for your hospitality. We need to go now. We're working under a deadline."

"No need to run off. Just when we're getting acquainted."

"I appreciate your kindness. But we got to get that little girl back to her pa."

"I was thinking I might take her into town. Show her the sights." He winked at me with a big broad grin that was like to make me sick.

"You have my regrets, but we must be on our way."

He came up real close, pushing up the short sleeves of his

undershirt, as if they weren't short enough already, and flexing his sweaty muscles. "Buddy, I say she stays, and I don't think you're tough enough to disagree with my decisions. Especially when I have all these friends and all you've got is a pansy driver."

That was when I realized how bad this predicament truly was. "Maybe you're one of them pansies, too," he said, laughing.

"Maybe that's why you two boys travel together. So you can amuse yourselves with each other while I amuse myself with that girl."

"Are you so blind you can't see that she is very, very with child?"

"Guess that means she likes it," he said, and again he flashed that repugnant smile.

My fists clenched. My legs trembled. I started to speak, but that boss man waved his big Popeye arms and five of his buddies circled 'round him.

"So what you gonna do about it, little man?" He shoved me back hard. "You wanna take a shot at me? Go ahead. I'll give you a free one. Then me and my boys will take five. Each." He laughed again. "There won't be enough of you left to carry to the hospital. Which is three hours from here."

Even though I wanted to turn tail and run, I stood my ground. At the same time, I knew I didn't have an angel's chance in hell of coming out of this scrape alive.

"Come on, pansy boy." He shoved me again. "Take your best shot."

I just exploded. It made no sense at all, but I lunged at him. Maybe I thought if I was gonna go down, I'd go down swinging my fists. But I really don't think I thought about it with anything resembling logic. My head burst and I went for him.

I got one shot in, but it didn't do him much hurt. He faked me out with his fist, then brought his foot up between my legs. I got caught by surprise and I crumpled, clutching my middle portions. I was out of the fight before it began. All five of his buddies moved in, pounding their fists together, and I figured I was done for.

twenty-four

I SWALLOWED hard and prepared myself for the pounding to come.

That's when we heard the gunshot.

Everyone jumped. The big boss crouched, looking just as scared as a jackrabbit.

I looked around to see what the heck was going on. "Get in the car."

Hart held a pistol, and he trained it on all those boys. Where did he get a pistol? I didn't know, but at the moment, all those questions seemed secondary to the more important matter of our escape.

I collected Maxine and tugged her toward the auto.

"We're leaving now," Hart said, keeping that gun between the men and himself. "You're not gonna follow us. 'Less you want a hole in your head."

He backed away. I got the auto started and made ready to blow just as soon as he boarded.

He was almost there when that stupid boss finally found a smidgeon of courage. He strutted up like a rooster, preening for his buddies. "I don't believe you'll shoot that gun," he said. "You're just a pansy boy. I can see your hands shaking."

"My hands are shaking," Hart said. From my angle, I could observe that his knees shook even more. "But I don't need to be that steady to hit a fat target like you."

The boss rediscovered his leer. "Then do it already."

"I will if I have to."

"You ain't gonna." He took two steps closer.

"There's no reason for you to die."

"I don't believe I will, pansy boy." He kept walking. "I'm gonna take your head off, then I'm gonna take that girl and give her—"

Hart blew a hole in him. Hit him in the leg, not the head, but it stopped him cold just the same. The other men looked stunned. I didn't know if this would scare them or inflame them. And I didn't want to hang around to find out.

Hart jumped into the passenger seat. "Go," he said succinctly.

I let out the clutch and pushed the accelerator to the floor. We sped away, spewing dust in our wake. Some of the men acted like they were gonna give chase—once it was clear we couldn't be caught—but it was too late. I could see them in my rear mirror. I noticed not a one of them went to help that big boss man. He was probably about as popular with his co-workers as he was with me.

Once we were a good, long ways from them, I relaxed a bit. It seemed we had cheated death once again. I felt much relieved—until I recollected that we were still off track and lost, with no idea where we were and little time to find out.

"I want to thank you boys for what you did back there," Maxine said.

I nodded in her general direction.

"I guess you ain't such bad men after all. As kidnappers go."

I thanked her right kindly. "Hart, where in tarnation did you get that gun?"

I think the excitement faded and he was back to being his despondent self. "Same place I got the car."

Well, now, that was informative.

"Given all we've been through on this trip, I thought it might come in handy," he added.

"You were thinking three moves ahead, right?"

"Yup."

We found our way back to the right road and drove several hours in peace, this time headed in the right direction. But that peace was shattered fast just as dusk set in.

"Boys, we have another problem." That came from the rear seat.

Good Lord, I thought, what could it possibly be this time? I heard a whooshing sound I couldn't identify.

"It's time."

"Could you be a mite less cryptic?"

"My water's done broke."

She still wasn't talking any language I understood.

"Your water? That ladleful you got from them migrant workers?"

"No, my waters. My mama waters."

"What in—"

Hart cut in. "She's trying to tell you she's going into labor."

"You mean—"

"That's what I mean." She was trying to be brave, but she wasn't very good at it. "I'm about to have this baby. Right here and now."

twenty-five

I **WILL BE** the first to admit that I didn't know anything about babies and never imagined that would ever be a problem. She did look plumb ripe, sure. But I didn't think any more of it. I guess I expected she'd have the courtesy to hold things up till we got back to Guymon. But it turned out the baby had other ideas. Probably all this stress and excitement didn't help any.

"Are you sure about this?" I asked her.

"'Course I'm sure. I've done this before, 'member?"

I did, though it wasn't the pleasantest memory I possessed. "And you're certain it's happening now?"

"I am one hundred percent absolutely certain." And then she give out with a piercing cry that shot through my head like a knife. If that was how she felt inside, I was impressed she could stay as calm as she did.

I looked at Hart. "You have any experience delivering babies?"

"That's one thing I haven't done."

"Me neither." I looked back at Maxine. "What do you need?"

"A midwife."

"Well, we don't seem to have one in the vehicle at the moment. What else?"

"You're supposed to have boiled water. Clean sheets."

"We don't even have a bed."

"Any flat surface will do."

I looked around. Didn't seem quite right to throw a pregnant lady out on the hard cold ground.

"Look," Hart said. "Over to the right."

I had to squint to see where Hart directed my attention. It didn't help that Maxine was gasping and crying, which had a tendency to disrupt a man's thinking. When I looked way off the road, I eventually detected a little bitty house, so small and set back that most folks probably drove right by without noticing it was there.

"You think we should pay them a visit?"

"We don't have any choice," Hart replied. "She can't have her baby in the backseat of this Dodge."

I couldn't disagree. I turned down the little private barely-a-road that took me to the front porch of the house. Before we even had a chance to get out of the auto, someone came to greet us.

He was an older man with lots of gray hair. He moved slow and seemed a bit befuddled. I wondered whether he could be much help in the current emergency. On the other hand, he didn't carry a rifle, so we were already off to a better start than we'd had during most of this journey.

I got out of the car but kept my distance so I wouldn't seem threatening. "'Scuse us for intruding on your privacy," I hollered. "We got us an emergency. There's a young gal in the backseat and she's about to have a baby."

He fiddled with his wire-rimmed glasses as if he were adjusting the focus. "You say someone's gonna have a baby?"

"That's what I said. You know anything about babies?"

"I don't. But my Flora worked as a midwife for something like twenty years."

I felt as if a gigantic weight had tumbled off my shoulders. "Praise the Lord. He must've brought us right to your doorstep."

"He must've." The man fiddled with his glasses some more.

"Most people never notice we're here. We kinda like it that way. That's one reason we moved out of town."

"I understand the desire for privacy, sir, but if you don't mind too much—"

"Don't be silly, man. That baby ain't gonna respect no one's privacy. You bring that gal on in. I'll tell my Flora so she can start getting things ready."

We did exactly as we were told. Hart and I led Maxine into that fairly ramshackle little house. She moved none too steady, weeping and screaming with each step, but we managed to get her inside.

By the time we arrived, they had a nice little daybed set up on what was normally the kitchen table. We briefly met Flora, a small woman with a sweet disposition. She was as old as her husband, if not older, but she managed to move around well enough.

"Are you folks hungry? I just made a nice stew."

"Thank you kindly, ma'am," I said, tipping an invisible hat. "But we have an emergency that needs to be dealt with before any of us chows down."

"Very well then. Let's get her on the table. I'll get more blankets and start the water boiling. Clarence, make sure she's comfortable."

She laid Maxine down and told her to relax, which seemed unlikely to me. Flora gave her instructions on how to breathe, which I suspected Maxine already knew how to do. And when the time came, she told the girl to start pushing.

"Please excuse us if our hospitality is wanting," Clarence said. "We don't get many visitors out this way, and the few that do come don't stay long."

"Doesn't mean we don't like visitors," Flora said as she scurried about. "Just don't get many."

"What kind of work do you do?" I asked, trying to be sociable despite the strained circumstances.

"I'm retired," Clarence explained. "Used to work in the oil patch. Take it easier these days. Have a nice nest egg saved up, and it's more than enough to take care of our meager needs. Can focus on my hobbies."

"Which would be?" Hart asked.

"Catching up on my reading. Lots of good books I never got around to enjoying. Flora plays the piano. We both enjoy taxidermy."

"Really?"

"More demand for that than you might imagine. I've made a few dollars, helping out folks. Mostly those real attached to their pets and not ready to let them go. I do the disemboweling and the stuffing, while Flora helps out with the stitching."

"I don't get the impression you menfolk are going to be much help to me here," Flora said. "And you're taking up this poor girl's air. Why don't you step outside? Have a smoke."

"I'll stay," Hart said. "You might need some help."

"I suppose I might at that," she replied. "Not quite as spry as I once was."

Clarence showed me to the door. Maxine screamed so much that I was glad to be out of there. She thrashed back and forth and used the most foul language I ever heard in my life, including from grown men who lacked education and spent long periods of time alone in the woods.

Clarence opened the screen door. "There's an outhouse in the back, and a porch for smoking if you got 'em."

"I don't."

"Here. Take one of mine." He placed a big cigar and a match-book in my hand. "Just don't go into the icehouse." He pointed in the general direction. "It's packed with meat for the winter. Cold as Siberia, and the smell is none too pleasant, neither." He disappeared back inside the house.

I nodded and stepped outside. Even on the porch, I had no trouble hearing the screaming. I felt a mite guilty, but I did need to relieve myself, and all that caterwauling and the thought of a baby popping out was making me more than a smidgeon uncomfortable.

I found the outhouse and utilized it. The odor was pungent, which made me wonder how much worse the icehouse could be. Even sitting on that cold wooden bench with the door shut, I could hear the screaming. Wondered how far I'd have to go to get away from that. Started to think the next county wouldn't be far enough.

I strolled outside and gazed up at the stars again. The night was cool, but not so much that a man could catch a chill. The stars were not so bright as before. Clouds masked the view from time to time. Perhaps those celestial shepherds weren't on the job tonight.

I was never much for smoking. Like I told Hart before, that noxious habit never appealed to me. But the old man had put the weed in my hand and I didn't have anything else to do, and I certainly didn't want to go back inside that house, so I used the matches he'd given me and lit up. Took a few puffs to get the cheroot going, and I coughed and sputtered all the way through the first inch. Eventually got the hang of it. Maybe it was just that my nerves had been jangling for so long, but it did seem to have a calming effect. Made a man more aware of his breathing, the gentle in and out. In through the mouth, down into the lungs, then out again. A pleasant sensation. I was sorry when I found I'd smoked the thing to the nub.

I suppose it was inevitable that I'd end up taking a look at that icehouse. I've never much cared for being told what to do and not to do. And after all the adventures we'd had and all the brushes with disaster I'd survived, I felt sufficiently mature to make decisions for myself. I'd heard about these icehouses some of the more well-heeled folks had. I don't think anyone ever had one in Guymon, though, not even Doc Bennett. Come to think, I didn't recall seeing one in Massachusetts, either. I know the university mess had some kind of icebox, but I was a bit sketchy on the details.

There was only one window, and it was fogged over. Or so I thought. On closer inspection, I saw that something had been smeared over it, making it impossible to see inside. I made my examination by starlight, so quite possibly I missed some of the details.

I could see a silhouette, though. Faint. Vague. But it looked like nothing so much as a man's head peeking up over the back of a chair.

My mind went back to Guymon and Pa. Coming all that distance to see him, spotting his head poking up over the top of the chair, only to learn he'd died before I arrived. He was dead and putrefying, and the smell . . .

The smell.

I tried the door to the icehouse. It had one of them metal handles, but it wouldn't budge. Maybe it was just frozen solid, given how cold it was in there. Even standing on the outside of the door, I felt the chill.

I pressed a little harder. It gave a mite but wouldn't open.

I glanced back at the house. No one was watching. They were absorbed in the drama inside, presumably. I still heard wailing, so I knew the excitement wasn't over yet.

I pressed the handle even harder. Still didn't budge.

I hit it with my shoulder, bringing all my weight to bear. The door snapped open.

I stepped inside the icehouse, careful to make sure the door didn't close behind me.

The cold hit just as solid as if I had walked into a wall. Stopped me in my tracks. My mouth dried up. Thought my nose might bleed.

As promised, meat hung from hooks all along the ceiling. Pretty much how I imagined it would look. But for some perverse reason, I kept walking inward.

Toward the back, not too far from the window, I found what I had glimpsed through the window. The chair. The head poking over the top.

"Pa?"

I was being stupid. I don't know what took hold of my brain.

It didn't make any sense. But at that moment, I thought for all the world like I was gazing at my pa again. That smoke was still in my lungs.

"Pa?"

The head did not turn in response to my inquiry.

I took a tentative step forward. Then another. I stepped around to face the figure in the chair.

It was a man, or used to be, sitting up, just like I'd found my pa. But it made me think of my ma. She used to sew, and I remembered the work she did whenever she could save a few cents by darning something instead of replacing it.

This man's eyes were stitched shut. Both of them.

His mouth was stitched as well. I could see the crisscross pattern going up and down across his lips.

His skin was blue and lifeless. The cold had preserved him, but this man had been dead a good long while.

Clarence told me he had taken up taxidermy . . .

I noticed his leg was missing. Cut off at the knee. Missing an arm as well. Cut off at the joint.

That's when I made the mistake of taking a closer look at that meat hanging from the hooks.

And all at once I was very damn glad I hadn't taken any of that old woman's stew.

I ran out of there as fast as it was possible for a man to move, part appalled, part disgusted.

And part terrified because I realized what I had left Hart and Maxine with.

I rushed into the house, not knocking, not stopping to announce myself. That woman Flora crouched in the corner, running her frail birdlike hands together, kinda like a vulture hovering over carrion.

Clarence held an axe. A big heavy one with a long handle.

Hart lay on the hardwood floor. Blood gushed out of the side of his head.

twenty-six

CLARENCE SAW me run in and adjusted his aim. I couldn't tell if he was about to hack into Hart or Maxine, but I was glad to intervene. Though not delighted to become his new target.

That axe's reach was longer than I realized, and Clarence swung it with a good deal more power than you might expect from a man of his years. He had the strength of Hercules once he got a weapon in his hands. Having seen his handiwork dangling from the hooks in the icehouse, I didn't doubt what he was capable of doing.

I jumped backward, but not quite quickly enough. I got the idea that the cheroot Clarence slipped me was drugged up with something. My head was thinkin' slow and crazy, and I just couldn't move like I normally do. The blade sliced open my shirt and traced a long red line across my abdomen. It stung like hell. I felt as if my guts were spilling out. They weren't—if that had been a serious blow, I wouldn't be standing. But pain does funny things to the logical parts of the brain.

My first impulse was to turn tail and run. But I knew that would be the end of Hart. And I wasn't sure Maxine would survive such a cowardly decision, either.

Clarence swung at me again, but this time he missed

completely, which caused him to lose his footing. While he was off-balance, I rushed in and grabbed his swinging arm. He tried to connect that axe with my flesh, but I managed to hold him at bay. I squeezed hard and eventually he dropped the weapon. It fell to the floor with a clatter. He was stronger than he looked, but no match for me, once we took the axe out of the equation.

Poor Maxine was still shouting and wailing. I couldn't see as she'd been hurt any, but that baby was still coming. I was too busy to pay much attention, till I heard her voice rise several pitches, screaming out my name.

"George! Behind you!"

Unfortunately, I didn't hear it quite soon enough. I moved, but not fast enough to prevent the skillet from connecting with my skull. I felt the thud on the back of my head. My brains rattled and I grunted in pain. I was on my knees before I knew what happened. If Maxine hadn't warned me, I expect that blow would've been my death. As it was, it just about crippled me.

That was sweet little Flora, of course, protecting her man with a swing Babe Ruth might've been proud of. Her husband followed up with a knee to my jaw, and then I was facedown and drooling on the hardwood floor. I tried to push myself up, but my body did not respond to its instructions. I thought about all the times I'd been beaten and punched since this misbegotten mission began. Some of them had been pretty rough, but I'd survived. How pathetic to finally be killed by a couple of cannibalistic old geezers.

Clarence kicked me again in the head. Felt like my jaw shattered. My mouth bled. I struggled to retain consciousness.

Before, when I'd been like to die, Hart had pulled my fat out of the fire. So it was only natural that my eyes wandered in that direction.

Hart still lay on the floor like a sack of manure.

Unless he rose again like some kinda zombie, he would not be saving me.

Clarence kicked and hit me so many times I couldn't count

them all. And I couldn't do anything to stop it. I just lay there and took it. I think even Flora got a few licks in. I was their private punching bag.

Maxine stopped wailing for a minute, and I had this fantasy that she got up and saved me. Maybe she grabbed the axe or the frying pan. Maybe threw the hot water into Clarence's face. But none of that happened. And as near as I could tell through blurry half-swollen eyes, she was still on the kitchen table, not even able to help herself, much less anyone else.

"I reckon we'll have enough stew to last the whole winter now," I heard that nasty old lady say.

"Nothing better than your stew, Flora. I'll make sure the meat is good and tender." He kicked me again in the ribcage. I was pretty sure I heard something snap.

"You're a good husband, Clarence. I respect you, just like the Bible says a woman should."

"And you're a good woman, Flora. Now hand me that axe so I can divide this carcass into more manageable pieces."

And that was the last thing I heard.

━━━

I'm not sure how long I was unconscious. Probably not all that long, but when I woke, I felt like I'd been to hell and back with several years spent in transit. My head throbbed and my body ached. It hurt to breathe, probably due to that last blow to the ribcage. Every time I inhaled it stung like someone poked a dagger into my side. I wasn't sure if I was still alive.

Only problem was, I felt cold as a snowball on a winter day. And if I'd gone to hell, I should be experiencing the opposite weather conditions, shouldn't I?

They'd brought me to the icehouse. That was the only possible explanation.

I opened my eyes with a gasp. I conducted a mental and physical inventory of all my parts, finding to my relief that I still had all four limbs and all fingers and toes, and my head was still attached to my neck. It didn't take me long to realize I was tied to the chair, exactly where I'd found the taxidermied corpse I initially mistook for my pa. My shoulders were strapped to a wooden chair. My feet were tied to the legs.

Clarence and Flora stood directly in front of me. Clarence held that damnable axe.

"Glad you're finally awake," Clarence said. "I was becoming somewhat impatient."

"Let me go," I growled. It hurt to speak.

Clarence turned angry fast. "Did I ask you to talk, food? I am not a man who cares to have his food talk back to him."

"You won't get away with this. I'm on a mission—" Clarence swung the axe around.

I shut up.

The axe blade stopped maybe an inch from my neck.

"That's more like it," Clarence said. "We've been waiting for you to awaken. But not so's we could hear your noise."

"We like to separate our meat while it's awake," Flora explained.

"Tastes better that way," Clarence added.

"I season it as we separate it. It's an old family secret." She spoke in a completely matter-of-fact manner that was the most chilling thing I ever heard, and not just because I was in an icehouse.

"We've tried killing the meat first," Clarence said. "But it don't come out as good. My theory is that when the meat is alive and knows what's happening to it, it gets all the juices flowing good. Which results in a choicer cut and a fuller flavor."

My mouth went dry and my whole body shivered. If I understood this man correctly, he was talking about cutting me up piece by piece while I could still feel every slice. So I could experience the removal of my own limbs, one after the other.

"Don't you worry," Clarence continued. "I'll take it nice and slow. Don't want to rush things. You might pass out again. And that would spoil all the fun."

"And dinner," Flora added.

I looked both ways at once, twisting my head as far around as possible.

"You looking for that friend of yours? The little fella?" Clarence chuckled. "Well, look no more."

He reached over to the wall and grabbed a lantern. He held it up and shone it toward the back.

Hart hung lifeless from a hook on the ceiling. Blood was smeared across his face. His skin was blue. His neck was twisted at a weird angle.

"Such a scrawny boy," Flora said. "Nothing worse than stringy meat."

Hart was already dinner. I was going to be dessert.

twenty-seven

IT'S funny how a man's head starts to race when he can see his own painful, torturous demise is only seconds away, and there's no one around who can come to his aid. A million thoughts run through your head at once. I remembered what Hart told me about staying three moves ahead of your opponent. I figured it was too late for that, but if I could maybe get one move ahead at least I'd have a fighting chance.

I was not gonna let this sorry couple of carnivores kill me.

Not if I could help it.

I couldn't move my arms much, but I found I could move from the elbow down, at least enough to reach around a bit. All my hands felt was the chair and ice. Lots of ice.

Ice.

I'd seen icicles so sharp they could hurt you. I'd even cut my fingers on them before, trying to break off a piece. And I'd heard about icicles falling down and impaling explorers. Could I turn this ice into a weapon? A weapon I could use again a man wielding an axe?

Odds seemed long. But it wasn't as if I had many options.

I kept chattering, keeping their eyes focused on my face, not my hands. Reaching under the chair, I found a good long ice shard dangling from the seat. It broke hard, which told me that it just might be solid enough to do some damage.

I kept it out of sight and waited for that man to come closer. Problem was—he didn't have to. That axe had a long reach. If he had any sense, he'd butcher me from a distance. There was a good likelihood he'd never get all that near to me.

Hart would never leave that matter to chance. So neither would I.

I laughed, loud and hearty. As obnoxious as possible. "Clarence, you are one sad sack of cow patties. You know that?"

Clarence appeared confused. He couldn't decide whether to ask a question or just lop my head off. "What the Sam Hill are you talking about?"

I tried to keep my teeth from chattering as I talked all bold and brash. "You think you're king of the heap. You think you're this sophisticated meat man." I made a scoffing sound. "You're a pathetic amateur."

I could see I'd riled him, at least a little. "Do you have any idea how many carcasses I've cut?"

I didn't want to know. "Amateur. Thinks he's the big man, picking on strangers here in Hicksville. You know what? I used to work in a slaughterhouse. I know how this job is done. And I never once seen anybody come into the packing house swinging some long axe like he's afraid to get close to the meat."

"I ain't afraid of nothing," he said. He slapped the axe handle in his hand. "This is my scalpel. My paintbrush."

"It's your cowardice, that's what it is."

"Clarence," Flora said, "don't let this boy get you heated up."

Nice try, but she was coming in too late. "You're a hack," I continued, cackling. "Not a soul on earth who knows nothing about cutting meat is gonna go about it with a big axe. When you cut meat, you gotta be clean and precise. You gotta get close to the bone."

"I know that."

"Then let's just see it in action, mister. Let's see you slice off my arm, can you? I don't mean hacking it off like some barbarian. Get close to the bone. Sever it in one piece."

Clarence raised the axe up, like he was aiming at a precise point. He squinted. I got the impression his vision was less than perfect. "Can you even see what you're aiming at from that distance, old man?"

He took a tentative step closer.

I kept goading him. "You're scared of me."

"I am not afraid of food."

"The hell you aren't. You got me all trussed up and you still can't get close enough to do a decent job."

He took another step forward.

"Clarence," Flora said, more insistently, "don't listen to him. Just start the cutting."

"Sure, just hack me up into teeny-tiny pieces like the third-rate butcher you are."

He took another step closer. He was maybe a foot away from me. Aiming the axe blade at my shoulder.

"Your sight's kinda poor, ain't it? From way back there, you're more likely to hit the wall than me."

He took another big step forward, and that's when I brought my hand up and stuck him in the gut like the sick pig he was. I don't think the icicle actually pierced his skin, but I hit hard enough to hurt him some.

Clarence doubled over and I launched my head into his, butting him like a goat. His nose broke. He cried out and staggered, falling forward almost into my lap.

I bit his ear off with my teeth.

He screamed and released the axe. I grabbed it by the square end of the blade and drove it right through the rope pinning my shoulders to the chair. I shoved Clarence back into his lovely wife. Then I cut my feet loose.

I was practically frozen, but at the time, I didn't even notice. I kicked that bastard hard against the wall. Then I turned my attention to Flora.

"Please don't hurt me," she said, holding up her hands. "I'm just an old woman."

"Make that an old dead woman." I swung the axe handle around, square end first, clubbing her on the head. She screamed and fell down, right on top of her beloved spouse.

I threw the axe down and ran back to Hart. I lifted him off the hook and pressed my ear against his chest. He was still breathing, though faintly. I hauled him out of that icehouse, shoving the door closed behind me, moving some rocks over to keep it shut. I toted Hart back to the kitchen. Maxine was still there, lying on the table. She looked like she'd been drugged, probably with the same stuff they used on me. I tossed Hart onto the sofa and rubbed him all over, trying to warm him up and get some circulation going. I got a warm wet rag from the kitchen and wiped the blood off his face. The cut wasn't that bad. Head wounds always bleed something fierce. I dabbed his face with boiled water. Eventually, his eyelids fluttered open.

"I'd swear we were in heaven," he said, voice crackling, "if I believed in such a thing."

"You're still alive and on earth," I informed him.

"I was afraid of that."

After he got his head together, he explained what happened after I disappeared. Once they'd sent away the only member of our party Clarence thought could be a threat to him, he side-swiped Hart. The kid never saw what hit him, but I'm betting on that infernal skillet.

"How do you feel?" I asked him.

"Like I was dead but some fool resurrected me."

"Other than that."

"My head's aching and I think I may have a concussion. Possibly permanent brain damage."

"That might render an improvement," I ventured.

He pursed his lips. "Let's take care of the girl."

I shared the same hot towel treatment with her and before you know it, she started coming around as well. Which was a good thing, because it seemed that baby wanted to pop some time ago and was sick of waiting around.

"Oh my God," she said. Nothing like extreme pain to bring a mother back to her senses. "Oh dear God, it hurts. It wasn't like this the last time."

I didn't know what could be different, but I did understand that the baby was on its way.

"I don't think Flora's midwifing skills are going to be any use to us," I told Hart. "And I have no idea what to do here."

"I read a book about delivering babies once."

"Why the hell would you read something like that? You planning to go to medical school?"

"No, it was research for a book I was—you know—I was editing. One of the Emerson Babylon tales. He's a doctor, among other things."

"A doctor who travels through time."

"Exactly."

"That's the stupidest idea I ever heard."

Hart pushed Maxine's skirt back and told her to spread her legs. That baby was already making its appearance.

"Are you boys gonna do something?" Maxine screamed. "Or are you just gonna stand there staring at my private parts?"

Hart gave me a sideways look. "Go boil some more water. Quick."

"You think we're gonna be her doctor?"

"No. I think I'm gonna be her doctor. You're gonna be my nurse." He spread the girl's legs a little farther. "Now listen to me, Maxine. We're gonna get through this. But you're gonna have to work with me. I'm tired and beat up and my head's throbbing, so you don't need to make this any more unpleasant than it's already gonna be."

"You're complaining about pain to me?" she screamed.

"If I had something to dull the hurt, I'd give it to you. But I don't. So unless you want me to bash you on the head, you're gonna have to muster through. And I'd appreciate it if you could keep the noise to a minimum."

To my surprise, she had no reply.

"For starters, you need to stop screaming and breathe."

"I am breathing!"

"You're not breathing right. You gotta breathe when I tell you to breathe. And when you exhale, you gotta push."

"Push what?"

"Push . . ." He had a hard time explaining this part. "You got to push down in your nether regions. Push that baby right out."

"That baby is coming out no matter what I do."

"That may or may not be, but you can make this go a lot quicker and make it hurt a lot less if you cooperate. Now take a deep breath. That's right. Exhale. And push!"

"I'm pushing!"

"That was a real good effort. Now push again."

She did, screaming the whole time.

"You're doing good, Maxine. Real good."

I brought the hot water, but I felt at loose ends, and to be honest, more than a little queasy.

Hart pulled that mindreading trick of his again. "Best thing you could do right now, George, would be to ransack the house and find some more blankets. Flora never did produce any, and when this baby arrives, it's gonna be cold."

Though I secretly was relieved to depart, I didn't want to leave Hart in the lurch. "You sure you don't need my help?"

"You'll be more help finding blankets than licking the hard-wood floor."

I took the hint.

"Maxine, you listen to me, girl. Bear down and push!"

twenty-eight

THAT LABOR WENT on for almost an hour, and that was by far the longest hour of my life. I felt bad about all the pain Maxine suffered and wondered why such a miraculous event had to be spoiled by so much suffering. But I was amazed at how quickly that mask of agony turned into an expression of sheer joy.

Hart handled all that post-birth business, cleaning up the baby and such. He tied off the cord while I was happy to watch from the sidelines. Except I really didn't watch too closely.

"Ten fingers," Hart said. "Ten toes. We have a perfectly normal baby here."

I could see Maxine's relief. I was considerably relieved, too. Given the child's parentage, I was afraid it might emerge with two heads or the like.

Maybe it was the light, but I thought I saw a tiny glint of water in Hart's eyes. "Yes, ma'am," he said. "Against all odds. A perfectly healthy baby girl."

With that one word—girl—all the light went out of Maxine's eyes.

"What's the matter?" I was such an idiot. "Were you hoping for a boy child?"

Hart jabbed me with his elbow.

"There's nothing wrong with being a girl," I protested.

"There is at my house."

And then all the pain and sorrow Maxine had held back came pouring out.

I finally got it through that dense head of mine what the problem was. As soon as Maxine heard the baby was a girl, she could see the child's destiny laid out. She'd be Doc Bennett's next victim, when the time came, when he was done with Stella. The next in a long line of womenfolk abused by that vile and disgusting man. The daughter who was also a wife. The mother who was also a sister. The father who was husband, father, and grandfather.

And it was my destiny to be the man who delivered Maxine and her baby into the hands of their defiler.

I didn't like it, but as far as I could see, I had no choice about the matter.

The only way to save my family was to destroy Maxine's.

⸻

Hart worked with Maxine a bit and got her settled in with the child. As it happened, she was experienced in these matters, which was good, 'cause I didn't think that, even for all the books Hart had read, he was qualified to give Maxine instructions on nursing her young'un. Baby was soon chowing down, and we found some food and drink in the kitchen for Maxine and ourselves.

While Maxine bonded with her newborn, Hart and I considered the delicate matter of what we were gonna do about those two old folks with a sweet tooth for human flesh. I didn't know if they were dead or alive and I wasn't planning to conduct a detailed inspection. My first instinct was to bring in the county sheriff. But I knew that would take hours, maybe even days, and we did not have time to spare. I also thought the sheriff might look askance at two strangers who dropped by the old folks place with the result that both of the old folks were now frozen or dead or possibly both. And I remembered the cops in Oxford claimed there was some kind of warrant out for me.

On the other hand, I was not prepared to take the risk that these two might employ their culinary skills on someone else.

So I burned down the icehouse.

Found some kerosene in the shed, sprinkled it all around the place, then dropped a match. One of Clarence's matches. Took out the main house, too, which I thought was just as well. I didn't want to leave any trace of the horrific activities that had occurred here.

Just before I dropped the match, Hart said, "Don't you want to see if they're still alive?"

"I do not."

"If they're still alive and you light—"

"Do you realize how many folks they've murdered? And eaten?"

"Doesn't your conventional morality insist: Thou shalt not kill?"

"If we don't do this, others might die."

"But the rule remains—"

"I'm more interested in people than rules."

So I lit the match and dropped it. Within five minutes, both the house and icehouse were consumed in flames. We stayed just long enough to make sure the fire didn't burn out of control, then the four of us climbed back into the stolen Dodge and continued our journey.

———

We behaved quite a bit smarter and more cautious from there on out. We never left the main road. Every time we stopped for gasoline, I made sure we had detailed instructions on where we were going next and how to get there. It appeared to me we could still make it back to Guymon just a hair ahead of the deadline if we didn't run into any more trouble and we didn't make any unnecessary stops. We didn't even stop at night. We took turns at the wheel and drove through the darkness.

Hart gassed on for some time about how he thought the drive was boring, but he enjoyed the intellectual challenge of navigating. "We're like Lewis and Clark," he said.

I had a vague memory of the two from American history, but I was fuzzy on the details. "How so?"

"We're bold explorers, making our way across the country, having grand adventures all along the way."

"We've definitely had adventures," I agreed. "Don't know how grand they've been."

"I've read several books about that duo. I particularly admire Meriwether Lewis. He was the brains of the operation, you know."

"I thought there was some Indian gal who showed them the way."

"Sacajawea. She was instrumental to their navigation. But Lewis was the one who kept the outfit going. He spent two years facing the unknown. Danger at every turn. But he never backed down. He said he was more alive during those two years than ever before or ever again. He was a great American."

"Guess he should've run for president. You'd have voted for him."

Hart's eyes turned downward. "He died not long after he got back. By his own hand. Big bloody mess. Horrible end to a heroic life."

We were maybe a day out from Guymon when Maxine announced, "I've made a decision. 'Bout the baby's name."

This was good news, if only because I was tired of referring to the baby as *the baby*. I also knew she was having some troubles with the whole concept of bringing another girl into the world, and I wondered if maybe declining to give the babe a name was a way of avoiding the reality of the situation.

"I had a lot of choices. Pa thought if it was a girl I should call her Henrietta. 'Cause he's named Henry."

"Figures," I said.

"But I'm not gonna do that."

"Good."

"I also considered Rose o' Sharon and Gilead and Esther and a bunch of other Biblical names. But I don't feel so strong about that any more."

I had no complaints on that score, either. "Hart says I should name her Gal—Gal-a-tee." "

Galatea," he corrected her.

"Why would you encourage this girl to give her poor defenseless baby such a name? What kind of name is that anyway?"

"It's Greek," he explained. "From mythology. It indicates that you made her and that you're gonna teach her and instruct her and see that she has a better time of it in this world than you did."

His words were pretty measured, but I think I knew what he was trying to get across.

"That's a nice thought. But no thanks."

"More's the pity."

She took in a deep breath. "I've decided to call her Hope."

We both fell silent.

———

Seemed like we spent most of the next day driving through the flattest, most boring countryside you ever saw in your life. At some point, while I drove, Hart let loose a soft, groaning noise.

"What's the matter?" I asked.

"My head hurts."

After what we'd been through, almost every part of my body ached, especially my ribcage. So what was the big deal?

And then I reflected that, throughout all the hardships we'd encountered, I'd never heard that boy complain once. Not once.

Until now.

Then I felt a chill do a tap dance on my spine. In a flash I recalled how bad the side of his head looked after he'd been hit. I recollected him saying he thought he might have a concussion. I should've taken him to see a doctor. But we didn't because I was in such a hurry to get home. I put my own priorities ahead of my friend. "How bad is it?"

"Fairly." I noticed he squinted.

"I'm gonna drive you to a doctor."

"Don't be stupid. We don't have time."

"I don't care if we do or we don't. I'm not gonna have you— you—"

"Yeah?"

I pressed my lips together. "Friends stick together, Hart. No matter what. When a friend is ailing, that's when he needs you most."

He reached out, and before I knew what was happening his hand rested on mine. "You're a special kinda person, George."

"I feel the same way about you." I stopped short. "I mean, not in a weird way or anything."

He closed his eyes. "Of course not."

"But I feel real . . . close to you, just the same. Don't recall ever feelin' this way before about anyone, boy or girl." I paused again. "Guess that's what it means to have a real friend."

"Couldn't be more proud than I am hearing you call me that. In another world, maybe—" He hesitated, then smiled. "But this ain't that world."

"This palaverin' ain't helping. I'm finding a hospital."

"You're making too much of this. After your sister is safe, I'll see a doctor."

"Hart, you're not listening to me."

"You're right, I'm not, and that's because you're not saying any—"

All at once, his body thrashed about like he was losing control of himself.

"Hart? What's going on?" I parked, leaped out of the car, and ran to his side. "Hart. Talk to me."

"Feels like my head's exploding." His eyes darted back and forth.

"Fight this thing. Stay awake."

"You're a good man, George. You collect your sister and take her someplace safe. Someplace like Massachusetts. Someplace far away from No Man's Land."

"Hart, don't you even think about dying. Hart—"

His eyes fluttered closed. And a few moments later, all I could hear was the wind blowing across the plains and that baby wailing in the backseat.

twenty-nine

ABOUT TWENTY HOURS LATER, just a few minutes before noon, I returned to Doc Bennett's fancy house on the outskirts of Guymon. Alone.

I don't know what I expected. I guess I thought he'd be waiting for me, maybe with a pack of friends toting big guns and the sheriff spitting his chewing tobacco and swaggering about. But, instead, I got absolutely nothing. I have to admit this was enormously anticlimactic. After all I'd been through, all the times I'd risked my neck to do this man's bidding, he wasn't even waiting at the appointed time.

I wandered about the grounds a little, but I didn't see any trace of him, so I knocked on the door.

His wife opened it. Maggie Faye. If I recalled correctly, today was her birthday, so I gave her the appropriate greeting.

"Can I help you?" she asked.

I wasn't sure she even remembered me. The smell of liquor hung heavy on her breath. "I, uh, have an appointment to see your husband. He felt strongly that he didn't want me to be late."

Over her shoulder, in the corner of the sitting room, I could see that younger girl, Stella, sitting quietly in the same chair, her head down and her hands folded in her lap. It was like nothing had changed in the entire time I'd been gone.

"I believe he's in the greenhouse." Her eyes were red and puffy and her hands shook a bit. "Tending to his rosebuds."

With her permission, I walked to the side of the house. Two black servants worked in the garden, watering plants and sprinkling them with store-bought fertilizers. I couldn't help but wonder how many of the folks I met on the road could've been fed with the money that was being used to raise flowers that only bloomed for the blink of an eye.

I eventually found Doc Bennett in the far corner, repotting what looked like a small magnolia tree. He acted busy, but something about his manner suggested that he wasn't. It was almost as if he were putting on a show, trying to look preoccupied and not all that concerned about my arrival.

"Doc Bennett?" I said as I approached.

He looked up, squinted, stared at me for a time. Then he snapped his fingers. "Oh, you're . . . you're that boy from the jail. Greg?"

"George."

"That's right. George." He pushed himself to his feet and brushed the potting soil off his apron. "How was your journey?"

"It contained some points of interest."

"I know you made it to Oxford."

"How do you know that?"

"The sheriff got a report from the local constabulary. Said you'd been seen in town. Said they tried to apprehend you but without success. How'd you manage to get away from those boys?"

"I'm a fast runner."

Bennett frowned, giving me the once-over. "Let's go back into the house."

He took off his apron and handed it to one of the servants, who bowed a bit as he took it and never made eye contact. I followed Bennett inside.

The sound of the door made that wife of his almost jump out of her tracks. Stella seemed to scrunch up even smaller into her chair. "Maggie Faye, look who's come to visit on your special day. The prodigal son has returned. Ulysses is back from his wanderings."

She made no reply.

"Stella, come give your daddy a hug." The girl sunk deeper into the cushions. "Stella, did you hear me?"

Her eyes turned up. She glanced at him, then at me, then back down again.

"Stella, do I need to take you into the back room and—"

The girl was on her feet faster than my heart could beat. She barely touched him, but he wrapped her up in his arms and pressed her tight against him. He squeezed and squeezed, then he bent down and kissed her tenderly on the cheek.

I was glad I had not eaten recently.

"That's more like it. Maggie Faye, it's time for some vittles." He turned back toward me. "Can you stay and break bread with us?"

"I'd just as soon not."

"You sure? Say, what happened to that friend of yours? Your cellmate."

"He died."

"I'm sorry to hear it. Sure you won't stay for grub? Maggie Faye makes a fine biscuit."

I drew in my breath, trying to steady myself. "Let's just get our business done, all right?"

"As you wish." He glanced at me nonchalantly. "Did you find my daughter?"

"I found Maxine."

"That's my daughter."

"Among other things."

His eyes narrowed. "Where is she?"

"Where's my sister?"

"In a safe place."

"So's Maxine."

"And where would that safe place be?"

"Someplace you'll never find her on your own."

"Don't play games with me, you half-wit farm boy. Turn over my daughter or I'll have you arrested and hanged on the spot."

"You could probably do that. But you'd never find your daughter."

"I'll turn this county upside down if I have to."

"You won't find her."

He took a step closer. He pursed his lips like I was a petulant sassy child who needed to be taught some manners. "You know, I got me a lot of men on this property. Maybe I should round them up and see if they can't persuade you to tell me what I want to know."

"I won't tell you anything."

"These boys can be awfully persuasive."

"It won't work."

"Just wait till we pound the stuffings out of you for an hour or two. Everybody talks, eventually. I bet we wouldn't have to work on you for ten minutes."

I shook my head, not arrogant but firm. "I've taken some serious poundings these past few days. I'm almost getting used to it." I squared my shoulders and looked him right back in the eye. "I won't talk."

The doctor stared at me a moment, then started to chuckle. "Well now, you just think you're the cock of the walk, don't you?"

I didn't take the bait.

"You know, the sheriff could throw you in jail and keep you there forever. And he'd do it if I asked him to."

"I am aware of that."

"And we don't have to go on feeding that scrawny piece of meat you call a sister, either."

My nostrils flared, but I kept it in check.

"Maybe I'll just bring her over to my house. I get kinda lonely some nights. Might be nice to have a new girl around."

I grabbed him by the shoulders and slammed his back against the wall. Two of his servants surged forward, but he waved them back.

"Well now, I got you riled up, didn't I? Seems I found the sweet spot." He chuckled some more.

I let him go. Much as I wanted to knock him into the next state, I knew this was not the time. I also knew that if I lost my temper, I would not be any good to anyone.

"I think I'll send for the sheriff now," Bennett said. "We'll continue this conversation later, after you've spent a week in jail and your sister has spent a week without food."

I looked at him levelly. "Then I'll be traveling to Weatherford. Before he gets here."

"Weatherford? That's almost two hours away. What's in Weatherford?"

"A newspaper."

He didn't blink for a long time. "You planning to place a classified ad?"

"No. Maxine's got a story to tell. About the house she grew up in. About the times she's spent with her daddy. And the times her little girl has spent with her daddy."

He pulled closer to me. "She wouldn't be so stupid."

"She would've done it already, if I hadn't stopped her." He didn't reply for once, which was my sign that I had finally gotten his attention. "You don't know this, but she gave birth to that baby of hers. A baby girl. And she's afraid you might end up doing to that little baby what you done to her and Stella. In fact, she thinks that was the whole reason you sent me out to fetch her, that you weren't so much concerned about her as you were desirous of having a new girl in the house to play with."

His teeth ground together. He wasn't used to being spoken to like this.

Good.

"Given that you're a prominent citizen and all, I'm thinking the fourth estate will be extremely interested in this story." I paused. "Think the county police might have more than a casual interest, too. Not the local sheriff, sure. But someone who's honest and hasn't taken any money from you."

The doctor's whole body shook. "What is it you want, you broke-dick paladin?"

"I want my sister."

"Then you should've done as I said."

"I did. Against considerable opposition. But when I got to thinking about how you treated me the first time we met, how you threatened to kill a young girl to get me to run your errand, I got the sneaking suspicion that you might have a few more schemes hatching. Like maybe if I'd shown up here with those two girls, I'd never see my sister. Or live to see the next sunrise."

He did not deny it. "Your sister will not be released till you've returned Maxine and her baby."

"And you're not getting the girls till I've gotten my sister."

"It seems this game is at a stalemate."

Yes, I thought. *Unless you're thinking three moves ahead.* "I propose a mutual exchange of prisoners."

"Very well. Seven this evening, just before sunset."

"That suits me."

"We'll do it right here in front of my house."

That sounded like about the worst possible location to me, but truth was, no other place would be any safer. He didn't want to do it where he could be seen by prying eyes, and come to think of it, neither did I. "I'll be here."

"With the girls."

"If you have my sister, I'll have the girls."

"I'll bring her." Along with, I suspected, numerous men bearing firearms. "Don't be late."

"I won't," I said. "I've been waiting for this a long time now."

thirty

I DIDN'T SEE any reason for being early, so I showed up at the appointed time at the appointed place in that beat-up Dodge. With Maxine and Hope in the backseat. She nursed during the drive, so I let them both finish before I plowed into the thick of things.

"You 'bout ready?"

"As I'll ever be," Maxine replied. "Should I bring the baby?"

"Definitely."

"I don't want her to get hurt."

"I don't want any of us to get hurt. And I think that girl of yours may be the only way to keep us all safe. Least in the short term."

I opened my car door. Maxine did the same. I felt like I was in one of them Tom Mix movies where the climactic scene is always a big shootout between the black hat and the white. I had a strong suspicion that not everyone in the cast would come out of this alive.

We walked down that long driveway to Doc Bennett's house. Doc Bennett waddled out of the house. He wore that gardening apron and his hands were dirty with soil. His face lit up when he saw what I brought him.

"Maxine! Thank the heavens you're home safe."

She didn't answer.

"And this must be little Henrietta."

"Her name is Hope."

"Oh, that will never do." He took a step forward. Maxine took several steps back, baby in tow, practically colliding with me.

"Just stay where you are," I told him. "Till you've kept up your end of the bargain. Where's my sister?"

He ignored me and kept coming. I reached out and wrapped my hand around Maxine's throat. "Stay right where you are."

He shined that big smirky smile that I had learned to despise so much. "You're not gonna kill her."

"You might be surprised."

"You're not the type, college boy. You don't know how to do a man's work."

I choked her tighter, jerking her hair back with my other hand. "You take one more step, she dies."

"He means it, Pa." Maxine's voice trembled. "He's a right mean bastard. He's been slapping me around and hurting me ever since he found me."

Doc Bennett's face contracted.

"He even . . . you know. He took advantages with me."

"What kind of advantages?" Bennett intoned gravely.

"You know. Like you used to do. 'Cept he ain't my pa so he's got no right." All lies of course. Lies I'd fed her to muddle the doctor's mind.

Bennett's lips pressed together. "You will release my daughter immediately."

"After you release my sister," I replied. "Then we can both go about our business."

"Surely you don't think that you will walk away from here alive."

"We can discuss that later. After you release my sister."

With a resigned expression he waved toward the house. The front door opened and someone shoved Callie out.

She still had on the clothes she wore when I saw her last, and she was no more clean. Looked just as skinny, too, but she wasn't dead, and that was what I cared about most.

Callie ran up and wrapped her arms around me. She started to speak, but I cut her off. "Git out of here."

"But George—"

"You listen to me." I tried to keep my voice down so the doctor and his legion of hidden friends couldn't hear. Callie had been a bit addled last I saw her, so I had to make sure she understood me. "Go right down that road and don't you stop."

"I want you to come with me."

"I can't do that right now."

"Then I'll stay with—"

I took her by the chin. "Callie, listen up and listen good. There's about to be a whole mess of trouble here. And I'm not gonna be able to do what I need to do if I'm worrying about you. So run. There's an automobile parked just where the driveway meets the road. You get in that car and wait. And if you see anyone but me coming toward you, start that auto and drive like hell and don't stop till you're somewhere safe."

"But—"

"Git!" I shouted, and she tore off running. I saw tears flying out of her eyes, but she scampered down the road and out of sight. I didn't speak again till she was where no one could see her.

"Well, that's settled," the doctor said. "Are you done with hiding behind the womenfolk?"

"As a matter of fact, I am." I stepped out from behind Maxine —affording him the first opportunity to see that I was holding a pistol.

Bennett just laughed. "If that don't beat all. The big man got him a little gun."

"You think this is funny?"

"I think this is pathetic. You truly suppose that peashooter is gonna save you?"

I turned my attention to Maxine. "You heard what I told Callie?"

"I did."

"Good. You and the baby do the exact same thing now."

She nodded and walked down that long gravel road, making impressive speed for a woman who recently gave birth.

"Wait just a minute," the doctor said.

"Keep going, Maxine."

She did.

Bennett's face flushed. "You listen to me, Maxine Gail. I'm your—"

I fired a shot into the air. The report of the gun made us both jump.

Bennett's lips curled up crooked. "You stupid son of a bitch. You are gonna be very sorry you decided to mess with me."

"I could shoot you where you stand, Doc. And the world would be a better place for it."

"There ain't gonna be none of that." The sheriff came strutting out the front door of the house, gun in hand. I knew he'd be lurking about somewhere. I just didn't know exactly where. "Put that firearm down, son. You are in violation of the law and disturbin' the peace."

I readjusted my aim to somewhere between the two men. "I believe I will decline to accept your advice."

"That wasn't advice. That was an order. From an officer of the law."

"You gave up the right to call yourself that a long time ago."

He was more taken aback by my remark than I expected. "You ain't got no right to judge. These are hard times. Lots of folk are . . ." His voice trailed off. ". . . are doing things they'd just as soon not be doing. A man has to survive, that's all."

"Not like this," I said. "Not at the cost of others. You're supposed to help folks. You're supposed to . . . to be a shepherd. Not a bully. Not a pawn on some rich man's chessboard."

The sheriff swallowed hard and, though he looked none too

happy about it, raised his pistol. He pointed it at me, and I got the distinct impression that his pointing was a lot more accurate than mine. "Put that gun down."

"How do I know you won't kill me if I do?"

The doc and the sheriff exchanged a look, but neither of them spoke. Which I guess was an answer in itself.

"Two against one ain't such bad odds," I said. "Especially when only one of you has a gun. I don't think the doctor can take me out with his trowel." I didn't know how long I could keep this banter going, but the longer it lasted the more time those three women had to find their way to safety.

"I don't think you 'preciate the situation you are in." The doctor snapped his fingers.

A man stepped out onto the upstairs balcony of the house.

Followed by another. They both had rifles.

Two men stepped out of the greenhouse. They were packing, too. Big guns that looked like they could blow a hole through the side of an automobile.

The side door of the hay barn swung open. Two more men stepped out. Both toting rifles.

"I see the odds have changed," I remarked.

"No," Doc Bennett said, "they were always like this. You were just too stupid to know it. And now you're gonna be too dead to know anything."

"You kill me. and you'll never find those girls."

"They can't have gone far. I got a lot of men. We'll get 'em." He drew in his breath slowly. "I think I will wound you but not kill you. Maybe I'll let you watch our activities for a little while. Maybe I'll let the boys cut on you some, never quite killing you. Maybe I'll listen to you scream and beg for weeks, pleading for mercy."

He took a step closer. "You will beg me, not to save you, but to kill you. But unfortunately, I am not a merciful man."

thirty-one

I STOOD MY GROUND. Wasn't that challenging, due to the lack of options. I'd come this far. I wasn't gonna back off now.

"Ready, boys?" the doctor said. "Aim careful now. No head shots. Get him in the leg. Get him in both legs. I don't care if he walks again. I just want to make sure he doesn't die right away."

Guns cocked. Rifles loaded. "On three, gentlemen. One—"

"Hear that noise?" I asked.

"What noise? Two."

"Don't pretend you don't hear that." The sound was distant at first, but it grew louder with impressive speed.

The doctor heard. "We got a thunderstorm coming in?"

"Nope."

He listened harder. "Sounds like a lawn mower. Or a thresher."

"You're getting warmer."

"What the hell are you up to?"

"The key word there was *up*."

I hit the ground, and a second later, before those boys could plug me, the monoplane soared up from behind the house. It swooped down in front, coming within inches of Doc Bennett's head. He hit the ground, and the others soon followed suit.

Bennett had his hands over his face. He peeked out between his fingers. "What in the Sam Hill—"

By that time, the plane was heading back for another run. I heard that lovely high-pitched laugh as it cruised by. The doctor hunkered down even more.

I saw the boys up on the balcony dive down headfirst. The plane soared over the house, barely missing the rooftop.

"You men stop acting like a pack of sissies!" That was the sheriff. "It's just a plane. It ain't gonna hit you."

The boys slowly pushed themselves up, looking as if they lacked his certainty.

Amy swooped in so close the wind was like to knock everybody down, and the house too. The doctor was as astonished as I ever saw anyone be. Crouched on all fours, he started crawling back to the house.

Up on the balcony, those two boys appeared to have figured out that she couldn't fly that close to them without hitting the house. I saw the man on the right pull his gun up and aim for the sky. He wanted to take down the plane, or at least the pilot.

Until a big heavy arrow slammed him in the chest and knocked him clear back against window.

"Geronimoooo!" I looked back to where Mo was hidden in the trees and gave him a wink.

The other gunslinger on the balcony raised his gun and waved it back and forth, trying to figure out where the arrow had come from.

About three seconds later, an arrow hit him in the neck. He crumpled like someone yanked the stuffings out of him.

The sheriff appeared fraught with indecision. The doctor gave him a mean glare, which forced him to continue the battle. He made a show of twisting his gun around as if he were looking for someone to shoot. He'd forgotten all about me. He was worried about what might come out of the sky next.

Which is why he didn't see the tractor till it was too late.

Now, I grew up in a farm town, but I still had no idea a

tractor could move that fast. Guess it wasn't pulling anything and it was in high gear. It seemed to be haunted, traveling without a driver—least that's what the men with the rifles thought.

Unlike me, they had not seen Jack jump off the rear just after he got it aimed proper.

The tractor was on a line drive toward the barn. The men shot at it a few times, but they didn't have the firepower to bring down a big metal piece of machinery. They had to run. The last one had to dive. The tractor smashed into the barn and kept on rolling.

"Stop this!" the doctor shouted. He was on his feet now, though in the relative safety of his front porch. "I don't care anymore where you hit that bastard. I want him dead. And everybody helping him!"

Guns fired. It was pure chaos. I managed to scramble behind some trees, hoping to ride out the firestorm. More than one bullet came much too close. I guess maybe I had a shepherd that day, because by all rights I should've been plugged and dead.

"Sheriff?" I heard the doctor yell. "Where the hell are you?"

"Right here." The man's voice sounded considerably feebler than the doctor's.

"Round up your men. You're gonna have to go out and get him."

And just when he said that, I sensed someone creeping up behind me.

I swiveled around, gun first. Hart smiled back at me.

"I see the reports of your death were greatly exaggerated," I said. "'Bout time you showed up."

"Sorry. Collected some friends."

"So I observed. As planned. What's it look like out there?"

"The sheriff 's scared to bits. He's only got two men left. Everyone else is down or ducked for cover. Mo's gonna drill anyone who shows their face."

"And the good doctor?"

"Still thinks he's invincible. But we're about to change his mind."

"Anyone comes out onto the lawn, the sheriff 'll plug him."

"Won't be necessary."

"You mean—"

"I do."

Another bullet whizzed over my head. "He did say he had the best arm in three counties."

At the outskirts of the property line, just as the road come over the hill, I saw a boy rise out of the asphalt.

He tipped his cap at me. "Gasoline?" I asked.

Hart nodded. "Your Rooshian ancestors called that a Molotov cocktail."

Jimmy reared back that wonderful right arm of his and threw. The bottle sailed across the front yard. Someone must've figured out what it was, or at least figured out it was bad news, because several men took shots at it. Fortunately, none of them were remotely good enough to hit a glass bottle sailing through space. It kept traveling . . .

. . . and crashed through the front of that fertilizer- filled greenhouse.

Which then exploded.

A huge fireball erupted. Everyone ducked behind anything available.

The heat was incredible. I thought I'd made a return visit to hell, except this time it was hot like it was supposed to be. Like I could feel the skin melting right off my face, that's how intense it was. Shards of glass flew through the air like bullets. I closed my eyes till the worst of the heat passed.

When I opened my eyes, everything was changed. The greenhouse did not exist anymore. All you could see was broken glass and burned greenery and a whole lot of black. The house was damaged, though still standing.

I heard someone creeping up behind me. "Nice job, Jimmy."

"Told you it would work," the boy said.

"Now get out of here. Get to safety with the others."

I couldn't detect any sign of movement. All the enemies

appeared to be eliminated, one way or the other. This was why I made my critical mistake.

I thought we'd won.

I cautiously rose to my feet. I searched all around, trying to figure out what was what. The sheriff was down on the ground, not moving. Looked like he'd been scorched.

He still managed to point his gun at me. I pointed my gun back at him.

"What purpose would this exchange of bullets serve?" I asked. His gun hand wavered.

"The superior man realizes when he has lost. And gives in so he can live another day."

His hand shook so much I was afraid he might shoot himself.

Hart spoke behind me. "Mo, you got another arrow?"

The reply emerged from the trees. "I do. Should I kill him?"

The sheriff lowered his gun.

"That goes for anyone else who might still be toting," Hart added.

"Let's go find the good doctor," I said.

We moved forward, spreading out. We wanted to make sure the doctor didn't slink off into the sunset.

We found him out back, trying to crawl over the fence and disappear into a grove of trees. His eyebrows were singed and his face was black, but he didn't appear to be mortally wounded. "If you're wondering whether I'll shoot you in the back," I said, my voice so calm I impressed myself, "I will."

He stopped. A moment later, he dropped to the ground, turned around and faced me. "You won't kill me in cold blood. You don't have what it takes."

I ignored what he apparently thought was a barb. "True, I ain't gonna kill you, 'less I have to. I'm gonna take you to the authorities."

The doctor laughed. "Do you know how much money I've spread around this state? There's not a lawman in all of Oklahoma that would touch me."

"I thought that might be the case," Hart said. "So I wired a friend of mine up north. Name of Eliot Ness. Used to be with the Treasury Department. He's made arrangements for us to deliver you into federal hands."

"For what?"

"Numerous crimes crossing state lines, thus making it federal. Conspiring with and bribing local law enforcement officials. Transportation of women across state lines for immoral purposes."

I think the doctor saw that we were serious. "You'll never make that stick."

"Well," I said, "we're gonna try, just the same. Walk."

I waved my gun toward the house. He did as I bid and walked, but made a point of chuckling the whole way, as if this didn't bother him a bit.

"Do you boys have any idea how many lawyers I employ? Do you know how many judges are indebted to me for their election?"

"Just walk," I said.

"Once I'm free again—and I will be—you'll both be marked men. I will hunt you down like the dogs you are."

"Maybe," I said. "But you're gonna spend tonight locked up."

"You fool. I won't be detained for two hours. I'll be home by midnight." He got this big ugly grin on his face. "Back home with my girls."

"No, you won't, Pa."

I had my attention so focused on the doctor that I didn't even notice Maxine coming up the road. I saw her now, though, and I saw that she had traded the baby for a gun, probably a weapon one of the sheriff's thugs abandoned.

"Maxine!" The doctor smiled like an angel. "You've come back to save me."

"No, Pa. I come back to kill you."

I wasn't sure if he took her serious or not, but I know I did. I saw the cold look in her eyes, and more than that, I knew what she was fighting for. The right of her newborn babe to live free of that monster.

"Maxine. Haven't I always taken care of you?"

"No, Pa. You've been mean and selfish. All you ever cared about was yourself."

"Didn't I feed you? Didn't I give you money when you needed it? You always had everything you ever wanted."

"No, Pa, I didn't." Her hand shook and tears welled up in her eyes. I thought about trying to rush her, but I was afraid that might make her shoot wild, and then anyone could've ended up dead. "All I wanted was a pa who loved me. In the right way, not the wrong way."

"These men have polluted your mind, I can see that. Sweet Maxine, put down that gun and we'll go inside and—"

"No!" Maxine's arms stiffened, and then I heard a gunshot that crackled like a bolt from the heavens. Doc Bennett's face went rigid. He rose up on his toes. Then blood welled up on his forehead, seeping through the slits around his eyes. And then he fell.

His wife stood in the doorway of the house. With a smoking gun in her hand.

"Ma!" Maxine cried. "Why'd you do that?"

"B—Because—" Her voice sounded funny. "Because if I hadn't done it, you would've. It would've ruined the rest of your life." Her head fell and the gun dropped out of her hand. "I think your life has been ruined enough already. It has to end sometime. So it ends now."

———

Once the doctor fell, everyone came out of their hidey-holes. We sent one of the servants into town to contact the coroner and Mr. Ness. Amy parked that plane somewhere, Mo came down from the trees, Jack pulled his tractor out of the brush, and Jimmy strutted like he was the most important actor in the play.

Amy gave Hart a huge hug. "I told you I'd come back. All you had to do was ask."

"Thank you," Hart replied. "Thanks, all of you. Especially for coming on such short notice."

"Gave me an excuse to fly, which is always welcome." She laid her finger on his shirt. "But make no mistake, you handsome boy. You owe me a favor now. And I intend to collect."

Everyone laughed. Hart looked supremely uncomfortable and I wasn't altogether sure why.

"I was glad to get the call," Mo said, making an Indian salute. "I heard tell you were dead."

"He did get his head hurt," I explained. "Fortunately, it wasn't fatal. We found a doctor who fixed him up with something. Told him to rest, which of course he didn't do. But that gave me an idea. Me and Maxine would go around telling people he was dead, while he went his separate way rounding up reinforcements for the fight we knew was coming. Amy got everyone here on time."

"How'd you ever find me?" Jimmy asked.

A small smile played on Hart's lips. "You left me a clue where you might be heading."

"You just love being mysterious, don't you?" He whistled. "Mighty risky plan you boys had."

"Yes, it was." I looked at Maxine holding her little baby. "But if I'd done what that man wanted me to do, I couldn't have lived with myself no more. This way, everyone gets what they want. Maxine is free—" I saw a familiar towhead poking up over the hill. "And I got what I wanted as well."

Callie wrapped her arms around me. A tiny sliver of light had returned to her eyes. "I hated bein' with those men. Thank you, George."

"No need to thank me. We're kin." I hugged Callie tight. "I'm not gonna leave you behind again, sister, not ever again. I'm gonna take care of you for as long as you need me. Maybe longer."

I glanced at Hart. His mood seemed to have changed. Just at

the moment of triumph, when everyone else was jubilant, he'd crashed. The black crow had descended.

It saddened me to see a man in pain when he should be celebrating. It saddened me that there was nothing I could do about it. That got me deep in thought, which is why I didn't realize what was happening until it was too late to do anything about it.

I heard a groaning, mumbling noise behind me, but it didn't register.

We were so busy congratulating ourselves that we'd forgotten about the sheriff. He'd been wounded in the explosion, but he was far from dead. And I guess he was still clear-headed enough to realize that if I survived to tell my tale, he was headed for prison.

"Damn you . . ."

The whole bunch of us got the drift all at once. The circle of friends parted right down the middle as we turned to look at the sheriff.

I've heard people say that at moments like this, time slowed down. I felt like it all happened too fast, so fast I couldn't think clearly or do what I should've done. This is what happened, all in less time than it takes to say hello.

The sheriff rolled over and raised his gun. Someone screamed.

The gun was pointed at me. Everyone moved at once.

Hart jumped right in front of me. The gun fired.

"No!" I hollered, but even as I did I knew it was too late, that whatever happened had already happened. I grabbed Hart and wrapped my arms around him.

Mo raised his bow and plugged the sheriff right through the chest. He collapsed, and I felt certain he would not rise again.

The bullet caught Hart in the neck. Blood spurted in all directions. I tried to clamp my hands down to stop it, but it was impossible. I was no doctor, but I knew he'd been shot fatally. He'd be dead in seconds.

"Goddamn it, Hart, why'd you have to go and do that?"

He just smiled.

"Did you forget what that Nietzsche said? 'Bout how stupid it all is . . . heroics . . . morality . . ." I had to fight to keep my voice steady. "You just got shot to save me. That's stupid!"

He kept on smiling, and I'll be damned if he didn't look more at peace than at any other moment I ever saw him.

"We've come through so much." I didn't want to be a crybaby, but there was no stopping it. "And we won. We *won*. I don't want it to end like this."

He clapped his hand over mine, still smiling. His last words were: "You're the best friend I ever had."

thirty-two

GEORGE WASN'T sure how long he sat there, thinking, staring at his grandfather, before he heard the guard enter.

"Ready to go?"

He surprised himself—and probably everyone else—with what he said next. "Could you hold up a few minutes? We're not quite finished here."

He heard his grandfather without even using the phone. "I can finish the story after they boot you out."

"You're just gonna leave me hanging at this dramatic moment?"

The old man's eyes traveled downward. "Not really much left to tell."

George reclaimed his meager belongings from a sour-faced jailhouse clerk, slipped back into his raggedy jeans and T-shirt, and stepped outside for the first time in a week.

His grandfather had his beat-up pickup waiting outside. He offered to drive, but his grandfather said he had something he wanted to show him.

"So Hart really was dead this time?" he asked.

"Yeah." He could see that the loss still stung the old man, even after so many years. "He took that bullet for me. Last thing on earth I wanted him to do. But it's the only reason I'm here talking to you today."

"Guess that put a damper on the celebration."

"Yeah. The jubilation drained away fast. Amy got truly shook up. She stayed past the funeral, then flew off again, looking like she'd left some essential part of her behind and didn't care what happened next. Mo and Jack hung around to pay their last respects. Mo said he thought Hart had the spirit of a great warrior in him, not to mention the sharpest strategic mind he'd ever encountered. Jimmy caught the next train north. Most of the men working for Doc Bennett escaped, but I didn't care. With the sheriff and the doctor dead, it didn't seem to matter much anymore. And no one gave a thought to prosecuting the doctor's wife for what she did.

"I was seriously messed up for a time. Didn't know what to do with myself. Took Callie back east and made sure she got healthier. But I couldn't get interested in architecture and engineering the way I once had. I kept thinking about poor Hart and what he done for me. The whole time we traveled together, I never understood how that man felt about me, not until the very last moment."

"Survivor's guilt?"

He pondered a moment. "My first surprise was realizing that I was the best friend he'd ever had. The second surprise was realizing he was the best friend I'd ever had, too. Whatever else might've been going on, those were the facts. And I never knew it till it was too late to do anything about it."

He stared at the road ahead.

"I've been a lucky man since then, and I've known my fair share of good people. But I never had a friend like that again, never shared that kind of adventure, and never for one moment thought someone would make the ultimate sacrifice on my behalf."

"How did you end up in law school?"

"I spent three years knocking about, trying to figure out what

I wanted to do with myself, till the scholarship money petered out. I lost all interest in tall buildings and big bridges and becoming a man of industry. All those great engineering projects I'd imagined just seemed like selfish steps on the road to inflating my own importance. I didn't want to be like that doctor, only doing things to impress people and benefit myself. While Hart and I were on the road, I'd seen how hard life can be for some folks. Skyscrapers don't seem so important after you've seen people huddled around a barrel struggling to get through the night, or seen workers fighting for a survival wage, or seen the hopes and dreams of an entire town shattered by a gust of wind. Those folks needed a shepherd."

"So you appointed yourself?"

"I wanted to help folks that needed it. Who knows, next day it might be me that needs help, but today it isn't, so I do what I can. I went to law school, so I'd be in a position to fight crooked cops and selfish employers and big shots like Doc Bennett. I didn't choose public-interest law because I thought I'd get rich. It chose me—'cause I suddenly realized there were more useful ways to live a man's life than the one I'd been contemplating."

George stared out the passenger-side window. "I figured this was all headed toward some preachy life lesson. So you want me to dedicate myself to helping others?"

"That would make me happy," his grandfather said, as he pulled off the highway. "But that's a decision you've got to make yourself. It's hard for a man to help others when he's in pain himself, or starving and frustrated or unable to do the work he knows he's supposed to do." He paused. "Don't think I don't understand what's been eating away at you, son. I been there myself. I know how hard it can be. And it has to be a thousand times worse for someone with your talent."

"I don't know what you're talking about." He felt a strange itching in his eyes. He'd always assumed his grandfather thought he was a complete screw-up.

Maybe the only person who thought that was him.

"The real breakthrough was when I met your grandmother. What a woman she was. I wish you'd had a chance to get to know her better."

"I would've liked that, too."

"She'd have been good for you. She excelled where I don't. Like knowing when a boy needs some attention." He sighed heavily. "After your pa got killed, it hurt her awful bad. I wasn't surprised she didn't last too much longer. And, of course, I lost Callie not long after that."

His grandfather made a left turn and slowed. "I know you're mad at me for leaving you in jail and probably a hundred other things that came before. But I didn't leave you there just to be mean. I thought that maybe if you spent a little time on the other side, with people who aren't privileged, aren't properly educated, who have to scrape and sweat just to get through the day, maybe you'd learn something from it. I sure did."

I couldn't believe it. "Do you know what kind of lowlife creeps are in there? I shared a cell with a guy who beat up his girlfriend. I ate next to a guy who led the cops on a three-city chase. Stabbings. Drug pushing. Pimps. No one was in that jail but the complete scum of the earth."

His grandfather's lips twitched. "And you."

"I was the exception to the rule. The only one."

"Some of the others might disagree with you. No one wants to be bad. Things happen, that's all." His wrinkled hands turned the steering wheel. "I met my best friend in jail. And I hoped maybe you'd meet someone or learn something. It's more valuable to understand people than to criticize them."

"Oh, please . . ."

The old man's voice dropped a notch. "None of us is perfect, so we'd damn well better help one another whenever we can. When someone screws up, that's not the time to get mean. That's the time to reach out and see if you can do something to make it better."

"I guess you're just a nobler person than I am."

His grandfather pulled into a driveway and parked. "I've known you your entire life. You've got a good heart. You've just gotten a little derailed. So now we're gonna do something about that. Get out of the car."

The one-story house sported orange-red brick with white trim around the door and green shutters. It was at best fifteen hundred square feet, with the plainest A-frame facade he could imagine and a strong need for a new coat of paint.

"Know what this is?"

"Local crack house?"

"No. First house my Jenny and I ever owned. And now—it's your studio."

His eyebrows rose. "Excuse me?"

"Oh, I figure you heard me well enough. You need a place to paint, you say. Here it is. I've been renting it ever since we moved out. Took me a few days to help the renters relocate, which is another reason I let you cool your heels in the slammer. But they're gone now. It's all yours."

"You're giving me a place to work?"

"And to live. If you want it. But there are some conditions."

His eyes narrowed. "Such as?"

"First, you only get it for five years. Period. No extensions. After that, it returns to me. So you've got five years to make this painting deal work. If it hasn't happened by then, I figure it ain't meant to be and it's time for you to move on to something else."

"Five years? Isn't that kind of arbitrary?"

"I think the men in our family work best with a deadline. Lord knows I did."

"What else?"

"I doubt you can paint all day every day, so in the odd moments, I want you to teach."

"Teach what?"

"That's up to you, but art would be the obvious choice. I've talked to people at the local middle school, and they would love to have someone qualified give private lessons to talented students who can't afford private lessons."

"What a minute. How would they pay—"

"They ain't gonna pay you, son. This is how you're giving back. This is how you're gonna learn more about real folks and reach out to people in need. This is how you're gonna do your shepherding. Or at least how it's gonna start."

"Then how can I afford—"

"You'll need a night job. To make ends meet. Pay for groceries and whatnot. Till you're selling your work."

"You got that all lined up, too?"

"No. Some things a man has got to do for himself."

"That will take away from my painting time."

"I doubt it. But it will keep you from getting lazy. Or developing self-indulgent habits. So what do you think?"

He didn't answer immediately. "Now can I ask you about that damn will?"

"I think you're entitled."

"I get why you're not leaving everything to me. You want me to stand on my own two feet."

"True."

"But who the hell is Gordon Irion? And why are you leaving him a huge chunk of change?"

"You don't know? I gave you all the clues."

"Is that Hart's real name?"

"No."

"Some descendant of his?"

"Good guess. But no. He died without issue. Probably just as well. The black crow ran deep in those veins."

"Okay, some descendant of Little Mo or Jack or Jimmy or . . . I don't know. Eliot Ness?"

"No."

"I give up. Who?"

His grandfather bent down and pulled a weed out of the lawn. "You remember the sheriff?"

"That sawed-off bastard who shot Hart? What about him?"

"Irion's the man's grandson."

His eyes bulged. "You've got to be kidding. Why the hell would you give your money to the offspring of that malignant viper?"

"Because there are no bad guys in the real world. That sheriff just wanted to survive the hard times. He went about it the wrong way, sure. But desperation drove him there. And who hasn't known desperation at one time or another?"

"Is this grandson a really great guy?"

"No. He's a walking horror story. Been in and out of prison— the real deal, not seven days in county. Dropped out of high school. Been involved in a variety of disreputable schemes. His father got shot by the cops while fleeing a robbery. And when you think about what that daddy had for a father, you can see there's a doomed streak running though those genes. I hoped that if I gave Irion a chance to turn his life around, it might end this ugly cycle."

"Or he might blow it all and the money will be gone."

"That's possible, of course. Though it's no reason not to help someone out."

"But—that man's grandfather killed your best friend!"

His grandfather nodded. "And in so doing, he may have shown Hart the greatest mercy that boy ever knew."

"Okay, now I'm really not following."

"Hart suffered from clinical depression. That's not what we called it then, but that's what it was. The black crow. The melancholy that shrouded him so bad it hurt. There was no way that was going to get any better, back when we had no treatment or medication for it."

"But still—"

"Did you notice who Hart's heroes were? Meriwether Lewis. Vincent van Gogh. All great men who suffered from acute depression. And ended up taking their own lives. Van Gogh shot himself in the chest. Lewis slashed himself up with a straight razor."

"You think Hart was headed the same direction?"

"More importantly, Hart thought he was headed the same direction. His father killed himself and Hart feared he'd be next. That fear haunted him. I sometimes wonder if that isn't in part why he jumped in front of the bullet. I know he wanted to save me. But I think maybe he also wanted to go out doing something fine, something heroic, rather than suffering through chronic misery till he finally gave in and took his life in some horrible way. He chose a better ending for his story."

"The sheriff murdered him."

"Maybe that was his intent. But what he did was a mercy killing. The only peace that smart, wonderful boy could ever find waited for him in heaven."

"So you believe there is a heaven?"

The old man stared up at the sky. "There damn well better be."

He began to see the situation more clearly than he had before.

But one puzzle remained unsolved. "What's with you leaving money to start some foundation to promote the work of a writer? I've made the connection. That's the writer Hart liked so much. The one he agented for, right?"

His grandfather smiled. "You should've paid closer attention in English class."

"I'm pretty sure we didn't study Edward H. Conrad."

"No, I mean so you could learn to read between the lines. Don't you get it, son? Hart didn't represent Edward H. Conrad. He *was* Edward H. Conrad. Edward Hart Conrad, to be precise. Sure, he didn't like to admit it. He was on the shy side, and back then no one had any respect for them pulp writers. Maybe he was saving his real name for the serious literary work he never got to write, I don't know. But I heard Hart tell those stories, and there's no way a man can tell a story like that, with so much power and passion, unless it's his own story. No one ever spun a better yarn than Hart."

He felt like an idiot. "And you don't want his work to be forgotten."

"It's more than that. Did you notice how, all along our journey, people loved those stories? How it took them away from their troubles? Made them feel better about themselves? People have been telling stories since cavemen sat around the campfire. We learn from stories. We're inspired by stories. Hart's tales helped a lot of people. Maybe they still can. I want to give other folks the same chance to benefit that I had. Can you understand that?"

"You want to create a living memorial for your best friend."

His grandfather looked away and wiped something out of his eye. "Yeah. I guess so."

"I do understand. And I hope—I hope—" His voice caught. He took a deep breath. "I hope someday I can do the same. With my painting. Or some other way, who knows?"

"You want to create a living memorial?"

He clasped the elderly man by the shoulders. "Yeah, for *my* best friend. And that would be you." He wrapped his arms around his grandfather and gave him a hug that seemed to last forever.

author's note

The descriptions in this book of historical events, the Dust Bowl, and the Great Depression, are accurate to the best of my knowledge. Everything pertaining to the fictional characters, of course, is invented. My previous book, *Nemesis*, was also set in 1935, and I enjoyed returning to the period, this time viewing it through a dramatically different prism. I consulted many sources in my research, but perhaps the most useful was *The Worst Hard Time* by Timothy Egan, a beautifully written book I highly recommend. James Michener really did ride the rails, but earlier than the setting of this book, which is why I omitted the last name. The Faulkner story about "Shakespeare's daughter" is reportedly true, though it occurred much later. Amelia Earhart did fly a Lockheed Vega 5B. Woody Guthrie traveled all over the country in the 1930s, but he didn't write "This Land Is Your Land" till 1940, so he must've been singing something else in this novel. The first recorded instance of someone shouting "Geronimo!" was in 1940, but I figure that since Mo was a relative, he was ahead of his time. Red Skelton hosted dance marathons (sometimes featuring Anita O'Day), Eliot Ness was in Cleveland in 1935 (he would be appointed Safety Director in December), that young man in Cleveland talking about comics was Jerry Siegel, the originator of

Superman, and the real Hugh Braddock was a pioneer in soil conservation. So it's all true. Except when it isn't.

I want to thank my wife, Lara, a superb editor and my shepherd in the sand. Thanks also to our spectacular children, and to James Vance and Hannah Buehler for reviewing and commenting on an early draft of this manuscript.

I invite readers to visit my website, www.williambernhardt.com, or to e-mail me at willbern@gmail.com.

about the author

WILLIAM BERNHARDT is the bestselling author of more than sixty books, including *The Florentine Poet*, *The Game Master*, the popular Ben Kincaid and Daniel Pike courtroom novels, and *Nemesis: The Final Case of Eliot Ness*. Bernhardt founded WriterCon, which hosts writing workshops and small-group retreats, an annual conference, and also offers a newsletter and magazine on Substack. His programs have educated more than three dozen now-published authors. He holds a master's degree in English literature, has won the Oklahoma Book Award twice, and has received the Southern Writers Guild's Gold Medal Award, the Royden B. Davis Distinguished Author Award (University of Pennsylvania), and the H. Louise Cobb Distinguished Author Award (Oklahoma State), which is given "in recognition of an outstanding body of work that has profoundly influenced the way in which we understand ourselves and American society at large." In addition to the novels, he has written plays, a musical (book and music), humor, nonfiction, children's books, biography, poetry, and crossword puzzles. He is a member of PEN International and the Academy of American Poets.

also by william bernhardt

The Daniel Pike Novels

Getting his client off death row could save his career . . . or make him the next victim.

After his courtroom career goes up in smoke, a mysterious job offer from a secretive boss gives Daniel Pike a second chance but lands him an impossible case with multiple lives at stake . . .

- **Court of Killers (Book 2)**
- **Trial by Blood (Book 3)**
- **Twisted Justice (Book 4)**
- **Judge and Jury (Book 5)**
- **Final Verdict (Book 6)**
- **Partners in Crime (with Ben Kincaid) (Book 7)**

- **Justice For All (with Kenzi Rivera)**

The Splitsville Legal Thrillers

A struggling lawyer. A bitter custody battle. A deadly fire. This case could cost Kenzi her career—and her life.

When a desperate scientist begs for help getting her daughter back, Kenzi can't resist . . . even though this client is involved in Hexitel, a group she calls her religion but others call a cult. After her client is charged with murder, the ambitious attorney knows there is more at stake than a simple custody dispute.

- **Exposed (Book 2)**
- **Shameless (Book 3)**

The Ben Kincaid Novels

"[William] Bernhardt skillfully combines a cast of richly drawn characters, multiple plots, a damning portrait of a big law firm, and a climax that will take most readers by surprise."—*Chicago Tribune*

Ben Kincaid wants to be a lawyer because he wants to do the right thing. But once he leaves the D.A.'s office for a hotshot spot in Tulsa's most prestigious law firm, Ben discovers that doing the right thing and representing his clients' interests can be mutually exclusive.

- **Blind Justice (Book 2)**
- **Deadly Justice (Book 3)**
- **Perfect Justice (Book 4)**
- **Cruel Justice (Book 5)**
- **Naked Justice (Book 6)**
- **Extreme Justice (Book 7)**
- **Dark Justice (Book 8)**

- Silent Justice (Book 9)
- Murder One (Book 10)
- Criminal Intent (Book 11)
- Death Row (Book 12)
- Hate Crime (Book 13)
- Capitol Murder (Book 14)
- Capitol Threat (Book 15)
- Capitol Conspiracy (Book 16)
- Capitol Offense (Book 17)
- Capitol Betrayal (Book 18)
- Justice Returns (Book 19)

Other Novels

- The Florentine Poet
- Plot/Counterplot
- Challengers of the Dust
- The Game Master
- Nemesis: The Final Case of Eliot Ness
- Dark Eye
- Strip Search
- Double Jeopardy
- The Midnight Before Christmas
- Final Round
- The Code of Buddyhood

The Red Sneaker Series on Writing

- Story Structure: The Key to Successful Fiction
- Creating Character: Bringing Your Story to Life
- Perfecting Plot: Charting the Hero's Journey
- Dynamic Dialogue: Letting Your Story Speak
- Sizzling Style: Every Word Matters
- Powerful Premise: Writing the Irresistible
- Excellent Editing: The Writing Process
- Thinking Theme: The Heart of the Matter
- What Writers Need to Know: Essential Topics

- Dazzling Description: Painting the Perfect Picture
- The Fundamentals of Fiction (video series)

Poetry

- The White Bird
- The Ocean's Edge
- Traveling Salesman's Son

For Young Readers

- Shine
- Princess Alice and the Dreadful Dragon
- Equal Justice: The Courage of Ada Sipuel
- The Black Sentry

Edited by William Bernhardt

- Legal Briefs: Short Stories by Today's Best Thriller Writers
- Natural Suspect: A Collaborative Novel of Suspense
- Christmas Tapestry